The Black Box

The cover is a portrait of The Duke Of Monmouth commanding the English army against the Dutch, painted by Jan Wyck in 1672.
　　　It is in the National Portrait Gallery.

The following historical novels are also
by David Macpherson

Defenders of Mai-dun.
A story of the Roman invasion of Dorset

Nomad.
A story of the Tibetan Uprising

A Zigzag Path.
A story of Smuggling in the 19th Century

All Lies
A story of the Portland Spies

Aquarius (pub in 2016)
A story of the building of the Dorchester Aqueduct

All are available through Amazon and Kindle

The Black Box

A Story of Monmouth's Rebellion and the Bloody Assizes

David Macpherson

Chapter 1
A Holiday Ruined

Caddie sat on the edge of her bed determined not to cry. *I'm nearly 16 and that's too old to be crying about a ruined holiday.* She had been looking forward to flying out to Bangkok to stay with her parents over the summer, but her mother's illness and the heat and humidity during the summer monsoon in Thailand had persuaded her father that Caddie should stay with her Uncle Robert and Aunt Ruth on their farm in Dorset. Uncle Robert was her mother Ellie's elder brother and Caddie recognised that he and his wife Ruth might not want a niece they hardly knew dumped on them for the summer. Also, despite their genuine kindness, at first meeting they didn't seem to have much understanding of 15-year-old girls.

Caddie was really called Camilla, but since she had been a baby, everyone, except her late grandmother, had called her Caddie. Five days earlier, Caddie had just finished her last GCSE paper when Mrs Templeton, the Housemistress at her boarding school, had asked to see her. 'Caddie, I have some bad news for you.' Caddie's stomach turned over and she felt sick. She was always terrified her parents were going to die in a plane crash or that her brother Ben, who was only five, might be bitten by a deadly snake or something. Mrs Templeton sat her down and explained that she had just received an e-mail from Mr Bentley, Caddie's father. 'Your mother is in hospital with malaria. She's not in any danger now, but your father thinks it best you don't fly out to join them. As soon as your mother is out of hospital the whole family will be flying back to England. He says the weather at home will be much more suitable for her convalescence. In the meantime, your father has asked your uncle and aunt to look after you on their farm in Dorset.'

Caddie had at first been quite relieved that any of the disasters she had been dreading hadn't happened. Then the truth hit her; the school holidays stuck in the back of beyond, on a Dorset farm, with no friends, no internet. In the last week she'd lost her mobile. She suspected one of the girls in her house had nicked it, but admitted to herself that it might well be hidden somewhere in the deep litter of her study at school. Without it there was no way she would be able to text her friends. *Did they even have electricity in Dorset?* she wondered. It sounded like a holiday from hell.

She sniffed and got up from the bed to look out of the high attic window. Aunt Ruth had apologised when she had led Caddie up the winding staircase into the tiny third-floor bedroom. 'I'm sorry I can't put you in the guest bedroom. The builders will be here on and off for the next few weeks to try to find out why the north wall in the room is damp. It's been like that for years. Your uncle has checked the gutters and slates, but they seem to be all right.'

However, Caddie had been thrilled. Up among the sloping roof beams her attic room was cosy and private. The family farm at Corton, five miles from Dorchester, was tucked into a fold of the South Dorset Ridgeway and her window looked out on fields of grazing cows and waving corn busy turning from green to yellow. Reluctantly she admitted to herself it could be worse. She shucked off her pyjamas and searched for the jeans and tee-shirt she had discarded on the floor last night. *At least there's no Mrs Templeton to boss me around,* she thought. *I'll wash after breakfast.* Picking up her hairbrush she moved over to the tall mirror fastened onto the back of the door and started to work her long coppery-red hair into some kind of order. *That'll do,* she thought, and studied the results of her effort. At five foot nine inches Caddie was one of the taller girls in her year group. She wrinkled her nose at the reflection that looked back at her. *Quite pretty, but not stunningly good looking like Amanda or Poppy.* She smoothed down her tee-shirt. *No real boobs yet as some of them have.* This didn't worry her. Her mother had told her that she had been a late developer, and anyhow, big breasts got in the way when you played lacrosse, one of Caddie's passions. Quite pleased with her reflection, she grabbed a sweater and went downstairs.

Uncle Robert, who looked as if he had been up for hours, smiled at her when she came into the low-ceilinged kitchen. Her aunt was busy at the Aga. Caddie had been much too tired to notice anything when she had arrived the previous evening, but now she appreciated the welcoming feel of the old room, the stone flags on the floor and the collection of glass jars on the shelf, all neatly labelled with various coloured liquids. Her uncle noticed her looking at them. 'That's your Aunt's collection of potions and patent medicines. She collects wild herbs from the fields and brews up these concoctions.' Her uncle had a long serious face, which was transformed when he smiled. Caddie recognised her mother's features in both his appearance and his awkward manner. His clothes smelled slightly of cow. 'Come and sit down, girl.' He indicated a chair at the long kitchen table. 'Ruth's cooking some breakfast, and a letter's just arrived from your father.'

Caddie thought he would hand over the letter for her to read and sat down at the table waiting, but instead her uncle held the envelope in both hands, studying it thoughtfully as if he was trying to guess what the message inside might say. She shuffled impatiently. Eventually he slit the envelope with his thumb and took out the letter. Even looking at it upside down, Caddie could recognise the headed notepaper as that of the aid agency where her father worked. Her uncle cleared his throat and began to read aloud.

Dear Robert and Ruth,
Many thanks for agreeing to look after Caddie until we can get back to England. I expect Ellie will be out of hospital in a couple of weeks. She should be fit to travel by the middle of August and we will then fly back with Ben to stay in our cottage in Hertfordshire. Please reassure Caddie that Ellie ...

'That's your mother,' he explained to the girl.

'She knows that, Rob,' Ruth said as she stirred the scrambled eggs on the Aga. 'Get on with it.'

Please reassure Caddie that Ellie is well on the way to recovery. The American Mission hospital has given her excellent treatment and she is over the fever now, though it did give us quite a scare. It would have been possible for Caddie to come out to join us, but I think it best that Ellie gets back to full fitness in England. It's pretty hot and sticky out here in the summer months. I will write again as soon as I have more news. Tell Caddie she can e-mail us, and give her a big kiss from me, and another from her mother.

With best wishes and thanks,
Greg.'

Robert carefully refolded the letter and put it back in the envelope, laying it on the table in front of him. He then picked up his mug of tea and started to drink.

'Isn't there a letter for me?' Caddie asked, disappointed.

Ruth picked up the envelope and placed it on the sideboard. 'I'm afraid not,' she answered, 'but I expect they think you will be contacting them by e-mail. Though your Uncle Robert uses a computer to help run the farm, we don't have a broadband connection here. There's an internet café in Dorchester, and when I go shopping tomorrow you can come with me.' She placed a large plate of bacon, scrambled eggs and tomatoes in front of Caddie who to her surprise found she was extremely hungry and had no trouble in eating the lot.

'What are you going to do today?' her aunt asked her. That was something that had been worrying Caddie quite a bit. *What today, tomorrow and every day?*

'Can I help you, Uncle Robert?' She'd never worked on a farm before, but the idea of helping with the house cleaning, like some character from a Dickens novel, made her shudder.

'I don't need any help this week, thanks,' he answered. 'Perhaps next week with the hay crop if it stays dry.' There was an awkward pause. The problem of how to fill Caddie's day was still to be solved.

The silence made Caddie squirm in embarrassment. Robert cleared his throat again. *I wonder if he does that every time he's about to speak,* she thought. *It could get irritating.*

Eventually her uncle put his mug down. 'Would you like to see where our family came from?' he asked. He pushed aside the plates on the breakfast table to make space and fetched a huge leather-bound Bible from the cupboard underneath the Welsh dresser. To Caddie it looked like something you would find on a refuse tip, but her uncle was obviously treating it with great respect.

The cover was badly stained and there was a ragged tear in the leather binding of the spine. Robert fetched a clean tea cloth from one of the drawers and, spreading it on the table, placed the book carefully on it. With some reverence he opened up the title page. 'Our family name, and your mother's too before she was married, is Jolliffe,' he said, pointing to the name written in beautiful calligraphy at the top of the page. 'There have been Jolliffes on this farm for nearly 400 years. The first date, 1653, is when I think the book was bought. The publishers have printed MDCL, which is 1650, on the title page. That was the time after the Civil War when Oliver Cromwell ruled England. The family were Congregationalists then, known as Protestant dissenters. This Bible was probably very important to them. Part of their belief was the sovereignty of God and the authority of the Bible.'

Her uncle turned back the title page to reveal the inside cover. He beckoned Caddie round so she could read the entry half way down the page. 'See, *Eleanor, born September 1975*. That's your mother. This is me, *Robert, born 1971, married Ruth Whittock of Portesham 1996.* That's your Aunty Ruth. Here's your grandfather, my father, see, born, married, died. All the dates are there. I must remember to put your father's name and yours and young Benjamin's in straight away.'

Caddie was fascinated. 'Who's the first in the book?' she asked. 'Whoever it was, it must have cost a fortune when he bought it.'

Robert pointed to a faded name right at the top. *Caleb Jolliffe, born 1608.* 'That's before the Authorised Version of the Bible was even written.' He traced down with his finger. 'He had two children, *Nathaniel Jolliffe, born 1646, married Sarah, and Anna, born 1648,* that's just after the first Civil War, *married Francis Langley, weaver of Bridport.* Look at all the children Nathaniel and Sarah had; *Ethan, Daniel, Katherine, Joshua.* Those last two were both born in 1673 so they must have been twins. As far as I can tell they are the only twins in our family.

It was the first time Caddie had learned where her mother's family had come from. Because she had spent most of her life either in boarding school or on school holiday with them in India, Sierra Leone or, most recently, Thailand, she had only vaguely known the family had a history in Dorset. 'What does this say?' Caddie pointed to some faded writing in the margin opposite Ethan's name.

'We think the first part is a date - 7th July 1685. After that your grandfather told me he thought it said *The Day of the Sacred Trust.* It's difficult to make out, as the ink then wasn't expected to last 300 years. In those days they used to write their 's's like our 'f's. That's why it looks like *Truft.* Then I think there are three initials – J S, then a gap, then R. No one has worked out what these stand for. This underneath is Latin: *Semper Fidelis.* It means *Always be Faithful.*'

'That's the motto of the American Marine Corps,' Caddie interrupted. 'In films they're always shouting "Semper Fi" at each other.'

'Fifty years ago that was the motto in England of the Dorset and Devonshire Regiment too and also the City of Exeter, but my father was never able to work out why it was written here,' Robert answered. 'All these bits after the date are in the same handwriting, but as far as I can make out it wasn't Nathaniel or even his son Ethan who wrote them.'

'What do you think *The Day of the Sacred Trust* refers to?' Caddie asked her uncle.

'No one has ever understood what that meant either. My grandfather, who spent a great deal of time on the family history, thought it might refer to the family stewardship of our little Chapel, which you might have seen near the back of the house when you arrived last night. Jolliffes have looked after the building ever since we lived here, and that's a pretty sacred trust!'

Ruth, washing up at the sink, looked across at the two heads, her husband and niece, bent over the book.

The family resemblance was strong. She felt a momentary pang of sadness. If the fates had been kinder and they had had children, Robert would have made a wonderful father.

'Who gets the Bible when ...?' Caddie stopped, embarrassed.

Robert laughed. 'When I die you mean? Well, as you know, Ruth and I have no children. This farm has been entailed since the 17th century. That's a legal term, which means the farm, and the Bible, will go to the eldest male Jolliffe. He lives in Yorkshire. So my grandfather's brother's grandson, called Martin, will inherit both. He's a good man and I'm sure he will be true to the family history. *Semper Fidelis.*'

There was an awkward pause. 'Show her the family heirloom, Rob. I know you're dying to,' Ruth said. Robert opened one of the drawers in the dresser and lifted out a long wooden box.

'The box isn't that old,' he explained. 'My great grandfather made it around 1867 from some oak he cut down on the farm.' He carefully opened the box and took out what looked to Caddie like an ordinary piece of writing paper. Robert read from the note.

> *Flintlock Pistol found under one of the floor joists when we were laying new boards in the small bedroom on the north side.*
> *Peter Jolliffe 10th May 1863.*
> *Mr Trumble of Dorset Archaeological Society estimates mid-17th century. Probably military originally. Monetary value unknown.*

'My father on one of his trips to London took it to the armaments expert in the British Museum. He was able to describe the firing mechanism more accurately as an English lock, which was in common usage at the time of the Civil War. See here what the expert has written.' He offered the piece of paper to Caddie.

'Hurry up,' Ruth butted in. 'She doesn't want all that history. Show her the gun.'

Robert carefully lifted the pistol from the box and unwrapped it from the piece of cloth protecting it. Caddie had expected to see a gleaming silver barrel with a polished mahogany stock inlaid with pearls, like the one Johnny Depp used in *Pirates of the Caribbean.* The reality was rather disappointing. The stock was rough, undecorated and looked to be made of cheap wood. The barrel was pitted and dull. The lock mechanism itself was too rusty to move. Caddie saw two initials burned into the butt. They looked like WO.

'What do you think of it, Caddie?' her uncle asked.

She managed to show a little enthusiasm, but in truth she couldn't find anything that was the slightest bit interesting in this museum piece. Robert, aware that this had not quite turned out as the grand show he had hoped, wrapped up the gun and returned it to its box and drawer. 'I wonder how it came to be here,' she said politely.

'That's the point,' her uncle exclaimed enthusiastically. 'It's a family secret to which we will never know the answer.' He stood up. 'I must go to work now, but you can look at the book if you like. Don't spill any food or drink on it and put it back in the cupboard when you're done.' He picked his cap off a row of pegs behind the door and left the kitchen, taking with him the slight smell of cow.

When Robert returned to the house for lunch three hours later he found Caddie still pouring over the Bible. Ruth had given her a big sheet of paper and she was trying to draw up the family tree. She asked her uncle what several of the names were, where the early ink was faded, and together they worked out most of the gaps in her chart. Around 1850, someone had tipped what looked like wine on the page and those names had to be left blank. Robert showed her how some names were repeated through the generations and was obviously delighted by her interest.

After lunch he asked her, 'Do you ride?' When she nodded enthusiastically he continued, 'Would you like to ride here?'

Caddie had taken riding lessons at school since she was 11 and loved it. She assured him it was a brilliant idea. The thought of hacking round the farm and some of the local bridleways was thrilling.

'She could take Monty,' Ruth chipped in. 'I don't ride him out nearly enough and he's nice and gentle. You can borrow my hat and boots, Caddie.'

An eager Caddie accompanied her uncle to the broad meadow below the farmhouse. Monty ambled over to greet them and Robert, clipping a leading rein onto his head collar, led the pony back to the stables. He helped Caddie saddle up. He was pleased and relieved to see she obviously knew what she was doing. 'If you go down the track below the house, cross the stream and up the other side, you can have a good canter along the top of the ridge. After about a mile you'll see tractor marks that'll lead you back to the lower barn. Follow the path back here and leave the saddle on the peg where we found it. Rub Monty down in the stable yard and then take him back to Lower Meadow. He'll be no problem. Go out and enjoy yourself'

Monty was a docile pony of about 14 hands. Over the next week Caddie had great fun exploring the Dorset countryside with him. One day she rode up onto the Ridgeway and along to Hardy's Monument, the next down to Martinstown and Maiden Castle. She discovered that the area around Corton Farm was crisscrossed with bridleways and tracks, some of them ancient, all waiting to be explored. She developed a comfortable routine of constructing a family tree at the kitchen table in the mornings and going out with Monty in the afternoons. She warmed to her aunt and uncle, who seemed to enjoy having her in their home. On a few days her uncle did find work for her and asked her to help him on the farm. On one occasion it was help with the combine harvester and on another artificially inseminating the cows.

She was fascinated as he explained the principles he employed in choosing which cows to breed with which bulls. 'Of course I don't need the bull itself to be here. I just need this little test tube. Not so much fun for the bull, I'm afraid.' He grinned at her and went on with his instruction, which she found considerably more interesting than any school biology or history lesson. 'The principles of breeding were not generally understood until Robert Bakewell published his ideas on selective breeding in the middle of the 18th century. For the first time he managed to control which traits were passed on in his cattle and sheep, long before the scientific ideas of genetics were understood. Neighbouring farmers couldn't understand why he had the fattest cattle and sheep in Leicestershire, while their herds and flocks were eating exactly the same grass.'

That afternoon when she had finished working with her uncle in the cowsheds she decided there was still time for a short ride on Monty. 'When you get back, I have something very interesting to show you,' Ruth said to her in the kitchen. 'Something the builders have discovered.' She refused to tell Caddie anything else till after her ride.

Monty seemed reluctant to put in much effort on such a hot summer afternoon. He had been ridden more in the last seven days than at any stage in his life, but with much kicking she managed to encourage him into a short, gentle canter along the ridge to the south of the farm. For the rest of the ride the two of them were content to amble along together in the sunshine. It was a happy girl and a weary animal that pulled up outside the stables at round 5 o'clock.

She patted Monty's neck and stroked his ear, pleased with the effort he had put in. Just as she was about to dismount, the braying of a motor horn shattered the peace of the countryside and the oil delivery tanker came round the corner. A startled Monty backed away from the unexpected noise, banging Caddie's head hard against an overhanging light bracket, which jutted out from the stable wall. She was knocked to the ground and sat on her bottom, leaning against the doorpost. Though dazed, she was experienced enough to hang on to Monty's reins.

'Are you all right, lass?' The tanker driver's worried face peered underneath the horse's belly at the seated girl.

Caddie scrambled to her feet unsteadily and leaned back against the wall. 'I think so. What did you do that for?' She felt her knees buckle and sat heavily down on the ground again.

'Give me those.' The driver took the reins from her hand and led an unprotesting Monty into the stable. He tied the horse to a ring on the wall and helped Caddie back to her feet. 'Let's get you to the house.'

Caddie grumbled that she was perfectly fit, but was still quite relieved by his strong right arm round her waist as they walked the short distance to the back door of the farmhouse.

'Oh, Caddie, whatever's happened to you?' Ruth's worried face greeted them at the door. The driver explained about the accident, and the two of them helped the wobbly girl to one of the kitchen chairs.

'Uncle Robert told me to leave Monty in Lower Meadow,' Caddie said, trying to struggle to her feet. 'We had to tie him up in the stable.'

'You stay there,' Ruth insisted, putting a hand on Caddie's shoulder. 'You're going nowhere except upstairs. Your uncle will sort out Monty when he comes in. Thanks, Bert,' she said to the driver. 'When you've filled our tank, you'll probably see Robert in the West Field. Will you tell him what's happened?'

A sorry-looking Bert left, still apologising to Caddie, who was relieved not to have to move from the chair, as she was feeling really woozy. 'Shall I ring for Doctor Ireson?' Ruth asked. But Caddie reassured her that this was unnecessary.

'What you need is one of my tonics, then bed.' Ruth reached up to the top shelf of the dresser and took down a bottle with a pale green liquid. 'This is poppy extract. I use it for headaches and period pains. It's absolutely safe, I promise, and will help you sleep.' She poured a little of the mixture into a measuring glass. Caddie looked at it doubtfully and then swigged it back. 'Now bed,' said her aunt and helped her up the steep stairs to the attic. She assisted Caddie into her pyjamas, folding her jeans and tee-shirt and putting them on the armchair. She tucked Caddie, now surprisingly docile, under the duvet. 'Sleep well, dear. I'll pop in at suppertime to see if you're awake and hungry.' She kissed her on the forehead and gently closed the door.

Chapter 2
A Call to Arms
10th June 1685

'And it came to pass when Joshua was by Jericho, that he lifted up his eyes and looked ....'

The sound of a horse's hooves clattering into the yard of Corton Farm made Nathaniel glance up from the Bible he was reading. The twins Joshua and Kate turned to look out of the window. Their father, Nathaniel, carried on in a stronger voice, trying to draw them back into the story, *'and, behold, there was a man with his sword drawn in his hand.'* The door was flung open.

'He's come, Father. He's come.' A sturdy boy of 15 or 16, fizzing with energy and with flaming red hair sticking out from beneath his cap, burst into the room. A woman, with an identical mop of red hair, stood up from the chair where she had been sitting and held out her arms to her eldest child.

'What is it, Son?'

Nathaniel gestured to Sarah. 'Be seated wife.' He turned to his son. 'You too, Ethan. We are reading from Holy Scriptures and nothing is more important than that. Please remove your cap.'

Ethan took off his cloth cap, using it to wipe the sweat and dust from his face, and sat down next to his mother. He winked at his 14-year-old brother Daniel, who was sitting on a stool in the corner, as his father continued reading.

And the Captain of the Lord's host said to Joshua, loose thy shoe from off thy foot, for the place where on thou standest is holy. And Joshua did so.'

He had intended to read them the story of the siege of Jericho but was wise enough to see that he had lost his audience. 'This is the word of the Lord.'

'Thanks be to God,' the family joined in.

Nathaniel closed the heavy family Bible and looked up at Ethan. 'Why have you left Forde Abbey, Son?'

Ethan looked round at the familiar family scene, pleased to be home, and as he gradually relaxed he realised how tired he was. He smiled across at his mother, who he loved without reservation. For his father, often the stern Presbyterian, he had respect and a strong desire to be worthy of him. He turned towards Nathaniel.

'Master lent me the horse and told me to come here.' He spoke with a strong Dorset burr and shrugged his shoulders as the tension began to seep out of him.

'Please refer to him by name, Ethan. You mean Sir Edmund?'

'Yes, Father. This morning two men came to the house and Sir Edmund called a meeting and told me to come here and then go on to Dorchester.'

'Stop there, Son. You must tell your story more slowly. Kate, go and get a mug of water for your brother. That will give you time to collect your thoughts, Ethan.' Kate was soon back with a pewter mug filled with water. The family sat in silence while the boy drank thirstily. 'Now, Son. What time did the men arrive and who were they?'

The break had allowed Ethan to gather himself and he continued his story, speaking more thoughtfully. 'The men arrived about 10 o'clock this morning. One was called Thomas Dare. He's a goldsmith from Taunton. I didn't catch the name of the other. They landed by rowing boat in Chideock Cove early this morning and came straight to Forde Abbey. They were with the Master, I mean Sir Edmund, for about an hour. He then called us all together, that's me and all the stable lads with the gardeners and those working in the house. Mr Dare and the other man were there and Sir Edmund said Mr Dare had an important announcement. Mr Dare said he had sailed from Holland on a Dutch frigate called *Helderenberg* or something like that. The Duke of Monmouth was on board and had come to claim his rightful crown as King of England. There were two other boats, Dutch doggers I think. The Duke had brought an army with him, but he wanted all honest and God-fearing men of the West to join him in a campaign to overthrow the usurper James Stuart.'

'Praise be to God. We have waited long enough for this day,' Nathaniel said. 'I am ever convinced that James, Duke of Monmouth, should be our lawful King. Where is he now, Son?'

'Mr Dare said he would be landing at Lyme Regis this evening if the tides were right. He had a bag with hundreds of copies of a Declaration already printed. Sir Edmund gave me some and said I had to bring one copy to you and then take the rest on to Dorchester. Other boys were given more copies to take to Beaminster, Bridport, Axminster and Taunton. Mr Dare and two of the stable lads took twenty of Sir

Edmund's horses with him back to Lyme for the Duke. It seems he doesn't have many horses of his own on the ships. Sir Edmund told all of us boys to be careful because if anyone saw us nailing up this Declaration we would be up before the magistrates. He told me I could sleep here tonight, but I have to be back at Forde by tomorrow. Sir Edmund will tell us then what we are to do.'

'Can I see the Declaration?' The boy opened his satchel that was still round his neck and drew out a roll of papers. He unwrapped one and handed it to his father. The family sat in silence while Nathaniel carefully read the document. 'The Duke does not maintain that he is King. He is happy to put his claim, along with others, for Parliament to decide, but he is prepared to fight for whatever decision Parliament might make. He also says that there should be freedom for all Protestants to worship however we please. That is all we Congregationalists, and all others they call Dissenters, have wanted ever since the Act of 1684 made it law that the whole country should worship as the Church of England.' He paused, screwing up his face, deep in thought.

After a moment he came to a decision. 'It is time you young ones were in bed. I wish to talk to your mother and Ethan alone. First we will join in prayer.' The family knelt on the rush floor and bowed their heads. 'Almighty God, protect and sanctify your servant James, Duke of Monmouth, in this enterprise, that his cause being just may also be triumphant. Then to you will be the glory. Amen. Now off to bed you three.'

The twins had enough experience of their stern father not to question his decision. Both of them kissed their father and mother and left the room. Daniel, usually mild and unconfrontational, stood his ground and looked at Nathaniel.

'Can I stay, Father?' he asked. He moved next to Ethan, trying to avoid his mother's concerned look. 'I am 14 now and that's old enough to fight. I must hear what Ethan has to say.'

'God knows we all hope it will not come to fighting.' Nathaniel looked at his second son, already taller than Ethan. *No longer a child, but not yet a man,* he thought. He sighed and nodded, trying to avoid Sarah's eyes. 'All right. You may stay and listen. Ethan's news is likely to affect all of us. Ethan, you and Daniel make sure Sir Edmund's horse is bedded down for the night. Rub him down well and put him in the little barn. You will find some fresh hay in the loft. Daniel, you know where it is.'

When the two boys had left Sarah moved over to her husband and took his two hands in hers. 'You're not going, are you husband? The children and I need you here. We cannot survive without you.' When her husband remained quiet she went on more urgently. 'Forbid the boys to get involved. They are little more than children. You know this is a foolish enterprise and destined to fail. You are a good man, Nathaniel Jolliffe, but no fighter. Let others go, others that are younger and without families.'

Nathaniel released his hands and stood up. 'We owe our farm here at Corton entirely to the goodness of old Sir Edmund. Remember, he leased it to my father as reward for his service at the Abbey.

Tomorrow I feel obliged to go and seek more information from young Sir Edmund, Ethan's present master. We must discuss matters further with the boys, but try not to frighten them. Tonight I shall pray for guidance and I hope by tomorrow the Lord will have told me what to do.' Just then, Ethan and Daniel came pushing back into the tiny front parlour. 'Did you give your horse a good rub down?'

'Yes, Father,' Ethan answered. 'I rubbed him down with straw while Daniel gave him some hay and water.'

The horse will survive the night, all right, thought Nathaniel. *I won't get any more work tonight out of these two.* 'Come and sit down, boys. There are things we need to talk about.'

'Father, who is the Duke of Monmouth?' Daniel asked.

'The Duke is the eldest son of our late King Charles. Some say he was born out of wedlock, others that his Majesty and the Duke's mother Lucy Walters were secretly wed. It seems certain that the King wanted his son to succeed him, but he died suddenly and now his papist brother James has called himself King. This King James has a mind to restore the Roman religion to England, and our family and our church will again be persecuted. The Duke has promised freedom of worship to all Protestants.'

'How do we know he really is the King's son?' Ethan asked.

Nathaniel scratched his head as he thought how best to answer his eldest son. 'Five years ago he made a tour of this part of the country. He came to Dorset, Somerset and Devon and one of the people he stayed with was your master, Sir Edmund Prideaux, at Forde Abbey. Just one night, mind you, but I know he made a big impression on Sir Edmund. Sometime later I heard what happened in Crewkerne market place. Lizzie Parcet, you know the youngest daughter of Old Bess Parcet of Hinton St George, she had this dreadful skin rash called scrofula. Some call this disease the King's Evil and many believe if a rightful King touches a person who suffers, they will be cured. Well, it was market day when Lizzie saw the Duke. She went up to him, whips off her gloves and touches Monmouth on the hand, saying, "God bless your Greatness." She was hustled away by some soldiers, but two days later she was cured. They say she has had skin as smooth as a baby's ever since. Only a King could do that. Everyone around Crewkerne knows the story and they all believe that the Duke should be King. I'll not be surprised if the West County, or at least all the Dissenters in the West, rise up and follow him.'

'I was listening to what Mr Dare said to Sir Edmund this morning, Father. Sir Edmund asked where the Duke would land and Mr Dare said Lyme Regis because it's known to be a Protestant town. Sir Edmund then said, "The town's new Member of Parliament, Sir Winston Churchill, won't like it. He's known to be for the King and is sure to call out the local militia." But Mr Dare shook his head, "Our spies have told us that he is safe away in London. There'll be no problem in Lyme." I didn't hear any more because all the stable boys were told to go and get the horses ready. That has nearly cleaned Sir Edmund out. With four of us taking this paper around, Sir Edmund now has only two or three horses left. There's no doubt which side he's on. What will you do, Father?'

'I shall pray tonight for God's guidance,' Nathaniel answered. 'Tomorrow I shall go to Forde Abbey to talk to Sir Edmund and find out what more he knows. Daniel, you will look after the farm and your mother. Ethan, I hope to see you tomorrow night at Forde. We all have to be careful now.'

'Son, who must you give the posters to?' Sarah asked.

'I cannot say, Mother. I swore to Sir Edmund on the Holy Bible that I would not speak the name to anyone. All I can tell you is I must leave tomorrow while it's still dark. There's one particular man in Dorchester I must meet before he starts work.'

'Then take care, Son.' Sarah looked worried and put her arm around him. 'If the militiamen in Dorchester catch you, you could be tried for treason. There's many who will suffer for this night's work.' She managed a smile. Nothing she could say was going to deter the boy. 'You can sleep in the top room so you don't disturb the rest of us tomorrow when you leave.'

Ethan was far too excited to take his mother's warning seriously. This adventure beat mucking out the horses at Forde Abbey. 'Can I put the Bible away for you, Father?'

'Thank you, Ethan. God speed you tomorrow.' Sarah went over to him and gave him a fierce hug. She then collected one of the lighted candlesticks and Nathaniel followed her into their downstairs bedroom. Ethan looked at the heavy family Bible lying on the kitchen table and stroked the fresh red leather. Then he carefully picked it up and returned it to the cupboard under the dresser. He was sorry he hadn't had any longer to talk to Daniel than a quick chat in the stable. Ethan got on well with his younger brother, who had grown since he had last seen him. Though now quite tall, Daniel was as skinny as a pea stick and a dreamy gentle sort of fellow. *Even though he's now a couple of inches taller than me, I expect I could still throw him if it came to a wrestle*, he thought with a grin. He was still in a state of suppressed anticipation as he carried the candle up two flights of stairs to the attic.

Chapter 3
A Grisly Discovery

Ruth drew the curtains in the attic bedroom. 'Good morning, Caddie. How are you feeling? It's a lovely day again and I didn't manage to tell you our exciting news yesterday because of your accident.'

If Ruth hadn't been so obviously a warm person, her fussing could have become quite irritating. As it was, Caddie, in the short time she had been at Corton Farm, had come to appreciate her aunt's kind-heartedness. She slowly surfaced from her deep sleep, still feeling a little woozy, but she wasn't sure if this was more the result of last night's dose of Aunt Ruth's medicine than the bang to her head. She stretched and smiled reassuringly at her aunt's anxious face. *She must have been really worried about me*, she thought, and decided to make an effort to be cheerful and positive. 'I'm fine thank you, Ruth.' (She had long since decided to drop 'Aunt' and 'Uncle'.) 'What is this news?'

'The builders yesterday found something really interesting in the spare bedroom. I told you about the damp patch that has been there for years. Well, they finally decided to strip all the plaster off the north wall to try to work out where it was coming from. They found a bricked-up doorway near the fireplace.'

'Perhaps it's a priest's hole,' Caddie said. 'I read about them in history. The Catholic families used to hide the Jesuit priests when Queen Elizabeth sent the magistrates to capture them. Lots of old houses had them.'

'We thought of that,' Ruth interrupted her, 'but this house wasn't built till Oliver Cromwell's time. I don't think there are many priest's holes built after that. As soon as the men have cleared up all the plaster mess from their work yesterday they are going to open it because there is no trace of a doorway or window on the outside wall. George, the foreman, thinks it is just an old cupboard.'

'I wonder if there will be any hidden treasure,' Caddie said, her imagination beginning to whirl.

'As far as I'm concerned the best treasure will be to find the leak where the rain has been getting in. Now hurry up and get dressed. The builders, George and Phil, will be here at 9 o'clock and I want to have breakfast cleared away by then.'

Even Robert had left his beloved cows to watch the wall being breached. The doorway, if it was a doorway, was only about four feet high, but it had been clearly blocked in at a later date using bricks, whereas the rest of the wall, like the house, was made of Portland stone. Phil was a large cheerful man whose boiler suit was already well covered with cement dust and paint. He was preparing to swing his pickaxe at the brickwork, as intrigued as the others by what might be behind it, when George stopped him.

'We'll take this down with hammer and chisel,' he said. 'We don't know what might be behind the wall, so none of the bricks must fall inwards.' He picked up his mason's hammer and started at the bricks at the top of the doorway, carefully chiselling out the mortar. The four watchers willed him on in their impatience, but George wasn't to be hurried. Eventually the top brick came loose and, like a dentist levering out a rotten tooth, he carefully drew it from the wall. Caddie thought that she could detect a musty smell coming with the draft through the hole, as George carefully laid the first brick on the ground and picked up his torch. He peered through the opening while the others stood waiting for his pronouncement. 'I can't see much,' he eventually said, 'but there's certainly a gap of sorts.'

The second brick proved quicker to remove as George was able to push his hand through the opening and work it from the inside. 'Not a very good building job,' he told them. 'The mortar's poorly mixed and the bricks aren't laid in courses properly.'

After ten minutes there was a sufficiently large hole for George to poke his head and shoulders through. 'It looks like a room, but very narrow,' he told them, his voice coming muffled through the wall. 'The outer wall's only three feet away, which must be why you can't tell there's a space from outside. There's something that looks like a bundle of blankets on the floor.'

He pulled his head back and offered the torch to Robert. 'You'd better take a look, Rob.'

Robert took a long time peering inside without saying anything. Eventually he pulled his head back into the room. 'I think your bundle of blankets, George, is a body. We shouldn't go any further until the police have had a look at this.'

Ruth and Caddie both tried looking through the hole, but despite having a vivid imagination Caddie could make out nothing but a bundle of blankets. She did notice that there were rushes on the floor, and it looked as if the roof of the tiny room was lined with bits of planking. Robert went off to phone the Dorchester police and came back to tell the others that a detective sergeant and a police photographer would be round immediately.

'Immediately' turned out to be three-quarters of an hour and it was an impatient trio who eventually accompanied Detective Sergeant Newton up the stairs to the back bedroom. He spent five minutes peering through the hole and decided he couldn't see anything, but everything should wait for the police photographer to arrive. Caddie asked if in the meantime they could take down the rest of the wall, but the sergeant shook his head.

'We must do everything properly, Caddie,' Robert explained.

'Your father is quite right, Miss,' the policeman said to her. 'This is a potential crime scene and we can't risk destroying any evidence that might be needed for an investigation. We must wait for the photographer.'

Caddie was about to correct the man, 'Uncle not father', when she noticed her uncle blushing and looking awkward. She decided it made no difference if the policeman thought Robert was her father or uncle.

It took another 45 minutes for the police photographer to arrive from the police headquarters at Winfrith, and Caddie grew more and more impatient as he took an age fiddling around adjusting his well-used Nikon. Eventually he decided he had a good enough shot of the wall, and George and Phil took it in turns to carefully prise out the remaining bricks. Every now and then the pedantic photographer insisted on another photo of the gradually lowering wall until the last brick was removed. Sergeant Newton now felt the hole was large enough for him to squeeze through without loss of dignity.

After five minutes, which seemed much longer to those waiting outside, he poked his head out into the bedroom and asked the photographer to join him. Caddie counted ten flashes as the bundle was photographed from every angle. There was a pause and the photographer and policeman, stooping through the low doorway, came back into the room. The sergeant looked solemn and not a little self-important.

'I have to tell you that it is a body, or at least a skeleton that was once a body lying on the floor. I am no expert but I believe it is very old. Until the police pathologist has had a chance to look at it, I must consider this space to be a potential crime scene, and I'm sorry, but none of you can go in there until authorised by a senior officer. Mr Broad!' He looked across to the builder. 'Grab some wooden battens and nail them across here. You can clear up the mess of bricks, but don't any of you go through the door.'

Robert and Ruth accompanied Sergeant Newton downstairs as he began to explain to them what was likely to happen next. Phil and George went off to the barn where Robert had said there were some planks they could use and Caddie suddenly found herself alone in the room.

Despite the very clear instructions from the policeman she could not resist the temptation to have a quick look though the doorway. George had left his torch lying on the floor and she went to pick it up, while listening to the fading drone of Sergeant Newton's voice as he went down the stairs to the kitchen with the photographer. Caddie shone the torch into the tiny room. The far wall was less than a metre away and the whole space was less than two metres high. She could see where Sergeant Newton had moved some of the clothing, exposing the bones of a foot and lower leg. Despite the musty smell, which she thought she had detected when the first brick was removed, the air seemed to be remarkably fresh. She flashed the torch up to the ceiling and could see clearly where the damp had run down from the ceiling onto the inside wall. *No wonder they couldn't fix it,* she thought. *It's not properly outside or in.* The roof of the little room was made of rough planking and in places she spotted odd bits of thatch pushing through the gaps.

Hearing George and Phil coming back up the stairs, she slipped quickly from the room, carefully putting the torch back where she had found it. She met them in the bedroom doorway trying not to look too guilty, but Phil grinned at her and she knew he guessed where she had been.

***

George and Phil had been told not to return until the house had been given the all clear by the police. It was four days before the forensic pathologist from Bournemouth phoned to say he would be coming the next day. He asked if he could bring a colleague who was an expert in old skeletons and Robert readily agreed. The pathologist, Dr Corbett, was old and wrinkled, but Caddie reckoned he looked wise enough. The expert who accompanied him was Dr Rachel Greenleaf from the Museum of London. She hardly looked old enough even to have gone to university, let alone earn a doctorate, but she was obviously full of energy and the venerable Dr Corbett seemed to hold her in some awe.

'Dr Greenleaf is one of the curators at the Centre for Human Bioarchaeology at the Museum of London,' Dr Corbett explained. 'Her specialism is osteology.

Caddie looked confused and Dr Corbett added kindly, 'Bones. It was Dr Greenleaf who dated the Viking skeletons found on the Dorset Ridgeway when they were building the Weymouth Relief Road. We really are very fortunate to have her here. There really is no one better.'

'Enough guff, Henry. Let's see the dead chap.' Caddie found Dr Greenleaf's relaxed manner refreshing after the ponderous attitude of Sergeant Newton, which she could see being echoed by Dr Corbett.

'You must be Caddie, daughter of the house. My name is Rachel.' She could see that Caddie was aching to be involved. 'Could you be our assistant? Henry and I will be messing around with the body and we need someone to act as our liaison. Caddie nodded her agreement. 'In the meantime, keep the coffees rolling our way. Mine's a Julie Andrews.' When Caddie looked confused Rachel roared with laughter at her own joke. 'Julie Andrews – White Nun. Get it? Henry's is black with no sugar.'

'I suppose that's a Whoopi Goldberg,' Caddie said and that made Rachel laugh again. Doctor Corbett hadn't a clue what they were talking about. In her new role, Caddie led the two scientists up to the bedroom and fetched them the first of many coffees.

'What we have here, Caddie, is a sort of walk-in wardrobe. The French word was *garderobe*, which roughly translated means *looking after clothes*. But *garderobe* was also a polite way of talking about an indoor toilet, what we still euphemistically call a cloakroom. Dr Corbett and I will look at the poor chap now, but I guess you could say he died in the loo.'

Caddie listened attentively as the two scientists discussed the body, never frivolously, but not pompously either. Before they entered the tiny chamber they put on white boiler suits and a pair of thin rubber gloves. Rachel handed a third pair of gloves to Caddie. There was not sufficient room for them both to work in there at the same time, so as Dr Corbett carefully uncovered the skeleton, Rachel photographed every step they took. When Dr Corbett tried to remove the jacket from the body, the material fell apart.

'We're lucky even to have this amount left,' Rachel explained to Caddie. 'The whole body has been covered in this white powder which I'm guessing is crushed limestone. It will certainly have hastened decomposition. The air in here is remarkably dry and there's no evidence of moths, but you can see here and here,' she pointed to two spots along the body's flank, 'where the rats have torn at the material to get to the flesh. Put these in one of those plastic bags, will you?' She passed Caddie a handful of small dull-looking round objects. 'They look like military buttons and with them we should be able to date this chap fairly accurately.'

Dr Corbett, on his knees, was working on the skeleton. 'Look at this, Rachel.' He carefully lifted the skull from the floor and passed it out.

'That's what probably killed him.' Rachel pointed out to Caddie the wide crack in the back of the skull where a piece of bone was missing. 'Could have been a blow from a club or some heavy object. We might be able to find out later. It certainly wasn't a sword cut or a bullet wound, and he didn't die in bed. On reflection, it seems more likely that he was hidden in here than died here. This might well be a murder victim.'

She placed the skull carefully on a plastic sheet and photographed it from several angles before popping it into another plastic bag. 'When we have had a chance to look at this in the lab we'll be able to tell much more.'

Dr Corbett came stooping out of the little room, pulling off his rubber gloves. 'Could you fetch your father please, Caddie?'

Caddie found Robert and Ruth sitting in the kitchen. 'The Doctors will see you now, father,' Caddie grinned at Robert. He gave her a playful shove as he went past and all three of them went upstairs. There they found Dr Corbett carefully packing the skull into a container padded with foam,

'Mr Jolliffe. An initial investigation would suggest that the body here is at least 300 to 400 years old. It is likely that the man died from a blow to the head, so technically this is still a crime scene, but I suspect that it's going to be more a matter for the archaeologists than for the police. I'll send two orderlies from the laboratory to collect the skeleton tomorrow. Please don't go into the room until the body is removed. You'll get a copy of the final report when it has been completed, but that's likely to take some weeks.' Caddie led them downstairs as Rachel asked about family history. When they reached the kitchen, Robert proudly showed her the great Bible, which she looked at with interest.

'When we've finished in the lab,' she told him, 'we'll have a pretty accurate idea of when he lived, how he died and how old he was when he died. I'd be grateful if I could come back and look at this again. We should be able to work out from the Bible if it was a family member. Oh, I should mention that news of this find is bound to get out. There will be plenty of people at the police headquarters with contacts in the local press. I'd prepare yourselves for an invasion from newspapers and possibly TV journos. You can chat to them as much as you like, but I would suggest you don't show them the room until after the body has been removed. I guess that will cause less of a problem. It will be a bit hectic for a couple of days but then it should die down.'

The next few days were in fact a nightmare for Robert. A reporter and photographer arrived from the *Echo* the next morning before they had finished breakfast. Robert explained that he would not show them the cupboard until the body had been removed, but he did give them an interview with the rest of the family round the kitchen table. Robert told Ruth and

Caddie that they should refer to the little room as a wardrobe. It would be far more sensational to describe it as an ancient toilet, but sensational was the last thing he wanted. When the van arrived from the laboratory, the *Echo* staff tried to follow the orderlies up the stairs, but Robert stopped them physically by blocking the way. However, he couldn't prevent them from photographing the bagged corpse as it was carried out of the farmhouse to the van. Only when the van had driven off did he allow the reporter and the photographer into the bedroom to see where the body had been found.

The following morning at breakfast Robert nervously opened the local paper.

MURDER AT CORTON FARM

The banner headline shrieked at him. There followed a lurid story, some of it based on facts gleaned from yesterday's interview, but most of it guesswork. Then the telephone started ringing. For the rest of the morning Robert and Ruth gave telephone interviews while Caddie answered the door to three local reporters.

In the afternoon a video journalist from Newsroom Southwest interviewed Robert, and Caddie showed her the room where the body had been found and told her what Dr Greenleaf had said.

'If I can't cut and edit it by 6.30 this will be on the lunchtime news tomorrow. It's such a good story the networks may want it. I do hope so because it'll be my first.'

The day after wasn't much better and Robert, Ruth and Caddie found themselves saying the same thing over and over again.

By suppertime Robert had had enough. 'No more,' he announced. 'I'm a farmer, not a bloody news story. Tomorrow and from now onwards we give no more interviews. I'll ring George first thing and ask him to fix the leak and fill in the damned door again.'

Ruth had never heard Robert swear before.

Chapter 4
An Unwelcome Companion
11th June 1685

Ethan could not think of a time when he had not loved horses. His father had bought him his first pony called Mini when he was three and it was on Mini that he and his brothers and sister had all learned to ride. Although it was some years since he had ridden her, it was always to Ethan that Mini came nuzzling when he entered the stables and it was only Ethan whom she allowed to treat a painful abscess on her hind leg. It was because of his love of horses and their obvious trust in him that he had been sent aged 13 to work in the stables at Forde Abbey. He knew that Daniel, his younger brother, was cleverer than he was. Daniel had already taught himself to read and write, but Ethan was determined that when he inherited Corton Farm he would breed horses. It was an ambition he had kept quiet from the rest of his family. You didn't need to know how to read in order to breed horses.

It was still dark when he left the house, scooping up a piece of his mother's pie and some bread from the larder on the way out. Tor whickered when he opened the stable door and looked round at him, blowing steam from his nostrils in the cold early morning air. Tor, a well-built black stallion, was Sir Edmund Prideaux's favourite of all the horses in his stable and only Ethan of the stable boys was allowed to ride him. It was a measure of Sir Edmund's trust in him that he had been allowed to take Tor away overnight. Ethan talked quietly to the horse as he ran his hands down his flanks and legs searching for any unexpected warm spots. 'You had a hard day yesterday and we've another long ride today, boy. We'll take it slowly enough and we should both be all right.' He stood in front of the beautiful animal and, taking one of Tor's hooves onto his lap, gently stretched his tendons. He then repeated this with the other leg. All the time Tor gently nuzzled at his shoulder.

Within ten minutes horse and rider were trotting the last few yards through the rough scrubland to the top of the Ridgeway. The sky was now light and the sun just peeping over the trees to the east when Ethan stopped to look back at the view. To the west he could see the great sweep of the pebble bank called Chesil Beach. Somewhere over there, given good fortune and fair weather, the Duke of Monmouth and his army would be landing at Lyme Regis. In front of him the dark and sinister finger of the Isle of Portland stretched out into the sea, with the sands of Weymouth Bay just visible. To the east the rising sun was striking the chalk cliff of White Nothe. This was a view Ethan knew well. He was aware that he had not yet seen much of the world, but he doubted if there could be a more beautiful sight anywhere. He turned Tor to the north and prepared to drop off the Ridgeway down the old Roman road into Dorchester. Sir Edmund had ordered him to hand over his package first thing in the morning while warning him that he might be in danger if he was caught by the militia. The boy had an address to go to, but for security he had only been given the man's name as John and told that he was a weaver.

Tor and Ethan stopped by the Winterbourne a couple of miles short of Dorchester. In the dry summer months the chalky land usually swallowed up the stream completely, but Ethan knew a pool where there was always water all year round. He had not wanted to disturb his family by his early start so, while Tor drank deeply from the clear water, Ethan took the opportunity to wash himself and eat his mother's pie and the bread for his breakfast. Though Ethan had no book-learning at all he was not a stupid boy. He was aware that the enterprise he was engaged in was hazardous and he had worked out rough plans of what to do if he was stopped. He fully expected there to be a guard at the town gate near Maumbury Rings, there usually was, but he hoped that it might be someone he knew and he had his reasons for travelling to Dorchester well prepared. It was still a shock when he saw that there was a pole stretched across the road and five or six members of the Dorsetshire Militia standing around, obviously prepared to challenge travellers. It was too late for him to change directions as he had already been spotted. He would have to bluff it out.

'Morning, Sergeant.' Ethan addressed the portly man who, he could see by the stripes on his jacket, was in charge.

'That's a good horse for a young lad like you. Whose is it and where are you going, boy?' The question seemed to be routine.

Ethan explained that the horse belonged to his employer Sir Edmund Prideaux of Forde Abbey who was an important magistrate. 'Sir Edmund told me to borrow Tor as he needed to send a message to my father.' He trotted out the story he had prepared just for such an eventuality as this.

'That's Ethan Jolliffe, Sarge.' One of the other soldiers got up from the little fire where he was brewing some tea. 'Morning, Ethan. The Jolliffes have the farm over Portesham way, Sarge. That's where my family gets their milk from. I heard that Ethan here was working somewhere near Chard.'

The sergeant seemed to be satisfied by this and was about to wave Ethan and Tor through when a further question occurred to him. He wrinkled his nose in thought, trying to put his thought into words. 'If you live near Portesham and you're going back towards Chard, why are you here? You should have gone by St Martinstown. That would be quickest. Why are you on this road?' His eyes narrowed suspiciously. 'What's in your bag there?' He pointed at the satchel slung over Ethan's shoulder.

Ten minutes ago Ethan had hoped that if there were a guard at the town gate he would be known to him. Now it seemed he could well be in trouble because the soldier had identified him so completely. He was horribly aware that he was in considerable danger, and not just him but his family too. He tried to keep calm and look unconcerned while his mind raced.

'Oh, that's something Sir Edmund told me to give to the priest at St Peter's.' He tried to remember what his father had read out the previous evening. 'It's some paper to do with the Duke of Monmouth who's supposed to be landing around here soon. I think it's a warning to all the people of Dorchester, which the Rector has to read out from his pulpit. I expect that's why you are all here, isn't it?'

The sergeant had no wish to admit he had no idea why he and his section had been told to check on all travellers. 'That's for me to know and you to guess at, boy. Show me the paper.

This was scary for Ethan, but he tried to pull one of the sheets out as casually as possible. 'Tell me what it says,' the fat sergeant ordered.

The other soldiers had drifted back to their fire and the brewing tea. 'I don't know how to read, Sir,' Ethan explained. He desperately hoped that the sergeant also was a poor reader, and it did seem that the man was reluctant to expose this ignorance to the other troopers by asking for help. He quickly glanced at the poster and handed it back. His orders were to look out for people, not posters. Ethan stuffed the paper back in his bag and gave the soldiers a cheery wave as the sergeant nodded him through the barrier.

Tor carefully picked his way through the mud and blood past the butchers' stalls of The Shambles, which led off the High Street near the site of the old priory. Ethan thought he knew Dorchester well, but this was not a part of town he was familiar with. The house of the weaver was towards the end of the road, just before the passage narrowed and dipped sharply down towards the corn mill and the river. The street refuse was piled high and Ethan compared the area unfavourably with his father's smart and well-swept yard at Corton. He secured Tor to a ring set in the wall of the house he had been told to go to. When he knocked on the door he identified himself to the weaver as coming from Sir Edmund Prideaux and he in his turn introduced himself as John Beavis.

'So the Duke is here at last.' His face lit up in a broad smile. 'We Congregationalists have been waiting for this moment,' he told Ethan. He quickly scanned the paper Ethan showed him. 'I see the Duke has promised freedom of worship to all Protestants, but is prepared to put his claim to the throne before Parliament. That is as it should be. Come in, Ethan. Mary!' he shouted over his shoulder, 'we have a visitor who looks as if he needs some breakfast.'

He led Ethan into the kitchen where Mary, his wife, was stirring something in a blackened pot hanging over the fire. 'Dorchester is a Dissenters town and I believe the Duke will be well received here.'

Mary Beavis was as serious and sad looking as her husband was cheerful and positive. *Like Jack Sprat and his wife,* thought Ethan. She carefully placed a bowl of porridge on the table in front of him and in silence returned to the fire and her cooking.

'Did you have any difficulty getting here?' the weaver asked him and Ethan told him what had happened at the town gate. For a moment the weaver's cheeriness left him. 'So they definitely knew who you were?' he asked.

Ethan explained how he had been recognised by one of the troopers. 'But I'm sure the sergeant wasn't able to read the pamphlet, and I definitely wasn't followed here, as I checked behind. No one knows your address.'

'These are posters. When they're put up all over Dorchester, Weymouth and up the Piddle valley,'

John Beavis pointed out, 'it won't take even the stupidest of soldiers long to realise how they arrived in the town. I'm afraid this will put you, your family and even possibly Sir Edmund in great danger.'

He thought for a while and then spoke quietly to his unhappy looking wife.

'She won't do it.' Mary Beavis whispered back angrily, though loud enough for Ethan to hear.

'She will if I order it so.' This time Ethan heard clearly what the agitated weaver said. 'Tell her to come down immediately.'

Mary left the room. John Beavis continued to pace up and down in the kitchen and in the silence Ethan could hear his wife climbing the stairs, followed by the sounds of conversation. Mary came back into the room followed by a girl who Ethan guessed must be 15 or 16 years old. She was wearing clothing he instantly recognised as Puritan. She walked with her eyes cast down and stood in front of John Beavis, her face in shadow from a white linen cap. Poking out below the puritan cap Ethan could see she had long black hair. Her floor-length dress was made of a dull brown woollen worsted, partially covered by a white linen apron and high collar. The weaver took one of her hands and turned her to face Ethan.

'This is my sister's child, Lucy. She came down from London to stay with us, as she has been unwell. Lucy, this is a new friend of ours called Ethan.'

The girl looked up. Her face was white and pinched looking. There seemed to be little sparkle in her eyes and her whole manner appeared listless and tired. She bobbed a small curtsey to Ethan, cast her eyes down again and said nothing.

'You are returning to Forde Abbey immediately?' John Beavis questioned Ethan.

'Yes, Mr Beavis. I promised Sir Edmund I would be back by nightfall.'

'You understand that you will be under suspicion as soon as I distribute the Duke's Declaration. To give you time to get clear, I will not post the copies you brought until tomorrow. I believe that Mary and I will be in great danger here, as the magistrates know that I am a leading Dissenter. I shall close up this house immediately. You must take Lucy with you to safety at Forde Abbey. Lady Prideaux is a friend of Dr Wells, Lucy's father, and will certainly look after her.'

Ethan's mind was in a whirl. He realised that his encounter with the militia had changed things, but he really had no wish to take this sulky, sickly girl with him the 20 miles to Forde.

'Can she ride?' he asked in the vague hope that the answer would be no.

'She rides well,' John Beavis told him, 'and she can borrow Mary's pony Becky. Sir Edmund will look after both Lucy and the horse until it is safe either for her to return here or to go back to London.'

'She's not coming with me in those clothes,' Ethan said rudely. 'It would take us days to get to Forde with her riding side-saddle and I promised to be back tonight. Anyhow, it's not seemly for a maid to travel with a farm lad. People would talk and that would put us both in danger.'

Up to now Lucy had said nothing and the conversation had proceeded as if she wasn't in the room. She looked up at Ethan and he noticed that her cheeks had reddened. Her sulkiness had gone. She was angry.

'If you will lend me some of Peter's clothes, Uncle, I'll travel dressed as a boy and I promise I will not hold him up. Aunt Mary, if you cut my hair, I believe I shall be adequately disguised.'

Ethan could think of nothing to say, but John Beavis was obviously shocked by her interruption. 'Your father would not wish you to cut your hair, my dear. Remember when St Paul said that a woman's long hair was her glory?'

'He also told the Corinthians, *If a woman be not covered let her also be shorn*,' Lucy answered, surprising Ethan with her firmness. 'I have decided that I shall go with him, Uncle. I will wear boy's clothes and I will cut my hair. Please come and help me get ready, Aunt. Let this boy know that I shall be ready shortly.' With that she left the room and went upstairs.

John Beavis shrugged his shoulders and smiled at Ethan. 'Lucy's mother, my sister, died of the plague in London in the spring. The girl also caught a fever and her father thought she would not survive. She had been very sick, so he asked us if she could stay here with us because he hoped the Dorset air would help her convalescence. She has been peaky and limp ever since she has been here. What you have just seen is the first spark of life I have seen in her since she arrived. From my experience of women, I don't think you will have much choice in the matter, lad.'

Ethan could think of nothing to say. He was annoyed that the matter had not been properly discussed. He had little enough experience with girls and the last thing he wanted was to nursemaid a sick and sullen girl back to Forde. But as John Beavis had said, it didn't look as if anyone was going to pay much attention to what he thought.

'Show me where Becky is stabled please.' If the horse was unsuitable to make the journey, he guessed that would give him a perfect excuse to say no. But Becky was a sturdy, healthy, chestnut pony, who certainly looked as if she could manage the trip to Forde easily. He patted her affectionately and inspected her hooves, hoping he would find there some reason for going back to Forde alone. But all four were well shoed and he couldn't think of anything else to prevent Lucy accompanying him.

'Which saddle shall I take?' he asked, and realised with that question the decision had been taken.

Chapter 5
The Notebook

Caddie had no qualms about going back into the little room. There was no skeleton, no unusual smell and, above all, no uneasy feelings. She decided to inspect the room thoroughly as if she was investigating an archaeological site, in the same way she had seen Dr Newton and Dr Greenleaf work when they had first gone in. She flashed her torch around the room … about two metres long by one metre wide she guessed. She cautiously went in and her head just touched the boards where the roof joined the wall. She was a little disappointed that it obviously wasn't a priest's hole. Even a small Jesuit would have found it difficult to live in there for any length of time. It was more likely to have been a wardrobe or even a *garderobe*, as Dr Greenleaf had said. She knew from her uncle that Corton Farm had once been thatched and that sometime in the early eighteenth century slates had been laid on top of the thatch. She wasn't surprised therefore to see old pieces of reed sticking through the gaps in the ceiling boards. The rushes on the floor were disintegrating where the two scientists had worked on the skeleton, and she could feel them crunch into dust as she carefully walked over them.

Caddie knew that George and Phil would be coming later to find the source of the damp patch and to brick the wall up again, so she was determined to discover everything she could while she had the chance. To her right the wall was badly discoloured where the rain had seeped in. Over her head she could see that one of the planks had become rotten and from here the water had run down the other planks onto the inside wall. She reached up to see if the damaged plank was loose and a rotten piece of wood came away in her hand. She looked around guiltily, but there was no one to see what she had done. She reckoned she could shove the piece back into the thatch and when George and Phil came to look for the leak she would tell them what had happened. She was sure no one would mind. The chunk of wood was reluctant to slide into the thatch and when she held the flashlight close she saw a black object blocking the way. She reached up and gently pulled at it and a small book fell to the floor as a shower of fragmented reeds and dust spattered onto her face. Caddie spat the dust from her mouth and picked up the book. Putting the rotten plank back in position was no longer important. She took the book up the attic stairs to her bedroom and went over to the window to inspect it. It wasn't black as she had first thought, but bound in brown leather and about the size of a paperback. The bottom corner was damp and had been discoloured over time. The pages of the book were stuck together and as she tried to open it she felt one of them begin to tear. *I'd better not damage it any further,* she thought. *I'll see what Robert and Sarah have to say. After all, this is their property.*

'I think I've found what might have been causing the rain to get in,' she told them as they sat down to lunch. 'This was shoved into the thatch and probably disturbed the tiles.'

She handed the book to her uncle who looked at it suspiciously, turning it over in his hands. 'I tried to open it up,' Caddie continued, 'but the pages are stuck together with damp and I'm afraid one of them tore a bit.'

Robert handed the little book to Sarah who inspected it much more thoroughly than he had. 'When it has dried out a little I think the pages will unstick,' she said. 'We had better send it to that helpful lady from London, Dr Greenleaf wasn't it? I'm sure she could tell us.'

'I'm not sending it anywhere,' Robert spoke fiercely. He was normally so mild mannered, Sarah had seldom seen him so agitated. 'If we do, we will either have to stop George bricking up the wall again, or take it all down as soon as the next team of experts arrive. No one has been any the worse off for all the time it has been in that room. As far as I am concerned it can go back in there and stay there.'

'What's the matter, Robert dear? Is it the publicity you're worried about?'

'I can't be doing with all that press and people coming to ask for interviews again,' he admitted. 'It was bad enough over the last few days, but once we get historians, treasure seekers and nosey-parkers coming here it will go on for weeks. I'll not have it.'

'As I found it, could I keep it, please uncle?' Caddie asked. 'I would like to see what is inside, and I promise to keep it a secret.' To Caddie's great pleasure her Uncle reluctantly consented, but they all had to agree that they would not even let George and Phil know what had been found.

'I'll put it in the airing cupboard, Caddie,' Sarah said. 'In a day or two it should be dry enough to separate the pages.'

Later that afternoon George reported that he had cut back some of the reeds from the thatch near a chimneybreast at the end of the cupboard. The source of the leak seemed to be the lead flashing round the chimney. He promised that with some roofing ladders he could fix it the next day. The roof would be secure enough now and the damp patch should disappear in the dry weather within the week. 'If you want me to brick up the doorway, Robert, I can do that this afternoon, and come back to replaster the wall next week.'

By nightfall the little room was once again sealed shut.

CHAPTER 6
Lucy Revealed
11th June 1685

Tor delicately picked his way through the mud and rotting vegetables of Dorchester High Street. The noise and bustle at midday contrasted with the quiet when Ethan had arrived that morning. Stall-holders in the market shouted at prospective customers as pigs and chickens scuttled between Tor's legs. A scabrous dog glanced up from the detritus it was searching through to bark at the two horses before returning to its scavenging. Ethan, in front, loved the commotion and energy of Dorchester on market day. Lucy, looking nervously around, followed on Becky much less certainly.

It had taken Lucy over two hours to get ready to leave; two hours that Ethan had spent chewing his nails in frustration at the delay. When dour Mary eventually brought her downstairs, he was hard put to recognise in the slim, short-haired youth that entered the kitchen the puritan maid who had gone up the stairs earlier. Mary had prepared some food for them both and packed a change of clothes and a water bottle in the saddlebag that was now slung across Becky's neck. John Beavis had hugged Lucy goodbye, with strict instructions to Ethan to look after her and keep her safe. It appeared to Ethan that Lucy was as anxious to set off on the journey as he was.

On the outskirts of Dorchester the horses forded the River Frome and Ethan slowed to let Becky catch up. The two continued side by side in silence.

'Who is Peter?' Ethan eventually asked.

'John and Mary's son.'

'Where is he now?'

'He's apprenticed to a weaver in Wimborne.'

'Those his clothes?'

'Yes.'

The conversation seemed pretty pointless to Ethan. Dragging answers out of Lucy was tougher than mucking out the stables on an icy February morning, and that wasn't much fun. He gave up and the two of them continued alongside each other in an unfriendly silence.

'Let's trot for a bit. The horses are properly warmed up now and it will be good for them to stretch their legs.' He didn't wait for a reply from Lucy but dug his heels into Tor's flanks. As he drew ahead he turned and shouted over his shoulder, 'Let me know if I'm going too fast.' Tor's controlled trotting was relaxed and comfortable. The big horse covered the ground in long, easy strides. At times like this Ethan felt he could ride for ever. He took savage pleasure in listening to Becky's chattering hooves falling further and further behind. It won't be long before the girl asks me to slow down he thought and the idea pleased him.

When he arrived at the road junction where the track to Forde left the Yeovil road he slowed down, realising that Lucy wouldn't know which road to take. He looked round and was surprised to see how far behind she was. Lucy and Becky plodded slowly along at a walk and it was some time before they pulled up next to him. Ethan was shocked to see that Lucy was quietly crying. He could think of nothing to say, but he quickly realised that his behaviour had been churlish and unreasonable.

'Sorry,' he mumbled and swung himself off Tor's back. 'It's time we ate something.' He offered to help her dismount, but Lucy shook her head and led Becky over to a patch of grass. She took down the saddlebag and unpacked some of Aunt Mary's food.

'You should have asked me to slow down a bit,' Ethan eventually said.

'If you are as good with horses as Uncle John says, you should know that Becky couldn't keep up with your horse,' she said bitterly.

This was so obviously true that Ethan could think of nothing to say that would possibly excuse his behaviour. He sat down on the ground and patted the grass next to him. 'Come over here. I have said sorry and I really mean it. I was angry, but it was unfair of me to take it out on you.'

Lucy sat on the rough grass far enough away from him to demonstrate that he was not entirely forgiven, but close enough to hold a reasonable conversation. She opened the saddlebag and handed across a lump of cold meat and some bread. She pulled out the water bottle, had a drink and handed the bottle to Ethan. 'Why were you so angry?'

Ethan scratched his head, figuring out the answer. 'I wanted to get back to Forde as quickly as possible. I had promised my master, he's Sir Edmund Prideaux, that I would be back before night and it is important to me that I do what I have promised so he will continue to trust me. This isn't my horse; it's his favourite, called Tor. I'm the only one of the stable boys he allows to ride him.'

'I'll try not to hold you up.' Lucy hoped that Ethan hadn't noticed her tears. She wasn't usually so feeble. 'I have not been very well and I am not as strong as usual. This is the first time I have been on a horse since my sickness.' She went on to explain to him how she had nursed her mother when she had caught the plague and how she had nearly died herself when she had become infected. 'My father is a doctor, quite a famous one, at St Bartholomew's Hospital. I don't exactly know what he did, but I think the treatment he gave me saved my life. He didn't want me to stay in London with so much illness around so he asked Uncle John if he would look after me till I was stronger. I have been at Dorchester for two weeks, and you might not believe it to look at me, but I am already stronger than I was.' Lucy would not have been human if she hadn't quietly enjoyed the look of discomfort obvious on Ethan's face. She let him suffer a while and then let him off the hook. 'You weren't to know all that, and I can see why you were angry.'

They ate in silence for a while, but somehow it seemed to be a much more companionable silence. 'I think you ought to be Luke while we are on the road to Forde,' Ethan said. 'If you're going to pretend to be a boy, I can't go on calling you Lucy.'

You haven't called me anything yet, Lucy thought. 'Fine, if you think it's for the best, Luke I will be,' was what she said. 'Do you think I can pass for a boy?'

Ethan studied her more closely. With short hair and without the horrid puritan cap she didn't look quite as sulky as she had in the kitchen. *If she wasn't so pasty faced she could be quite pretty,* he thought. 'You'll do.'

If Lucy had expected a compliment she didn't show it. 'I have dressed as a boy before,' she told him. 'I think my father wanted a son to follow him as a doctor, but I turned out to be his only child. I expect he was disappointed in having a daughter, but he never loved me any the less. Instead he taught me astronomy, logic and medicine, things that most girls don't have a chance to study. For the last two years he has let me into the operating theatre with the other students. Even though he is very senior, he wouldn't have been allowed to let a girl in, so he dressed me in boy's clothes and told me not to speak. I would like to be a doctor, but the church will never, never allow it.'

'What about your hair?' Ethan asked. 'I saw back in Dorchester that it was long enough. Didn't the others recognise you were a girl?'

'When I went into the hospital I tied it up and hid it under the scholar's cap that all the students wear. I had a black gown also. Anyhow, the other students were so wrapped up in making a good impression on my father that they never looked at me.'

'What's logic?' Ethan asked nervously as if fearing a snubbing.

Lucy was not a vindictive person. Although she had been hurt by Ethan's mean behaviour she could see that it would be unkind to humiliate him just because he was uneducated. She decided to try to explain what her father had been teaching her. 'It's a way of thinking; a way of deciding what is true and what is false. I didn't completely understand it,' she admitted, 'nor could I see why it was important, but

Father said it was part of understanding something called the Scientific Method. My father is a follower of the ideas of Francis Bacon. He said that a scientist should observe, measure and experiment to arrive at the truth. That is what he has been teaching me to do.'

'I think I understand,' Ethan said. 'It's what I do with horses when they aren't well. I look carefully what the symptoms are and then try different medicines to see which of them produce a good result. Then next time I know better what to try first. If I could read and write, I know I could keep a good record of what cures had worked for which symptoms. This would help the other stable lads when I'm not around.'

'Oh, can't you read?' As soon as she had spoken Lucy regretted it. She saw Ethan's face close up and the sullen expression she had noticed in the Beavis house returned.

'It's time we got going,' Ethan said swinging himself onto Tor's back. Lucy scrambled over to Becky and, hastily remounting, trotted over to where Ethan was waiting for her. The two jogged along side by side in silence for a while, but he was far too good-natured a person to sulk for long. Lucy had plenty of time to study Ethan. At first she had thought he was an ill-mannered oaf, then she had thought he was just stupid, but as he talked about his family, his pride in them shone through everything he said. But it was when he discussed horses that he became really alive. It became obvious to her that despite his inability to read, it was lack of opportunity rather than lack of intelligence that held him back.

It was a hot June afternoon and they ambled alongside green cornfields and through meadows newly cut for hay. Lucy felt relaxed for the first time since her mother had fallen ill. To her surprise she found Ethan to be a much easier travelling companion than she had anticipated. The long silences were no longer uncomfortable. Though he wasn't handsome, his stocky frame, unruly red hair and cheerful face were unexpectedly attractive to her. Ethan told her at great length about the magnificence of Forde Abbey, though she doubted that someone who had been brought up within sight of Westminster Abbey and the Palace at Whitehall would find it impressive. At first she had found his Dorset burr faintly irritating, but as she had become used to his accent she found his voice comforting and reassuring. Ethan wanted to know why she had been wearing the clothes of a puritan maid and she explained how her father had met her mother at the Dissenters' Meeting House in Chelsea and they had brought her up as a strict Congregationalist.

'I try to read my Bible every day,' she told him, 'and to live by the words of Jesus.'

It was after eight in the evening that they waded the horses across the River Axe to the south of Forde Abbey. As Ethan explained, 'Sir Edmund doesn't like it if servants pass in front of the main house, and we'll waken the gleanies on the front lawn and when they cry out that might make Lady Prideaux angry. Let the horses drink as much as they want,' he instructed Lucy. 'They need to cool down a bit and it has been a long day for them.'

'What on earth is a gleanie?' she asked.

'Folk in the big house call them guinea fowl, but in Dorset we call them gleanies.'

Despite all Ethan's boasting Lucy was unprepared for her first sight of the superb building. Some parts, with tall honey-coloured walls and tiny slit windows showed clearly that it had once been a monastery before it became a private house. In the evening light it looked impressively grand and peaceful. Her exclamation 'Gracious heaven' was one of genuine admiration.

Despite his outward composure, Ethan had suffered a feeling of inferiority all day to this sharp and confident maid. He was quietly satisfied that the place where he now lived had come up to expectations. He led Lucy under a low arch into the stable courtyard.

'We'll leave the horses here. There's plenty of spare space for Becky, as the Duke has taken most of Sir Edmund's horses. Us lads live in the room above the stables.'

Ethan reported to Geoffrey Ostler who was in charge of the stables. 'Sir Edmund is away from the house but returning early tomorrow,' he was told. 'As soon as he's back I'll let him know of your return. I know he wants to see all of you lads who have been away. In the meantime you and the boy can have some food in the kitchen and there's plenty of space in the top chamber.'

'It's probably best that I stay as Luke tonight,' Lucy whispered, and it was as Luke of Dorchester that the two of them rubbed down and fed the horses, then made their way to the kitchen. After an excellent mutton stew, Ethan led Lucy through the stables to the loft known as top chamber, which was usually home for fifteen stable lads. They climbed the wooden ladder and both took a blanket from the pile stacked in the corner. Ethan whispered a warning to Lucy to steer clear of Foxy who was the unofficial leader of the hayloft. Christened George after the leader of the new religious sect, the Quakers, Foxy was far from being a pacifist like other members of the Society of Friends. His position as leader was confirmed not by intelligence or good looks, but by big fists and nasty temper.

'Hi, Foxy. This is Luke,' Ethan introduced Lucy. 'I've got to take him to see the master tomorrow morning.' *This should be enough to protect both of us from his vicious bullying for tonight,* he thought.

George Fox gave the two of them only a passing glance. He had another victim lined up this evening. Oliver, a whey-faced fourteen-year-old, was snivelling in the corner. Sir Edmund had taken him on to work in the stables as an act of charity when the boy's mother had recently died. Foxy, surrounded by other lads who were all too afraid to interfere, was taunting him about his dead mother. 'Just as well your ma died, Olly. She was so ugly ... face like a pig's arse ... no one would ever have fancied her again.'

This last comment was too much for Oliver who flew at Foxy in a rage, just the reaction George Fox had been hoping for. He held the younger boy away from him at arm's length, laughing at his feeble attempts to hit him. He then clattered him on the side of his face with a stinging open right hand. Oliver cried out, stumbled and fell to the ground. As Foxy advanced on him, still laughing, the frightened boy scrambled to the top of the stairway, trying to escape the advancing bully. Oliver unfortunately, still dazed by the blow, missed his footing, slipped and fell ten feet to the floor of the stables below. There was silence in the hayloft as the boys looked down on the body lying still on the ground.

'You've killed him, Foxy!' one of them said, as the other boys instinctively drew away from the tormenter.

Lucy, who was nearest to the top of the stairs, was one of the first to react. She cautiously climbed down the steps and knelt beside Oliver's body. 'He's not dead. He's knocked himself out. I think he's dislocated his shoulder as well.'

By this time some of the other boys had joined her in the stables. 'What do you know about it?' Foxy asked rudely.

Lucy, whose heart was beating rapidly, knew it would not do to show how scared she was. She stood up and faced George Fox. 'I've had training in how to deal with injuries like this from my father, who's a doctor.' She turned her back on him and spoke to the other boys. 'If you don't want him to die, you lot carry him carefully upstairs and lay him on a blanket. You,' she pointed at one of the boys standing next to her, 'get me some cold water.' They all seemed happy to accept Lucy's direction and four of them gently picked up Oliver, who was rapidly coming round, and carried him up the steps and took him to the far end of the hay loft.

George was fussing around like an old granny. He knew that if Geoffrey Ostler discovered his part in the incident he, George, would be kicked out immediately. He had no wish to lose this comfy job, as he had nowhere else to live. 'There's no need for Geoffrey to hear of this, is there?' He stood there, wringing his hands like an undertaker at a funeral.

Lucy could see that Oliver was coming round and she bent down over him. 'Keep your eyes closed and don't say anything,' she whispered in his ear. She turned to look at George. 'He's still breathing. There's no need to tell Geoffrey anything as long as he lives. Now all of you except Ethan clear off and give me some space.' She was quite surprised that all of them seemed to accept her authority quite naturally and shuffled off to the other end of the long loft.

Ethan knelt down next to her. 'Do you know what you're doing?' he whispered anxiously.

'I think so,' she answered quietly. She was pretty certain that the shoulder joint was dislocated and she knew it was important to put it back immediately. 'This one's a ball and socket joint and if the arm bone doesn't go straight back into the cup in the collar bone the muscles stretch, or something, and then it's much more difficult,' she told Ethan. 'Oliver has come round now and I told him to pretend to be unconscious, so I don't think he's in any actual danger.' She turned to the boy who was still lying on his back with his eyes closed. 'Oliver, your shoulder joint has come out and it needs to go back immediately. My name is Luke and I think I know what to do to help you. Do you want me to have a try?'

The boy opened his eyes and gave her a scared look. 'Will it hurt?' he asked.

'I honestly think it will hurt quite a bit, but I know it will hurt much more later if we don't do something now.' She looked down the room and saw all the boys were staring at her. She turned to Ethan. 'Help me to sit him up.' The two of them lifted Oliver into a sitting position. The boy tried hard to stifle a groan but was obviously in pain.

'Feel this bump here.' Lucy put her hand onto Oliver's right shoulder and Ethan felt where she directed. 'I don't think anything's broken, but this is where the joint has come out. If you get behind him and push on the knob when I say "now" and I pull at the same time, it should go back in.'

She put her face close to Oliver's ear. 'We're going to do it on the count of three. It will hurt and I want you to scream really loudly. That'll scare bloody Mr Fox.' Oliver gave her a wan smile. 'Lean his weight against your body, Ethan, and hold his shoulder back when I pull. Oliver, lift your arm onto my shoulder.' She helped the boy gently raise his arm. 'Ready, Ethan? One, two, three, now!'

No one could fault Oliver for the quality of his scream. Ethan felt the arm snap back into the socket, as Lucy sat back on the straw, shaking. Some of the other boys crowded round, but Ethan pushed them back.

'Foxy, thanks to Luke here, Oliver will probably be all right. If you have another go at him I'll personally tell Geoffrey exactly what happened here tonight. Instead, we'll tell him that Olly fell down stairs. The boy won't be fit to work for a few days. You'll offer to cover his work. As some of the lads are away at Lyme, Geoffrey will probably accept your offer without question.'

A very subdued George Fox agreed. Ethan wasn't sure how long this new Foxy would last, but at least Olly should be safe for a few days. Lucy bound the boy's arm to his chest with a piece of cloth, gave him a drink of water and then tucked the blanket round him. The other lads drifted off to their mattresses, chatting about what had happened. When Lucy had finished with Oliver, Ethan led her to the corner of the room where he had his mattress. He collected together some straw for her and the two lay down close to each other. The noise in the hayloft gently subsided into sleep.

Chapter 7
A Trip to London

15th July

Dear Mr Jolliffe,

I promised I would let you know as soon as I had some results from examining the skeleton of the poor chap you found in the cupboard. It will be some time before I have completed all my enquiries, but at least I am able to give you a little information, which should answer some of your questions. I am sure you will be pleased to know that as a result of my initial findings the police are no longer concerned about the case.

The skeleton is that of a male between the ages of 30 and 35. He was probably about five foot eight inches tall and had no apparent weaknesses in his bones, apart from a basilar fracture of the skull (more of that later) and a broken bone in the ankle, which had healed reasonably well. It was likely that the man still walked with a limp. From the bones I can tell he died sometime between 1655 and 1745. Despite all the newspaper and TV accounts about the accuracy of carbon dating, it is not possible to be more exact than that. The white powder turned out to be lime. Someone knew about its caustic properties and must have used it to cover the smell of decomposition.

There was enough of the cloth retained for me to establish that he was wearing a blue woollen jacket and I was able to identify the buttons that Caddie collected for me. Though they were badly discoloured, there is no doubt that they came from a jacket of someone in the Queen's Regiment of Foot. The symbol on the button is that of a walking lamb, carrying a flag over its shoulder and with a halo over its head. (There are still several pubs called the Lamb and Flag around today.) This regiment came to the West Country in 1685 and were known as Kirke's Lambs after their commanding officer Colonel Percy Kirke and the regimental badge. If you Google K's L you will see why our soldier chum might have been in your area.

As to cause of death, there is little doubt he died as a result of a single blow, which caused a fracture at the base of the skull (occipital bone). Such a blow would not always cause death, but a portion of bone dangerously close to the hole through which the spinal cord enters the skull had been dislodged. I have consulted a specialist at Barts, and showed him the skull. He told me that 9 times out of 10 such a blow would have caused instant death.

There you have it. In your cupboard was a 30-something-year-old soldier from Kirke's Lambs who died as a result of a single blow to the head. I have more measurement to do before I can begin to guess how the blow was delivered, but I thought you and your family would like to know my preliminary findings.

Tell Caddie she can compare the dates in the family Bible to see if it he was a Jolliffe. It would certainly be useful to be able to give the skeleton a name. Should she want to come and look round the

*Museum of London I would be very pleased to be her guide. She has my e-mail address.
Yours sincerely,
Rachel Greenleaf*

After a few days in Ruth's airing cupboard the little leather-bound book had dried out completely. Caddie had been itching to see what was inside the covers and Rachel's letter gave her the spur she needed. In her attic bedroom she set a small table under the window to give herself maximum light. The pages at the back of the book appeared to be damaged the least so she decided to start off there. Using her uncle's letter opener she gently worked the knife between the back page and the cover. The book opened and on the back page there was ... nothing. The last page was absolutely blank. But not quite nothing. The jagged edge next to the spine was evidence that a page had been torn out from the back of the book. Lucy carefully slipped the knife under the next page ... again nothing. She had been so certain that her little book was going to be an important discovery that she could have wept at the nothingness. She gazed at the book in disappointment. Then she realised, *of course. Any writing will be at the front of the book. Most of my notebooks are only half filled and I haven't often managed to get past February writing in diaries.*

The pages at the front of the book were much more tightly welded together by the damp, but she worked slowly and carefully with the letter knife until she was able to look at the first page. There was some writing there but it was too faint for her to make out words. She rushed downstairs to her uncle's desk where she had noticed a magnifying glass and sprinted back to her room. The faint lettering leapt towards her under the glass but was still too indistinct to be readable.

Robert was interested by the discovery. 'Shame we can't read it. I would like to find what was there. Is there any way of bringing the faded writing back to life?'

Neither Caddie nor her aunt could offer a helpful suggestion, but Caddie suddenly remembered that there was someone who would know. As she had promised to keep quiet about the book, one of the conditions her uncle had insisted on if she was to keep it, she decided not to tell him what she was thinking.

On the train journey up to London Caddie had rehearsed several conversations she might have with Rachel Greenleaf. She was nervous about the meeting, unsure if the invitation to visit had been sincerely meant. After Waterloo she had intended to take the underground to Monument and then, in good time for the suggested appointment, walk to the Museum from there. She became confused as Monument Station on the District Line was closed for some reason. She was worried that she would now be late and in a panic studied her tube map and A–Z to see how she could get to the Museum of London as quickly as possible. At Tower Hill she changed to the Circle Line and from Barbican Station she ran down Aldergate towards London Wall where she knew the Museum to be. Some steps signed to the High Walks and Museum of London led her to the front doors.

At first sight the Museum of London was a disappointment to Caddie. The dull flat-roofed building in amongst the glass-fronted office blocks of The Barbican was not as impressive as the Natural History Museum or the British Museum, both of which she had visited with her school. Inside the sliding doors, the atrium was dominated by a long white plastic desk shaped like a sea-slug. Groups of foreign students were sitting round the edges of the reception area eating their egg sandwiches and crisps and the young receptionist behind the desk, in best GCSE French, was trying to make herself understood to two young girls. Caddie waited impatiently till they had finished.

'I've an appointment with Dr Greenleaf. Sorry I'm a bit late.'

The girl smiled at her. 'You must be Caddie. Don't worry. Rachel told me you were coming. She's tied up with some reporter from *The Standard* at present, but she will come and collect you as soon as she is free. While you're waiting, why don't you look at the exhibition over there called *London before London*? It's really interesting and I'll find you somewhere when Rachel comes up.'

Caddie was engrossed in the drawings of wild animals feeding on the grasslands that would thousands of years later become the Thames Basin when the girl called her over. 'I'm Miranda by the way. Rachel has asked me to show you down to *Dem Bones*. I know it's a silly name, but that's what we call the area in the Rotunda where she works. It's much easier than saying the Centre for Human Osteoarchaeology.'

They took the lift down two floors and the girl led Caddie through a swing door into a low-ceilinged area lit entirely with strip lighting. 'She's over there,' Miranda said, 'Rachel, your visitor,' and she left to return to Reception.

Caddie had no need to have worried.

'Hi, Caddie. Glad you could make it.' Rachel came over, peeling off the inevitable latex gloves. 'I am pleased your father let you come.'

'He's my uncle actually. My parents are in Thailand.' Caddie was pleased she had at last corrected that mistake.

Rachel laughed. 'Silly me. I just assumed … you look so alike. Come and see your soldier flat out.'

They passed between shelves and boxes of bones to the far end of the room where several skeletons were laid out on a huge table. 'These are some of the skeletons found on Maiden Castle near your uncle's farm. They were dug up over 70 years ago by a famous archaeologist called Mortimer Wheeler, and I've been trying to work out exactly how they died. See this one? These cuts on the ulna,' she pointed at the arm of a skeleton near the edge of the table, 'the damage to this bone was I believe caused by a sword slash as she was trying to protect her head. That wouldn't have killed her. Look here at these broken ribs. That was a sword thrust to the heart. That certainly did for her.'

Caddie looked at the skeleton. 'How do you know it was a woman? I can't see any differences.'

'There are lots of small differences. After a while you learn to recognise them quite quickly. The most obvious is the female pelvis,' she pointed at the large flat bone which Caddie could see joined the legs to the rest of the body, 'women's are flatter and more rounded, probably to make it easier to have babies. This girl was about your age, and most likely a warrior killed in battle.'

Caddie wished that Rachel was her science teacher at school. Every single thing she said was more interesting than anything Mrs Buckley had tried to teach in two years of biology.

At the end of the table Rachel pointed out another skeleton. 'This is your soldier. Of course I realise he might not actually have been a soldier, he could have been wearing a jacket he had stolen, but I'm guessing he was one of Kirke's Lambs. See this bit missing at the back?' She held up the soldier's skull. 'This is undoubtedly what killed him. A blow caused the fracture, but it is an unusual injury. The blow seems to have come from below. Perhaps he was killed by a dwarf.' She laughed, putting the skull back on the table. 'Did you bring a record from the family tree?'

Caddie pulled out the family tree she had drawn and Rachel laid it on the table, moving some random teeth to make room.

'I couldn't see anyone who might have fitted your dates,' she said, and Rachel, quickly scanning the dates, agreed.

'Not a Jolliffe, by the looks of things. Sad, but we shall probably never know who he was.'

Caddie had prepared several artful ways she might ask Rachel some questions about the book without giving away her secret. But Rachel wasn't only sharp with bones. 'What have you found, Caddie?' It was quite a relief to Caddie that she didn't need to lie. She told Rachel the story of finding the book and the promise she had made to her uncle not to tell anyone. 'Please let me look at it. I can't believe you wouldn't have brought it with you.'

Caddie ferreted about in her bag and brought out the little book, carefully cocooned in bubble-wrap. 'I don't think I have done any damage to it.'

Rachel once again put on her latex gloves and studied the leather binding. She opened the book at page one and carefully laid it on the table. 'Let's look at it under a lamp. We'll try infrared first.' She brought over something that looked to Caddie like a hairdryer. 'If infrared, doesn't work we'll try ultraviolet.' She switched on the lamp, and immediately writing leapt from the page. 'Ah, that's good. See, Caddie, when the agent binding the ink has dried out there are usually traces of carbon left on the page and these are picked up by the infrared light. Now let's see what it says.' The two of them peered at the page. Rachel Greenleaf read out loud:

To my Dearest Daughter.

Caddie noticed that the *s* of dearest was written as an *f* just as her uncle had told her. Under that she could make out the words

Gather observable, measurable evidence, experiment, formulate hypotheses and modify by testing.

Then there was a gap on the page and around the middle she read:

If I have seen further it is by standing on the shoulders of giants.

There was something else written on the bottom of the page but it had become unreadable because of the discolouration caused by the damp.

'What does it mean?' Caddie asked.

'The first bit's easy,' Rachel answered. This is a nice expensive present from daddy. Expensive because the leather binding is calfskin. Daddy was probably a scientist and could have been a disciple of Francis Bacon.' She pointed at the words at the top. 'This is the basis of what we call the Scientific Method. These are near enough Bacon's word. We were taught at college *systematic observation, measurement, experiment*, but it means the same as this. Now this second bit is a quotation from Isaac Newton:

"Standing on the shoulders of giants."

'Isn't that carved on the edge of the £2 coin? One of the teachers at school told us about it,' Caddie interrupted.

'Yes, Newton wrote this in a letter to Robert Hooke in 1675,' Rachel said, pointing to the writing on the page, 'and at the time it was taken to be an insult to Hooke, who was a tiny little chap. From this we know definitely that your book can be dated post 1675. Pity that we will never know what was at the bottom here. The damp has ruined that.'

'Can this writing be recovered?' Caddie asked.

''Fraid not. Once gone it has gone for ever. It can only be read under a lamp. Let's see what Dearest Daughter has written.'

Carefully she inserted a thin blade between the first and second pages and slowly, using minimal effort, eased the blade from bottom to top. As before, the pages appeared blank, but under the hairdryer lamp a very faint drawing of a plant appeared. Underneath was the caption *Sweet Gale (called Bog Myrtle in Dorset). Found by the River Frome.* On the opposite page was another flower with just a tiny fleck of blue on one of the petals. This was captioned *Periwinkle*.

'These are pretty good drawings,' Rachel said. 'Now let's see how they do under ultraviolet light.' She fetched what was much more like a recognisable table lamp and plugged it in. The effect was the same. Once more the letters and drawings jumped up from the page. 'Good,' Rachel said. 'UV is much easier to manage and means you can do this at home with less risk of setting fire to the farm. You should be able to buy a UV lamp on e-bay for about a tenner. Actually I think we've got a spare one in the odds and sods cupboard, which I can let you have. It'll save you spending your pocket money.' She turned back to the book. 'This looks like a young girl's notebook to make simple nature recordings for daddy. I'm perfectly happy for you to do this at home. Open the pages carefully like you've seen me doing and let me know if you discover anything interesting.'

Chapter 8
Further Responsibility
12th June 1685

It was still dark when the other stable lads left the hayloft and made ready to start work. Ethan and Lucy lay for a while on their mattresses, listening to the sounds of a busy household waking. They could hear the boys larking around by the pump as they washed. When it became quiet Ethan told her that they would have gone to the kitchen to get their breakfast. Lucy couldn't strip off like the boys but she washed herself as best she could while Ethan worked the pump for her. She took her turn on the handle while Ethan doused himself with the cold water. She couldn't help noticing, with his shirt off, that he had a powerful and well-muscled body.

The two made their way to the main house where, in the staff parlour, Cook served them with a generous helping of ham and eggs. Half way through breakfast a young footman, correct and serious in his grey jacket and breeches, came in to let them know that Sir Edmund was waiting to receive them. Even though Ethan had lived for four years at Forde Abbey he now entered a part of the house that was entirely new to him. He felt scruffy and awkward walking through so much wealth and grandeur. He glanced across at Lucy who looked remarkably relaxed. The footman led them up the grand staircase, warning them to keep their dirty feet clear of the carved balustrade, which the housemaids had to dust every morning. They waited at the top of the stairs while he knocked and entered the highly carved double doors. A few minutes later he came out and gestured with his head. 'Sir Edmund'll see you now.'

The saloon was the largest private room that Ethan had ever seen. Two of the walls were covered in vast brightly coloured tapestries illuminated by the early summer sunshine streaming through the three windows on the south wall. Despite it being summer, a log fire was blazing in the marble fireplace. Sir Edmund Prideaux was standing comfortably in front of the fire with his hands behind his back. Ethan moved over towards him and managed a sketchy bow. 'Welcome back, Ethan. Who is this you have brought to see me?'

Lucy stepped forward and introduced herself. 'My father is Dr Gideon Wells. I am told he is a friend of yours in London. I have been staying in Dorchester with my uncle and aunt, John and Mary Beavis. I believe my uncle is acquainted with you. Uncle thought, given the present uncertainties, I would be safer if I came to stay with you.'

Sir Edmund smiled. 'I hope he is right, my dear. You are welcome to stay with us for as long as is necessary.' He turned to Ethan. 'Now, young man, tell me how you got on.'

Ethan told Sir Edmund about the encounter with the militia on the outskirts of Dorchester, and how unfortunately he had been identified by one of the pickets, and the decision taken for Lucy to accompany him back to Forde. 'I think John Beavis thought Lucy would be in considerable danger staying in Dorchester. He felt that as soon as the

Proclamation was posted things would start warming up there and he and his wife might need to go into hiding. It was Mr Beavis's idea that Lucy would be safer on the journey over here dressed s a boy.'

'Lucy, I am sure my wife will be delighted to have a female companion in the house.' He rang a small hand bell and when the footman appeared asked him to request Lady Prideaux's presence in the saloon. 'I am uncertain though how much safer you will be here than in Dorchester. I fear my position has been compromised and I know the Chard magistrates suspect my loyalty to the Crown.'

After only a few awkward moments, Lady Prideaux arrived in the saloon. She was a small, timid-looking woman, some years younger than her husband. Ethan knew her quite well as he had, on occasions, been delegated to accompany her on her rides round the estate. He knew her to be a cautious horsewoman, and gossip from the chambermaids said she found managing the household a problem as she disliked taking decisions. She nodded to Ethan as she passed him and went to stand next to her husband. He quickly explained Lucy's situation to her.

'You poor child. We must get you out of those frightful clothes immediately. Do you mean you spent last night in the stables? You should have sent a message to me as soon as you arrived.'

Ethan could see that Lucy was uncomfortable with all the fussing, and he had no chance even to say goodbye to her as she was whisked away to another part of the big house unknown to him.

As the door closed Sir Edmund addressed himself once more to Ethan. 'You have done well. I regret that in carrying out my orders you may well have put yourself and your family in danger. John Beavis will never betray us, but it is possible that one of the soldiers might well remember that it was you who brought the Duke's Proclamation into Dorchester. I must speak to your father as soon as possible.' When Ethan assured him that Nathaniel was in all likelihood already on his way over to Forde, Sir Edmund looked relieved. 'I will send for you again when he arrives. It may well be that I have further work for you.'

Late in the afternoon Ethan was grooming Tor in long sweeping circles with the curry comb when he heard horses arriving in the yard. A few minutes later Daniel came into the stables, leading two of the Corton farm horses. Daniel grinned at his elder brother. 'Father and I are going to fight with the Duke of Monmouth. At least I think we are. Father is talking to your master now to get his agreement.' His words bubbled out in his excitement. 'Mother wasn't happy about it, but Father and I wore her down and in the end she agreed. She made Father promise that he would look after me, but I don't mind that. The main thing is I'm off to join the army.'

Ethan smiled at his brother's enthusiasm. *How absurdly young he is to be a soldier*, he thought. *I guess he should be safe enough with Father to keep an eye on him.*

The same young footman, who had fetched Ethan earlier, came to the door of the stables. He looked disdainfully at the muck on the floor and chose not to come inside. 'Sir Edmund wants to see you straight away.' Ethan spent a couple of minutes rinsing his hands, face and boots under the pump and then followed the young man once more up the grand staircase.

His father, sitting upright on one of the two settees, nodded a greeting to him, but it was Sir Edmund who spoke. 'If you are willing, Ethan, I have another task for you, which might prove to be equally dangerous. Your father is taking your brother Daniel to Taunton. I have asked him to make sure that town is ready for the Duke's arrival in a few days. I'm hoping that Somerset will be able to raise a sizeable army for him. They leave in the morning. I have a different task for you. Tomorrow I would like you to take a message from your father to your aunt and uncle in Bridport and then next day ride on to find the Duke. I don't know if he will still be in Lyme Regis but you will certainly find news of his whereabouts when you get close. Your father has a letter for you to give to his sister, my message to Monmouth I will not write down. That you must deliver in person.'

He stood for a while gazing out of the window while Ethan shifted uncomfortably from one foot to another. Then he sighed and turned back to face Ethan. 'Tell his Grace that though my heart is with him, I cannot afford to join him in person. Because he came to stay with me five years ago I am already suspect and have heard rumours to expect my arrest any day now. Tom Dare has already taken to him most of my horses. He also has my prayers and best wishes for the success of his venture. Can you remember that boy?'

'Yes, sir,' Ethan nodded and repeated the message. He was disappointed not to be going to Taunton where there was likely to be action.

However, this adventure had possibilities. Though he was keen enough to go, he didn't actually remember having been given the chance to say yes or no.

'I want you to take this to him.' He handed Ethan a leather moneybag, which by its weight must contain a great many coins. 'Tell him I will send more as soon as I can raise it.' He looked across to Ethan's father. 'Can the boy be trusted to do this, Nathaniel?'

'I'd trust him with my life.' Ethan felt a glow of pride at his father's words. 'Take care, Son. It's more important that you arrive safely than swiftly. Don't travel at night and travel in company if possible.' He handed Ethan a letter. 'Give this to your Aunt Anne. She'll put you up for the night. God go with you.' He went over to Ethan and put his arms round him in a fierce hug, something he had not done for many years.

Ethan hid the moneybag inside his shirt and returned to the stables. There he found Daniel grooming the Corton horses, watched by an admiring group of off-duty chambermaids who often sneaked down to the stables to chat to the lads. Evie, who Ethan was uncomfortably aware had a soft spot for him, was questioning his brother. Her companions tugged at her dress till she looked round and saw Ethan standing in the doorway. 'He's much taller than you,' she told him pertly, 'and more handsome too.'

Ethan grinned. He had plenty of experience as to how to deal with Evie and her friends. He picked up a pitchfork, stabbed at a pile of dirty straw and threw it towards them.

'Your lardy-dardy girl friend is all sweetness with Lady P now,' Evie shouted over her shoulder.

'Dressed up like a proper toff she is.' The three girls ran squealing from the stable yard as Ethan loaded the pitchfork again.

'You're going on to Taunton tomorrow with Father,' Ethan told his brother. 'Sir Edmund told me so himself. I'm off to give a message to the Duke of Monmouth in Lyme.' Though the two brothers had always been fond of each other, they were not used to showing affection. Ethan suddenly realised that Daniel, who looked so young and innocent, might well be about to face considerable danger. 'Look after yourself, Dan.' He put an arm over his brother's shoulder and ruffled his hair. 'I expect I'll see you in Taunton.'

Chapter 9
The Battle of Bridport
13th June 1685

Next morning Ethan and Tor jogged along the narrow lane towards Bridport. He had said goodbye to his father and brother and was looking forward to another day in the saddle with Tor. The track, grassy in places, was narrow and bounded on both sides by the white heads of the cow parsley and the delicate pink of the dog roses. *The sun seems to be shining every day this summer*, he thought. *There's nowhere I would rather be.* A red deer, startled by the approach of horse and rider, scrambled to safety through the hawthorn hedge and stood in the field staring suspiciously as Ethan rode past. He was glad to be on his own again and quietly eager about the mission Sir Edmund had sent him on. Once more he put his hand into the pocket of his leather jerkin to feel the reassuring bulk of the bag of coins he had been entrusted with. He slowed Tor to a walk, realising he had all day to reach Bridport, and started to whistle.

Some little time later, Ethan became aware of the sound of another horse behind him. This by itself did not surprise him. He had met several other travellers that morning going about their business, and once he had been forced off the track as a heavy hay wain, filling the whole pathway, had rumble passed. The horseman behind him, however, never seemed to get any closer. When Tor trotted, so did the following horse. Ethan pulled onto the bank and let Tor nibble at the grass. Almost immediately, the sound of hooves from behind him stopped. He was being followed. *I wonder if the magistrates have found out what I did in Dorchester,* he thought. *Maybe it's a footpad. Surely no one could know I'm carrying coins.* Ahead there was a small coppice of beech trees on the left side of the road. This was dense enough to hide him. He would let the mystery follower overtake him and decide then what to do next. He urged Tor forward and, once hidden in the wood, dismounted and waited.

He recognised the horse straight away as Becky. Lucy, dressed once more in her cousin Peter's clothes, was peering anxiously ahead trying to see where Ethan had gone. He led Tor back onto the track and stood there waiting for her to reach him. 'Why are you following me?' he asked roughly. 'I've been hearing you for some while now, and I know it's not chance that has brought you here.'

Lucy pulled up Becky next to Tor. 'Please help me down,' she said.

Ethan noticed that she looked pale, unhappy and a little scared. Though he was angry that his peaceful ride had been disturbed, he was intrigued to find out why she was there. He held Becky's head while Lucy swung herself to the ground. 'Now tell me what you're doing.'

'I was following you. I want to go with you,' she said defiantly. She was miserable enough, but still managed to look straight at him in challenge.

'You can't come with me. I'm on important business for Sir Edmund.' He had a sudden bleak thought. 'Does he even know you are here?'

'I left a note for Lady Prideaux. I told her you would be looking after me and that she was not to worry,' she answered. 'I know you are going to Bridport to stay with your Aunt and then going on to Lyme Regis. She told me all about it last night.' Lucy paused to let him take in what she had said so far. 'I want to go with you.'

'That's not possible,' Ethan told her.

'It has to be possible,' Lucy answered. 'I'm not going back there.' Ethan could see in the girl's face a complicated mixture of defiance, unhappiness and entreaty. 'I didn't know that kindness could be so smothering. When Lady Prideaux whisked me away from the saloon she overwhelmed me with attention and new clothes. She's determined that I shall look pretty and wants me to smear my face with powder and rouge. I am to be her new best friend. The dress that she gave me to wear was made of taffeta. I remember my mama always dressed me in linen and used to tell me that excessive dresses were evidence of a mind that has strayed from God. I don't want to slip away from God's grace. I remembered the night before last; the energy and noise in the hayloft and the thrill I got from helping Ollie. Yesterday I spent all day sewing a sampler and gossiping about neighbours' love affairs.'

Ethan admitted to himself that he couldn't think of anything worse.

'I'm not going back,' Lucy said with growing confidence, perhaps detecting a spark of sympathy in Ethan's manner. 'Either we go on together, or you can leave me to whatever dangers there might be for girls alone in the Dorset countryside. What would Sir

Edmund say to that?' she finished with a note of triumph in her voice.

Ethan could not immediately see a way out of the problem. There wasn't sufficient time before nightfall to ride back to Forde and then set off again for Bridport. Sir Edmund might be angry with him for letting Lucy ride with him, but he knew he would be much angrier if he just abandoned the girl in the middle of the unknown. 'All right. You can come as far as my Aunt's house with me, and I will see what she says then.'

They covered the remaining miles to Bridport in silence. Ethan remembered the advice his father had given him about not travelling alone, but he was angry that she had forced him into a position where he was extremely uncomfortable. She was upset that he had been so churlish and had not, as she had hoped, welcomed her as a travelling companion.

Anne Langley threw her arms around Ethan. 'Welcome, Nephew.' She was a large, smiling woman and, though Ethan had not seen her for a while, from his warm memory of her, he had never doubted that he would be cheerfully received in her house.

'I have a letter for you from Father. He gave it to me yesterday and asked that you would put us up for the night.'

'Us? Who's us?' she asked.

Ethan led Lucy forward. 'This is Lucy. I know she looks like a boy, but she really is a girl and could be quite pretty.' He hoped that comment would hurt just a little. 'It's a long story but she's a friend of Lady

Prideaux. We would both like to spend the night here please, before Lucy goes back to Forde Abbey.'

'You are both welcome. Ethan, you can sleep in Peter's bed. He's away on his apprenticeship in Weymouth. Lucy, you can sleep with my daughter Jane. She is down by the market cross at present. There's been some ruckus in the town today and she and her friends have gone to look at the soldiers. Now, let me see what my elder brother has to say.' She opened Nathaniel's letter and carefully read it. 'The man's not being very clever,' she muttered, giving the letter to Ethan.

'I haven't learned to read yet, Aunt Anne,' he mumbled, handing it to Lucy.

'It's very short. He tells his sister that he's going to Taunton with Daniel to fight for the Duke because he thinks Monmouth's cause is just. Then there is something about doing God's work. At the end he asks your Aunt and Uncle to look after his family if anything should happen to him.'

'We heard here in Bridport that the Duke had landed at Lyme Regis and the Dorset Militia has been called out,' Anne said. 'Many of the young want to join Monmouth's army, but the King's soldiers led by General John Churchill could well arrive here tomorrow and the farm hands and shop boys will be no match for them. There will be many tears in Dorset before this enterprise is finished. My brother is a foolish man. I have forbidden my Francis to consider joining the Duke's cause. He also may well think it's God's will, but I suspect he is more afeared of me than God,' she said laughing.

'Tomorrow I must take a message to the Duke,' Ethan said. 'I understand what you're saying, but I must go because I promised Father and Sir Edmund I would.' Ethan felt depressed by his aunt's words. He had thrilled by the thought of joining Monmouth's army, but his aunt's warning and his father's letter had shown him that he had not thought about the possible consequences that war might bring.

'Lucy, you come with me.' Anne Langley took Lucy by the hand and led her into the parlour, firmly closing the door behind her. 'Now tell me what your story is and why Ethan is angry with you. He's a good lad and usually gets on well with everyone.'

Lucy poured her heart out to this understanding woman. 'I know Ethan doesn't want me with him, but I'll be no trouble and I am not going back to Forde. I know everyone says Lady Prideaux is a kindly person, but I think I would go mad if I had to stay in that house. Please persuade Ethan to let me go with him. I'll even continue as a boy if it will make a difference.'

Anne Langley had little enough out of the ordinary in her life. Her husband, Francis, was a dour and serious man, while her daughter Jane was of an age where she had not much to say to her mother and certainly didn't need her help in anything. Lucy's predicament and her plea for help appealed to her. 'Let's get you out of those clothes and washed. If you are to continue dressed as a boy, I am sure I can find some clothes of my Adam's that will be more suitable.' As she fussed over Lucy the girl started to relax. Perhaps her foolish flight from Forde Abbey might turn out for the best after all. 'What you need is a nice hot bath. Within a short while she was lying relaxed in a hot tub, while kindly Aunt Anne poured more and more warm water over her stubbly hair. Her cousin Peter's trousers and jerkin were steaming on a line in front of the fire.

Just before supper Francis came down from the attic where he had been working on his loom. He was naturally a gloomy man, but though he was tired from his day's work he was friendly enough to Lucy and Ethan. They were both washed and wearing clean clothes, though whether Francis recognised his son's clothes, which Lucy was wearing, or even recognised that she was a girl, he gave no indication. They all listened to the stories Ethan's cousin Jane told of the Dorset Militia who she had watched drilling in the market square. Ethan told them of his commission for Sir Edmund to meet the Duke of Monmouth in Lyme and showed them the bag of coins he had to give him. After supper Francis read to them from the Bible and finished with a prayer for Lucy and Ethan. This was supposed to be encouraging for them, but the overall effect was to make everyone a little gloomier.

After a good night's sleep, full stomachs and clean clothes, Lucy and Ethan left before dawn the next morning in excellent spirits. Ethan was anxious to complete his mission to Monmouth as soon as possible and, under pressure from Aunt Anne, he had agreed that Lucy could accompany him to Lyme Regis and with any luck they would both be back at Forde by nightfall. At just short of 5 o'clock it was beginning to get light and a low mist hung over the houses. As they reached the edge of the town they came across the soldiers of the militia. Drums were sounding and men were marching backwards and forwards. It all looked very confusing, but the officers were obviously expecting some action. Ethan and Lucy passed through the picket line and started up the hill towards Chideock. As they neared the top the mist cleared and they saw a band of horsemen jogging towards them. Alongside marched the strangest army Lucy had ever seen. Most of the soldiers were wearing rough ploughmen's smocks. All of them were wearing bunches of green leaves in their hats. Later she learned that this was the only uniform that the rebels used to identify their own side. Those on horseback carried swords, but the marchers were carrying a mixture of farm implements, pitchforks, hoes and rakes, with a few muskets dotted through the ranks.

The officer who led the cavalry pulled up next to Ethan. 'Have you come from Bridport?'

'Yes, Sir.'

One of the other cavalrymen poked at Ethan with his sword. 'That's Baron Grey of Warke you're talking to, oaf. You should call him My Lord.'

Lord Grey spoke again to Ethan. 'Are there any soldiers in the town?'

'Yes, My Lord. We passed through a line of them about ten minutes ago, just at the bottom of this hill. There were about fifty of them and I think they were waiting for you.'

'Damnation. I thought we would take them by surprise. I suppose we had better go on.' He looked dispirited and turned to his raggedy army. 'Onwards, men. Forward.'

Ethan and Lucy reached the top of the hill and looked across the bay towards Lyme as a spluttering of shots broke out behind them. For about five minutes the firing continued and then stopped.

'What do you think is happening now?' Lucy asked nervously.

This was answered immediately by the sound of galloping horses as Monmouth's cavalry led by Lord Grey crested the hill, and dashed down the other side to Chideock in full retreat. Tor and Becky, infected by the panic of the other horses and the shouts of the men, galloped along with them through the village street and up the hill the far side. No one pulled up until they reached the hill above Charmouth. Later Ethan was to learn that when the cavalry arrived at the picket line just outside Bridport, they had managed to seize the few horses they had found tied up near a bridge. But when the militia had opened fire, Monmouth's poorly trained cavalry had bolted and panic had spread through the whole force. While the horses regained their composure, the infantry, who had in fact been quite successful in the engagement, drifted into Charmouth, cursing the cavalry in general and Lord Grey in particular, branding him a coward. It was a very despondent remnant that trudged into Lyme Regis around midday. Neither side appeared to have lost many men in the battle of Bridport, but about fifty men had deserted from the Duke's army on the march back to their camp, having decided the military life was not for them.

A picket on the edge of the town stopped Ethan and Lucy. There was some small resemblance to soldiers by those on guard. They wore a ragbag collection of military uniforms, but all carried muskets and had white scarves tied around their arms and green sprays in their hats.

'We've a message for the Duke,' Ethan said to the leader and they were waved through. Over to the right in a grass field next to a makeshift camp they could see another group being drilled by a despairing officer. They looked like farm hands, which is what they probably were. The main street of Lyme Regis was overcrowded with lines of horses tied to the house railings. More men were drilling on the beach and a few drunken soldiers plundered the houses, emerging into the street with arms full of clothing, food, and pots and pans. The two had no problem being directed to the Golden Hart Inn where they were told the Duke was waiting to be told the result of this morning's foray. *I don't suppose he will be very encouraged by what he hears*, Ethan thought.

Chapter 10

From: caddie@gmail.com
To: Dr Rachel Greenleaf
Date: Thursday 21st July
Subject: Mystery man

Rachel,
First page successfully viewed. Think I have read it all properly.
D – FA   15m   4h
FA – B   12m   5h
B – L   10m   2h
L – T   25m
Can't make head or tail of it. Any help?
Love Caddie

From: Rachel Greenleaf
To: caddie@gmail.com
Date: Thursday 21st July
Subject: Mystery man

Hi,
Looks to me as if these might be journey times. If m are miles, h could be hours. 10 miles in 2 hours is going some on foot. Could it be distances travelled on a horse?
Good luck
Rachel

From: caddie@gmail.com
To: Dr Rachel Greenleaf
Date: Thursday 21st July
Subject: Mystery man

Hi,
If you are right, I guess **D** might be Dorchester. I cannot yet find any town called **FA** that is 15 miles away from Dorchester. Perhaps the figures are a journey to Dorchester, in which case I have the whole of England to look at! Letter could be **FM** not **FA,** which might stand for Fifehead Magdalene but this is about 35 miles from D.
Caddie.

From: Rachel Greenleaf
To: caddie@gmail.com
Date: Friday 22nd July
Subject: Mystery man

Hi Caddie,
Don't worry if the answer doesn't come from the first page. I often find that a few more clues will start to unravel things, which have earlier been a complete mystery.
Stick at it.
Rachel

Chapter 11
The Duke
13th June 1685

Monmouth's headquarters in the Golden Hart Inn were close to the beach in Lyme Regis. A small crowd of local people had collected round the front door and men and women pushed, shoved and jostled each other to get the best view of the comings and goings. Almost none of the local people had gone to work that day, as this was the most extraordinary thing that had happened in the small fishing village since the building of the Cobb three hundred years earlier. Outside the inn fluttered a red and golden banner bearing Monmouth's motto *Fear Nothing but God.*

Ethan, followed by Lucy, went up to the soldier who appeared to be guarding the door and told him that he had an important message for the Duke. The man, more bumpkin than soldier, nodded them through without giving them more than a glance. The front room was packed with soldiers, courtiers and citizens of Lyme, all trying to get close to the Duke. Ethan started wheedling his way through the crowd and quickly lost contact with Lucy. In the far corner next to the fireplace a tall man sat lounging in an armchair. He was wearing a purple jacket and trousers and his dark, flowing curls framed a pale and strangely empty face. *That must be the Duke,* Ethan thought, edging himself closer and closer through the crush. Standing next to the Duke was the cavalry officer Ethan recognised as Lord Grey. A fat, red-faced soldier was accusing him of cowardice and desertion in the face of the enemy. Grey vainly tried to defend himself against this verbal assault, though even to Ethan his excuses sounded feeble. Eventually, the Duke, looking bored, raised a hand and the others fell silent.

'Now Fletcher has sailed away, Lord Grey is our most experienced officer. He is also my friend.' He looked at the fat officer who squirmed uncomfortably. 'Thomas, we must learn from this disaster and look forward not backwards. Where should we go from here?'

The man he addressed as Thomas composed himself and spoke with conviction. 'Lord Albemarle has raised the Devonshire Militia and is advancing from Exeter. Informers tell us that most of them will desert to our cause if we march to meet them with sufficient force. If we can defeat this enemy, the South West will be ours and many more will join us. If we sit here arguing we will be trapped like a stag surrounded by hounds. With our backs to the sea there will be no escape.' His arguments drew nods of approval from others around.

'Ford,' he said to Lord Grey, using his Christian name as a signal to others of his privileged position, 'please take some of our horse to find out what Albemarle is up to. If your report is favourable, we will send over the rest of the army.'

This languid instruction wasn't exactly inspirational leadership, Ethan thought. A grim-faced Lord Grey forced his way towards the door and Ethan took the opportunity to wriggle through until he was standing in front of the Duke. 'Sir, I come with a message from my master, Sir Edmund Prideaux.'

The Duke looked at Ethan, but, before he could speak, the man who Ethan had just pushed past cuffed him on the side of his head. 'You should address him as *Your Grace*, oaf. God's truth! Haven't I taught you any manners yet?' This was the same officer who had spoken rudely to him outside Bridport. Angry and humiliated, Ethan was just about to reply hotly when the Duke held up his hand.

'Enough, Venner. I have warned you about your oaths. I am anxious to hear what my old companion Prideaux has to say. This boy comes as a friend, and God knows our cause needs all the friends it can get.' He beckoned Ethan closer. 'What does Sir Edmund say? Why is he not here in person to welcome me?'

Ethan had carefully memorised the message his master had given him yesterday morning. He didn't want to bring any more bad news to this sad-looking man seated in front of him, and he knew his master's words were not what the Duke wanted to hear. 'He told me he could not write down his message in case I was captured. His heart is with you, Sir, I mean Your Grace, but he is closely watched and expects to be arrested any day. I believe the reason for that is because you came to stay with him at Forde Abbey five years ago. He cannot at this moment leave the Abbey, as his greater duty lies there.'

Ethan expected the Duke to explode with anger, but the news seemed to produce little reaction. Monmouth flicked a piece of fluff from the lapel of his jacket and sunk even lower into his chair. 'Why do they not join us … the gentlemen, I mean? We have plenty of support from the common folk but the gentlemen are stuck in their comfortable houses. If they will not risk anything, I suppose we must try and win without them.'

The Duke looked even sadder at Ethan's news than before. Ethan suddenly remembered the second part of his commission. 'Sir, he asked me to give you this.' He handed over the leather bag, which Monmouth weighed in his hand. 'He said there would be more as soon as he could raise it.'

'What is your name, boy?'

'Ethan Jolliffe, Your Grace.'

'How much is there in this bag, Ethan Jolliffe?'

'I don't know, Sir.' Ethan wondered if he had made a mistake in not counting the coins.

Monmouth signalled to one of his aides who handed over his hat. He untied the string and emptied a stream of gold coins into the hat. 'The bag was not sealed in any way. Why did you not look inside and count the coins? Did Sir Edmund threaten you with punishment if you opened it?'

'No, Your Grace. He didn't mention it at all. I didn't believe it was my business to open the bag.'

'There must be a hundred gold guineas here,' Monmouth went on. 'More money than you will earn in your entire life. I thank you, Ethan Jolliffe. The news you bring is not welcome, but the content of this bag is. As Sir Edmund obviously trusted you, so will we. It is my request to you that you ride now with Lord Grey and bring back his news as quickly as possible. Venner,' He waved at the man standing behind Ethan, 'please tell Ford what I have decided.' He turned away from the two of them to talk to the aide standing by the fireplace holding the hat full of coins. Obviously dismissed, Ethan turned to follow the man called Venner from the room.

***

Once Lucy had lost contact with Ethan she quickly found herself eased backwards by the crush, through the doorway of the inn and out into the street. At first she decided to wait for Ethan just outside the Golden Hart, but the heaving crowd and the noise and smell of drunken and sweaty people was so unpleasant she decided it would be better to wait on the beach. She was confident that Ethan would come to look for her, so she was not particularly worried being on her own. She decided to do some exploring. To her right was the Cobb, a jumble of boulders heaped on top of each other providing some shelter, she assumed, from any south-westerly gale. There was little enough breeze that day and, as the tide was out, Monmouth's two ships lay on the sandy bed of the harbour with their masts angled towards the houses on the hills behind the town. In front of her she noticed six or seven soldiers, obviously wounded, being tipped unceremoniously out of a cart onto the pebbles. 'Good luck!' the carter shouted out to them and whipped his horse back onto the street.

The wounded men, in various states of distress, tried to organise themselves into a more comfortable position on the ground. She guessed that these were the injured from the morning's failed expedition. No one seemed particularly interested in their well-being.

'Fetch us some water, lad.' The man closest to her held out a leather bottle. With a jolt she realised she was the lad being spoken to. 'There's a pump round the back of the Hart which usually works.'

Pleased to be able to do something useful, Lucy collected water bottles from four of the men and assured them she would to do what she could. She had no difficulty finding the pump, but however hard she worked the handle no water came out. *It may usually work but it's not working today*, she thought.

'You must prime it first.' An old man smoking a long clay pipe was sitting on a wall watching her. 'It won't work unless you prime it first.' He puffed at his pipe. 'See the jug laid on the step? Tip the water into the pump and then it will draw.' She emptied the jug into the top of the pump and worked the handle up and down. Sure enough she quickly got a good flow of water and started to fill the water bottles. 'Don't forget to fill the jug before you finish.' She waved to the old man that she understood, collected the bottles and walked back to the beach.

The men were absurdly grateful to her for what she had done. They all drank thirstily from the bottles except the young man at the end who appeared to be unconscious. 'Shall I fetch some more?' she asked the man who had first spoken to her.

'Aye, lad. If you don't, no one else will.' When she returned with the second load of water the wounded men seemed more relaxed. A large woman was holding the hand of the unconscious young man and quietly weeping.

One of the others, who had not spoken before, asked her to sit down on the pebbles. 'What's your name, boy?' Lucy remembered that she was Luke from Dorchester and that was what she had told him. 'Well, thank you, Luke from Dorchester. I'm George Willmott from Lyme here and I'm grateful to you.' The others, even those too injured to sit up, all mumble their thanks.

'What's wrong with you?' Lucy asked George Willmott, greatly daring. He pulled aside his tattered and stained shirt to show her a huge gash crossing the front of his stomach.

'Cavalry sword did that just outside Bridport this morning. The carter brought us all back here and dumped us on the beach. If he hadn't done that we'd all have been picked up by the King's men and no doubt by tomorrow we'd be hanged'. His gloomy manner suggested that his present situation was only a marginally better alternative to the hangman's rope. One of the other men opened his jacket to reveal where a musket bullet had entered his shoulder. A third had obviously broken his ankle. They were pathetically eager to let Lucy see their wounds as apparently no one else had shown any interest in them.

'Has anyone gone to fetch a doctor?' she asked.

George laughed. 'Pah! There's no doctors in this god-forsaken army. The Lyme doctor is a King's man and has fled to Exeter. No one's bothered with us as we're no use to the officers now.'

Lucy looked more closely at George's wound. The cut had stopped bleeding but it was certainly dirty. There had been no attempt to clean it and flies buzzed around the dried blood. She had watched her father at work in the operating room of St

Bartholomew's often enough and she screwed up her face remembering the lessons he had tried to drum into her. An ancient Greek doctor called Hippocrates had used wine or vinegar when dressing wounds as, for some unknown reason, these seemed to help a body to heal. Her father had told her that there was a growing belief in his hospital that putrefaction could be delayed by basic cleanliness. He and some of his colleagues had started to wash their hands before operating. The results of this, though not hugely significant, had encouraged him to believe that dirt was in some way responsible for infection. Flesh seemed more likely to corrupt in open wounds, and this corruption invariably led to death.

She knelt down next to George. 'Has anyone got a piece of cloth?' The weeping woman looked up and then tore a strip from the bottom of her petticoat. Lucy crossed the pebbles to the sea and washed her hands and wet the cloth. She gently began to wipe away the encrusted blood. The wound began to bleed again, but George seemed hardened against pain and encouraged her to carry on. *This wound is not going to close by itself,* Lucy thought. She remembered her father telling her that for a wound to heal, the sides must be brought together within the first 24 hours. She turned to the woman again. 'Do you have a needle?'

The woman fetched her leather hussif from the pocket of her apron and handed it to Lucy. 'My Walter's gone,' was all she said. In the little wallet there were three needles, a thimble and a reel of thread.

'This wound needs to be closed,' she said to George.

'Go to it, lad. You seem to know what you're about. I prefer you trying to do something than everyone else choosing to do nothing.' *Perhaps those ghastly hours spent sewing my sampler Bless this House won't be wasted after all,* she thought. 'Don't mind me, lad. Do what you have to,' said George. Lucy threaded the needle and tried to think of George's stomach as the last thing she had sewn, the piece of linen Lady Prideaux had given her. So deep was her concentration that for a time she forgot that she was in the middle of a rebel army.

'There.' She patted George's stomach. Her stitches were rough but at least they were holding George's guts in and he looked pleased enough. She went down to the sea and rinsed the cloth until it was fairly clean. She wrapped it carefully over George's wound. 'Keep that in place until the two sides have knitted together,' she told him. 'When you are certain that it's holding, get a friend to cut the stitches out.' She felt secretly pleased with herself. However queasy she had been at the start, there was no doubt that George was now better off than if she had done nothing.

'I'm next, lad.' The man who had first spoken to her, whose name she had discovered was Jonas, awkwardly pulled off his jacket. There was a bloody hole just below his shoulder blade, but when he leaned forward Lucy could see no exit wound. She supposed the musket ball was still inside.

'The bullet's still in there. I'm sorry but I can't do anything about it. I'll just clean it up a bit,' she said.

She felt like crying in frustration, but just in time realised that would not be in Luke's character.

'In the Bible, Luke the Evangelist was a doctor,' Jonas said to her. 'I think the good Lord sent you to us, Luke of Dorchester. As George said before, if you do nothing, no one else is going help me. I will either die of the wound or, if by chance it heals with the shot in me, I will be useless as a pig-man, which for me means the same as an early death. Do what you can, lad.'

Very tentatively Lucy prodded at the wound. Jonas merely smiled at her and told her, 'You need to go in harder than that, boy.' The entry wound of the bullet was quite a neat hole just below the shoulder blade. Lucy guessed the bullet must lie somewhere near one of the bones. It might even have smashed the collarbone. She had no idea where to start. If the bullet was lying on a bone she assumed it would hurt if she pressed at it.

'I don't want you to be brave, Jonas. Let me know when I hurt you.' Using her thumbs she pressed at the areas around the wound. Jonas continued to look unconcerned. She pressed harder and managed to get a yelp of pain out of him. Although the wound was near his neck the area that hurt him was much closer to the shoulder joint. 'I think the bullet must have come in at an angle,' she told Jonas. 'It needs a proper surgeon to take it out. I can't do it. Anyhow, I don't have any instruments.'

The mother of the dead Walter fished in her son's trouser pocket and brought out a small knife in a tattered leather sheath. 'Will this help?' Lucy pulled out the short filthy blade. *At least it's sharp,* she thought.

'If you don't do anything I'll have to do it myself,' Jonas said, 'and that will be messy.'

Lucy looked wildly around, but there was no one to help her. 'I'll try,' she said. First she collected another piece of petticoat from Walter's mother, then took the knife and the cloth to the sea and cleaned both as best she could. Further along the beach she could see a small group of soldiers had a fire. She went over to try to persuade one of them to come and look at Jonas, but no one moved and one of them rudely told her to shove off. They did allow her to heat the knife in their fire, as she had heard that flames would help to clean the dirty blade.

'Come here and hold him still,' she ordered Walter's mother. The woman, used to receiving orders, came over immediately and sat on the pebbles behind Jonas. She laid his head in her lap and helped Lucy wipe the wound clean. Once again, Lucy felt around the shoulder till she came to the spot where Jonas felt most pain. She pricked the place with the tip of the knife to mark it. Her hands were shaking so she pulled back to steady her nerve.

'Cut quick and cut deep,' Jonas said. 'Try to forget about me and just go for it.'

Lucy made a small cut and Walter's mother wiped away the blood that oozed out. The lips of the cut opened out and she could see the flesh inside. She cut again and more blood appeared. She had hoped that the musket ball would just be lying there below the skin but there was nothing to see except red meat. In panic she cut again and Jonas groaned. That time she felt the blade of her knife grate on something. She prodded into the cut with the tip. There it was again. Something hard. Perhaps it was the shoulder blade. She dug the knife in again and felt sure that she had located the musket ball. How to get it out? She felt a little calmer now, as she was sure she had found what she was looking for. She cut into the flesh around where the bullet lay. When Walter's mother dabbed away the blood, Lucy could just see the piece of grey metal. She was beginning to feel faint with tension but knew she couldn't stop now. George passed her one of the water bottles and she took a long swig, which helped a little. *If I can get the tip of the blade under the musket ball perhaps I can flip it out,* she thought. Walter's mother again wiped the blood away, but Lucy was dismayed to see it was flowing more freely now. Hurriedly she pushed in the knife, trying to slip it behind and underneath the ball. She felt the blade grate against the shoulder blade and Jonas cried out with shock so she quickly pulled it out again.

'Sorry about that, lad,' Jonas said to her. 'Keep at it. I feel you're nearly there.' Though he was white and sweating he managed to give her a wan smile of encouragement.

That wasn't going to budge it, Lucy thought. *I'll have to try something else.* 'I'm going to try to hook it out,' she told Jonas. She knew she wasn't going to be able to make many more efforts. This one had to be decisive. She pushed her finger and thumb into the wound, felt the roundness of the ball, grasped it and pulled. Jonas let out a long, involuntary groan, as

Lucy looked at the small, round object in her bloody hand. She felt sick and exhausted.

'Please, you sew him up,' she said to Walter's mother, thrusting the leather wallet at her. I must go and wash.' She went down to the water's edge and rinsed her hands, arms and face, standing shaking in the water as the waves gently lapped over her soft leather boots.

It was several minutes before she felt composed enough to return to the wounded men. Walter's mother was tying off the last of the stitches and Jonas, though still grey in the face, gave her a smile. 'Thank you, boy. You did well. Goody Hebditch here has said I can rest at her house until I'm recovered enough to go back to the farm. I reckon you've saved my life.'

'What about my leg?' the man with the broken ankle said to her.

'I can't do any more.' Lucy was almost crying now. 'I must find my friend.' She ran from the beach back to the Golden Hart. There was no longer a crowd round the front door. The guard had gone and the saloon was empty. Ethan was nowhere to be seen.

Chapter 12
Am I a Spy?
13th June 1685

Following close behind Colonel Henry Venner, Ethan forced his way through the crush waiting outside the Golden Hart. He looked around for Lucy, expecting her to be near the door or at least on the edge of the crowd. He knew she would not want to lose contact with him.

'What are you waiting for? Hurry up. We need to catch Lord Grey before he rides off.' Venner grabbed Ethan's arm and started to drag him towards the line of horses in the main street.

'Give me a few minutes. I need to find a friend of mine.' Ethan shook his arm free.

'When Monmouth gives an order,' Venner snarled, 'no one, not even you, farm boy, waits a few minutes.'

Ethan was angry at the repeated insults from this man. 'Don't you mean His Grace rather than Monmouth?' He knew his answer was impertinent but he had had enough of this fat bully.

Venner hit him hard on the side of the head. 'Don't try to be clever with me, pig boy. You had better learn some manners quickly or it will be hard for you.'

'If you lay one finger on me again, I will tell His Grace the Duke of Monmouth that I have detected you spying for King James.' He reached Tor and swung himself into the saddle. 'He may not entirely believe me but I can give enough details so there will be sufficient doubt to ruin your chance of a position. You will never again be entirely trusted by either side.' Ethan rode past him towards Lord Grey who he could see mounted on his horse in the High Street. Colonel Venner, who had occasionally wondered if his interests might be better served by siding with the King, was silenced by Ethan's remark. He followed the boy without saying anything more, but Ethan knew he had made a dangerous enemy.

'Your Lordship,' Ethan said to Lord Grey, 'the Duke has ordered me to accompany you on your reconnaissance expedition and to bring a report back to him as soon as you have assessed the situation.' His temper had made him bold and his boldness had taken Venner by surprise. 'His Grace has ordered Colonel Venner to find you. He will confirm this.'

Venner growled his agreement, but added, 'I'm to come along too.' Ethan knew that this was not what Monmouth had ordered. He was determined to be very watchful.

There were twenty cavalrymen in the small troop that accompanied Lord Grey; enough to give protection should there be a surprise attack, but not sufficient to think of attacking themselves. They travelled swiftly along the coast road towards Exeter and just outside Beer they met the first of Lord Albemarle's pickets. When they saw the horsemen approaching the nine or ten members of the Devonshire Militia scattered. 'If this is an example of their so-called professional army,' Lord Grey said, laughing to Venner, 'I don't think we have all that much to fear. We do need to discover what their morale is like and if they will come over to our side. Any suggestions, Harry?'

'Send the farm boy to find out. They're his sort, so it shouldn't be too difficult even for him. If necessary I can take your initial report back to James at Lyme.' He smirked over his shoulder at Ethan. *With any luck*, thought Venner, *they will arrest him as a rebel and he will hang by nightfall.*

Certainly Ethan did not look a particularly military figure as he plodded towards the village of Beer on Tor. He had decided to say that he was visiting a make-believe aunt in Exeter who wasn't very well. In case he was questioned heavily he decided to tell the truth about his own family back in Corton. The fewer lies he told the less likely he was to be caught out. Lord Grey had told him exactly what he was to find out. How large was the enemy force? Where were they camped and how many of them would come over to the Duke's cause? It wasn't long before he saw soldiers in front of him and he decided on a bold approach. Ethan cantered towards them and he pulled Tor to a halt by the guard post. 'Help me,' he called out. 'There's a group of horsemen behind me who are trying to steal my horse.'

The soldiers started running about, as far as Ethan could see, in total disorder. He was taken to an officer and told his story. He described Lord Grey's band of horsemen but denied knowing who they were. 'They said they wanted my horse for the Cause, but I don't know what that means.' Ethan was bright enough to play dumb when it was necessary. A soldier was detailed to escort him to the major who was stationed in Beer and he soon found himself waiting once more in the saloon bar of an inn surrounded by militiamen. His escort left him to join his mates. As no one seemed to be particularly concerned about him, Ethan decided to sit quiet, say nothing and listen. He quickly gathered that the men were not very enthusiastic about their commanding officers. None of them thought Lord Albemarle was half the soldier his father had been. It appeared he had little military experience and was a ditherer. Some of the men in the saloon had read one of Monmouth's posters and were talking about his offer of freedom of religion. When the major came out of the snug they stopped talking until he had left the room.

'What's the major's name?' Ethan asked one group.

'That's Major Cartwright,' he was told in a broad Devon accent. 'You oughtn't to mess with him. He's in a right pet.' It appeared that Major Cartwright and his regiment were stuck guarding the coast while Lord Albemarle and the rest of the army (about one thousand militiamen he was told) had marched to Honiton to try to cut the enemy off. Major Cartwright was 'in a right pet' because he wanted to be in the fighting where glory was to be found. The major had already sent off two riders requesting permission to join the main army. His men, on the other hand, were perfectly happy to be as far away from any fighting as possible. Most of them, like Monmouth's army, were farmers who wanted to get back to their fields. Ethan decided it was time to leave.

Outside he found Major Cartwright looking over Tor. 'Boy, how did you acquire this horse? It's far too good an animal for a young 'un like you.'

At no time since he had arrived in Beer had Ethan been asked what he was doing there. His escort was drinking in the inn so he decided to risk reversing his story. 'It's not my horse, sir. It belongs to Sir Edmund Prideaux who is a magistrate in Dorset. I've been taking a message to a relative of his in Exeter and now I'm on the way home back to Forde Abbey.' He hoped that enough titles and names would be sufficient to convince the major.

But Major Cartwright was not so easily satisfied. 'Come here, lad.' He quickly searched Ethan's clothing and then ordered him to take his boots off and searched them too. He found nothing compromising but was still suspicious. Ethan began to worry that if he tried to check up on his story his lies would be discovered. 'I think you're hiding something, boy, though I don't know what. I'll send you back to Exeter.'

Just then a militiaman galloped up and handed Major Cartwright a letter. He looked at the address. 'At last,' he muttered. 'I hope this means ….' He stopped and strode back into the inn to read what his commander had said.

Ethan quickly swung himself into Tor's saddle. His instinct was to get out of Beer as fast as he could, but, trying to keep calm, he walked the horse up the main street and out of the town. At the guard post the lieutenant stopped him again. 'What are you doing back here?'

'Major Cartwright told me I couldn't go any further for security reasons. He told me to go home. He said I'd be in trouble if I didn't do what I was told.' Ethan tried to look frightened which wasn't very difficult.

'Where's Dick who I sent with you?' Ethan could honestly say he had last seen him drinking in the inn. This did not make the lieutenant's temper any better. 'Blast him. Those horsemen you saw seem to have gone. You had better do what the major told you.'

Ethan found Lord Grey and his cavalry camped in a small copse drinking tea. Henry Venner was far from pleased to see the boy return. He had tried to persuade Lord Grey that Ethan must have been captured and they should move on. Grey was delighted with Ethan's report. 'You must take this information back to the Duke straight away, Jolliffe.' He thought for a moment, knowing that after the debacle at Bridport, his military reputation was compromised in the army. He suspected that some would always think him a coward. He sighed. 'Tell him the road to Exeter is open. If he marches there he will control the West. However, he should expect the enemy's militia to desert and not to count on many soldiers being left to join his army. I will take my troop towards Honiton and find out what young Albemarle is up to. I will anticipate meeting His Grace's army near Axminster or Chard.'

'What did the soldier mean by saying Lord Albemarle wasn't half the man his father had been?' Ethan asked.

'George Monck, the first Duke, was one of the finest parliamentary generals in the Civil War. If he had still been Lord Lieutenant of Devon today I don't suppose we would have landed in the West Country at all. The second duke, this Lord Albemarle, has no experience of commanding an army. As long as he is in charge the odds are with us. Remind His Grace what the militia think of their officers.'

'I will go with the boy,' Venner spoke to Lord Grey, trying hard to keep the menace out of his voice. 'After all, he's a valuable spy now and we don't want anything to happen to him.'

His words scared Ethan. 'Am I a spy?' he asked Lord Grey. 'I thought I was just finding out some things for you.'

'That's what spies do,' Venner sneered. He was delighted to see the effect his words had on Ethan. 'If they catch you now, you will certainly hang.'

This time there was no attempt to disguise the hatred. Lord Grey guessed that any journey back to Lyme would be hazardous enough for the boy, but suspected it would be even more dangerous if Venner accompanied him. 'You stay with me, Harry, I need your experience. Go quickly, Jolliffe.'

Ethan made rapid time back to Lyme. A mile short of the town Tor cast a shoe and Ethan, anxious not to damage the horse's hoof, walked him the last bit of the journey. He tied Tor outside the Golden Hart, but before he made his report he hurried up the main street to see if he could find Lucy. *By now she'll be worried about me. Probably a little frightened as well. If only I'd been able to see her before I was whisked away by that bully, Venner*, he thought. There was no sign of her on the beach or in the High Street, and Becky was no longer tied up where they had left her. *I'll make my report to the Duke, then I can make a proper search for her.*

Ethan found Monmouth still surrounded by his officers, holding court in the saloon. He gave a full account of all he had seen and tried as accurately as possible to repeat what Lord Grey had told him to say.

'Albermarle has one thousand militiamen, you say? You're sure of that?' Monmouth asked him.

'Yes, Sir.' Now Henry Venner wasn't here, no one else seemed to mind the use of 'sir'. 'I also believe many of them want to join your cause, Sir.'

Monmouth looked at one of his officers. 'What do you think, George?'

'We've twice that number, My Lord. While Albemarle is dithering around we can take him at Axminster. Then there won't be any other troops but ours between here and Bristol. Take Bristol, and the West is yours.'

Albemarle was not the only ditherer. 'These militiamen from Devon are our friends. If I am to be King I don't want it remembered that my first action was slaughtering my subjects. Perhaps it will be safer to march to Exeter and secure a base there.'

The argument bounced from one possible action to another. The Duke of Monmouth listened to what everyone had to say and took first one side and then changed to the other, then back again. 'Can't make his mind up,' Ethan heard one officer whisper behind his hand. 'Just like his father and grandfather. Typical Stuart.' Eventually a decision, or at least a compromise, was reached. They would march early the next day towards Axminster and see what Lord Grey had to say.

'You can go now, Jolliffe,' Monmouth said, turning back to Ethan. 'Be back here and report to me at 5 o'clock tomorrow morning. I can make good use of you as a messenger boy.' Ethan slipped quietly from the room, determined to find Lucy.

The guard, who had been listening to Monmouth's remarks, stopped him as he left. 'You're Jolliffe?' Ethan admitted he was. 'The officer said to tell you the other lad had gone to the camp up the hill.'

'What for?'

'I dunno. That's what I was to tell you.'

It was still puzzling him why Lucy hadn't waited, but at least he knew where she was.

Chapter 13
The Army Camp
13th June 1685

Lucy waited for two hours outside the Golden Hart and had begun to worry that Ethan might never turn up. She was sitting on a low wall, hungry and just a little frightened, when a young man approached her. 'Are you Luke, the boy from Dorchester?'

Just in time she remembered that was who she was supposed to be. 'Yes, I am,' she said.

The man was dressed in a military uniform of sorts. His tight-fitting blue jacket had gold flashings and buttons but was faded, worn and patched. His trousers appeared to be ordinary riding jodhpurs, but his boots were magnificently long, made of shiny black leather. He introduced himself. 'My name is Andrew Crompton and I'm a Captain-Lieutenant in the White Regiment of the Duke's army. We are camped just up the hill on the edge of the town.'

He must be about nineteen or twenty, Lucy thought, *but his face is so smooth and babyish he looks more like a schoolboy.*

In an attempt to appear older Andrew Crompton had tried to grow a moustache, but the thin wisp of fair hair on his upper lip made him look faintly comic. 'Two of my injured soldiers, George Willmott and Jonas Thatcher, tell me that you have been operating on them.'

Lucy was aware that although in many cases medicines were dispensed by women, surgery was a preserve still jealously guarded by men. She started to make excuses before remembering that as far as Lieutenant Crompton was concerned she was male. However, before she could speak he shushed her quiet.

'If you hadn't acted, I don't know what would have happened to those men. I should have done something about them, but you know how it is …,' he waved vaguely in the air to indicate important matters that couldn't be overlooked. 'I really would be awfully grateful if you would come up to the camp to look at some of the other sick men we have.' Lucy started to object but Lieutenant Crompton just carried on, disregarding her protests. 'I know you're not qualified, but we have no one else and my men swore by you. They say you are better than any doctor they've met.'

Lucy started to explain that she had to wait for her cousin, but Andrew Crompton just gave an order to the guard standing outside the inn, telling him that anyone asking for Luke should be directed to the army camp. Without really being given a choice, Lucy found herself whisked away, first to the horse lines where Becky was still tied up and then to the camp on the outer fringe of the town.

'I can't do any more operations,' Lucy explained as they rode together. 'I was nearly sick over what I did to Jonas. It just seems a shame that simple wounds aren't kept clean.'

'That's it,' the young officer said with enthusiasm. 'That's just what I'm looking for. Surgery won't be necessary. I don't have any idea what to do and I just need your advice.' He looked embarrassed. 'I've not been in the army very long. I came over from Holland with others of the Duke's supporters. Lord Grey, who is my uncle, was in exile over there. The Duke has appointed him the regimental colonel and Uncle put me in charge of the first company. He just told me to look after the men and to carry out his orders. I have never done any actual fighting before today. Some of my men were injured at Bridport. Those who you helped on the beach I'd ... er mislaid.' He did look pretty helpless and miserable.

If it really is just advice, I ought to be able to manage that, Lucy thought. As they neared the camp she noticed that the avenue of holm oaks, planted so carefully years ago to give shade to travellers on the road, had been hacked at and dismembered. Some of the trees had been chopped down altogether. Hedges too had been despoiled. The crude barbarism of the sight made her even more apprehensive. It was with some nervousness that Lucy followed Andrew into the field.

Lucy had never been in an army camp before. This camp was a mess. At first glance the rough row of tents in the middle of the field gave the appearance of order, but a second glace round the edge of the field showed her several hundred rough little bivouacs made of woven branches and leaves. 'We have over five hundred soldiers in this regiment,' Crompton told her. Many of these so-called soldiers, lolling around on the grass, looked like farm labourers to Lucy. There seemed to be little of the organization, energy or bustle that she had expected. Men relieved themselves with no attempt at modesty or hygiene. A drunken brawl against the eastern hedge had drawn a big crowd of spectators who jeered and cheered as punches were thrown and kicks landed, but even that seemed a half-hearted affair. If it had rained, Lucy thought, the squalor would have been even worse. Many of the little shelters had fires burning outside with an assortment of kettles and pans boiling and brewing away. *This camp can only have been here for three days at the most*, Lucy thought, *but already there is a smell of decay*.

They passed close to the brawl and Lucy pulled Becky up next to Lieutenant Crompton's horse, scared by the raw brutality of what was happening. 'They won't touch you as long as you're with me,' the Lieutenant said, trying to reassure her. 'We're not much of an army, I'm afraid, but once we get on the march, things should improve. I hope so, or we're in for a drubbing. What you see here is about a quarter of our forces, but we expect to raise hundreds more in Taunton and Bristol.'

In the top corner of the field they passed a group of soldiers sitting around a campfire chopping wood. Andrew Crompton rode up to them and started berating them, threatening all sorts of dire punishments. The men scowled at him and turned away in silence. Their obvious antagonism frightened Lucy. Andrew explained to her what the problem was. 'These men are being trained as pike men for our army. The 18-foot pike is the best defence there is against an enemy cavalry charge, but it is also heavy for them to carry while we are on the march, even when they trail it. Those fools think they are being clever and making their lives easier by cutting lengths off their pikes and using the wood on their campfires. When it comes to battle and they have to face the

King's pike men and cavalry, they will find, with their shortened pikes, the enemy can skewer them without them having any means of defending themselves. With the Dutch army it was a hanging offence to shorten your pike, but we don't have that sort of discipline here.'

The injured and wounded men Lucy had come to see were collected under a canvas awning at the far end of the field. No one seemed to be attending them and they lay on the ground in a cloud of apathy and despair. Even if she wasn't going to do any operations Lucy could see that their situation could very easily be improved. She remembered what the men on the beach had needed. 'These men must have plenty of water to drink.'

Crompton shouted at two farm worker soldiers who were passing. 'Fill these bottles and bring them back straightway.' The men ambled off to do as they had been ordered.

This encouraged Lucy. Having water to drink must be good for the wounded. At least it couldn't do any harm. 'A few bottles won't be enough,' she told Crompton. He dismounted and roused a few of the men from the nearest bivvy to fetch more water. Lucy counted ten injured men under the awning who began to show a little interest in her. So far, since they had been ill, they had been largely ignored. She went down the row, examining each of them to see if she could find out what was wrong. Five of them had bad diarrhoea and told her that they couldn't hold any food down; two had sword cuts similar to the ones she had seen on George Willmott. There was a broken leg, what looked to her like a fractured skull and one man lifted a bandage from his head to show her that he was now missing an eye.

'What do you want next?' Crompton asked Lucy.

She had no illusions about her lack of skill. Even regular attendance with her father in the hospital had not equipped her to deal with these problems. The best she could hope for was to improve their conditions. No one seemed to have any idea of basic hygiene or cleanliness. She also remembered that when her mother had been ill with the bloody flux on an earlier occasion, her father had told them not to feed her anything for days, but to drink plenty of water mixed with either sugar or salt. She explained this to the Lieutenant.

'I doubt if there's much sugar in the camp,' he said with a smile, 'but I expect we can scrounge a little salt. Anything else?'

I can't have done much harm so far, she thought. 'I want this tent moved to a clean area. Those five men,' she pointed out the ones who had stomach cramps and diarrhoea, 'tell them …,' she hesitated. *Oh well, here goes,* she thought, 'tell them they're not to shit here.' She noticed a gap in the hedge. 'They must go through that hedge. I want water, warm if possible, and some clean bandages. I also want a needle and some thread. The men will need blankets tonight. As they're injured they will feel the cold.'

The Lieutenant was galvanised into activity. He was a kindly man but totally lacking in initiative. There was nothing she had said that he could not have worked out for himself, but lacking medical experience and confidence he had been paralysed into inactivity. He quickly rounded up a squad of men who began to take down the awning and re-erect it where Lucy directed. Some dirty bandages arrived and she sent them away to be washed. She told Crompton that the five men with diarrhoea had to be cleaned up. She had already made up her mind that this was not something she was prepared to do. Fortunately most of the sick had friends around and it was they who rolled up their sleeves and set to. 'No food for two days for you lot and drink plenty of water.' A small crowd had gathered, fascinated by the sight of this young boy issuing orders. She sensed that they not only were interested in what she was doing, but also approved. *After all, it might be any of them next*, she thought.

It wasn't all straightforward. When she told the man with the missing eye that she couldn't do anything for him, his wife (at least Lucy assumed she was his wife) came up to her and started shouting abuse. Lucy feared she was about to be assaulted, but some of the men grabbed the woman and led her away. She could do little for the soldier with what she guessed was a fractured skull, so she put a bandage round his head and told him to lie still. She sewed up one of the wounds, a man with a gashed arm, quite neatly, but when she tried to do the same for the leg wound the stitches started tearing through the flesh. She had already cleaned the cut, so at least it looked better than before. All she could manage there was a fresh bandage.

When she had finished, Lucy had been working for nearly two hours and was shaking with tiredness. It didn't seem to her that she had done much, but she did notice that there was a more cheerful atmosphere (and it smelled less) under the canvas. Lieutenant Crompton was absurdly grateful and it did look as if his men were regarding him in a more favourable light. She was just wondering what to do next when Ethan walked up, leading Tor. She was so relieved to see him she nearly flung her arms around him. Just in time she remembered that this would be unsuitable behaviour for Luke of Dorchester. Ethan was grinning with relief.

Lucy introduced Lieutenant Crompton to Ethan and told him what she had been up to. When he could get a word in he told them both his story since he had left Lucy at the inn that morning. He was proud to have been made Monmouth's personal messenger. Andrew Crompton commented that he would have much preferred Ethan's role to his commanding a company. Ethan finished by telling them that the Duke required him again the next day, early before they moved out. 'The latest decision was that we should march towards Axminster, but that could easily have changed by the morning. I should have told the Duke about Tor's hoof,' he added. 'I can't ride tomorrow unless I manage to get him re-shoed.'

'My regiment has managed to get hold of a farrier,' Andrew told him. 'He has set up near the horse-lines. So far he has always been terribly busy, but if I take you there and explain that you're on urgent business for the Duke, I expect you can jump the queue.'

The farrier was a surly man and grumbled how overworked he was, but Andrew, showing surprising authority, ordered him to deal with Tor immediately. Reluctantly, still grumbling, the man agreed. Ethan was reassured when, after inspecting Tor's hoof, the farrier confirmed that there was no damage. Andrew passed him a silver coin, which the bad-tempered man slipped into the pocket of his apron without a word. He promised that he would tie Tor up in the horse-lines when he had finished. There he would be safe under guard all night. Ethan was grateful, but concerned enough to decide that he would check on Tor later that evening.

Andrew, who was a friendly enough young man, invited them both back to his tent for some food, where his servant, Otto, had a kettle of water boiling and a pot of chicken stew bubbling away over the fire.

'I need to get clean,' Lucy said.

'Me too,' Ethan added.

When Otto brought over a bucket of water for them both Andrew, who, though gauche, was both intelligent and observant, noticed that Ethan stripped off while Lucy more modestly washed hands and face but definitely kept her shirt on. 'I bet you're not called Luke at all,' he said to Lucy. 'My guess is you're a maid, not a boy. What's your real name?'

Lucy felt panicky, but Ethan was an intuitive judge of character. He quickly decided that Andrew Crompton could be trusted. 'You're right, but please don't tell anyone else. She'll be in far more danger in the army if people know she's a girl. Her real name is Lucy, but please, go on calling her Luke and treat her like a boy.'

Having been impressed by Ethan's apparently important position and Lucy's obvious competence Andrew was pleased to be back in a position where his decision counted for something. 'That's fine,' he said, 'Luke it is. Sometime I'd like to hear why you've chosen to dress like that, but I'm so grateful for what you have done for my men that I'm happy for you to be whoever you want. I won't tell a soul.'

'What gave me away?' Lucy asked.

'I noticed your hands when you were sewing up the soldier's arm. Your fingers are long and delicate. Anyhow, you're far too pretty to be a boy, even if your hair is frightful.' Lucy blushed. In London, wearing her puritan clothes, she had been unused to compliments. Also it was sinful to think oneself pretty. Andrew, noticing she was uncomfortable, hurried on to suggest that while Ethan carried messages for Monmouth, Lucy (or Luke rather) should act as medical orderly for the regiment. 'This should keep you together, but means that Lucy won't be expected to do any fighting. Otto will look after you. He's Dutch and doesn't understand much English, but knows enough to keep us fed. You can both sleep in my tent, if you like.'

A rough plan having been agreed, the three of them spent a satisfactory evening exchanging stories about their respective families. Before turning in for the night Lucy showed the two young men the logbook she was keeping. 'My father gave me this so that I could keep a record of all the unusual things I might see.'

Ethan admired the flower sketches on the first page, which she had made by the River Frome. 'You are a brilliant artist, Lucy.' He could make nothing of the inky scrawl on the next pages, which to him resembled the trail of a drunken spider. 'Why have you only done two drawings?'

'I had intended to keep the sort of record my father wanted, but since we started to travel I have been too tired in the evenings to do much writing. I have recorded the length of our journeys so far, and today I am keeping a record of the men I have treated. I think some sort of medical record might be important, though I doubt if anyone except my father will ever read it.' She showed Ethan the little bottle of ink. 'I make this from charcoal dust and oil. It's not as good as the ink I can buy in London, but I hope it will last long enough for my father to read this. Uncle John gave me three swan feathers for writing, and I keep them sharpened with this little knife.'

'You had best not put any more names, particularly ours, in your book. If the King's men were to get hold of it, it could be used as evidence against us.'

Lucy agreed. She noticed that Ethan had raised no objection to the suggestion that she should continue with the army. With his new responsibilities there was no way he could escort her back to Forde Abbey and the matter was not mentioned. Andrew and Ethan spent the rest of the evening discussing their families, while Lucy scratched away in the logbook, content enough.

Chapter 14

From: caddie@gmail.com
To: Rachel Greenleaf
Date: Saturday 23rd July
Subject: Mystery man

You were right, Rachel. When I was able to unscramble the next page I found the clue I was looking for. There was nothing on the page opposite the list of mileages. This is what was on page 6:
FA Stables
Ollie   dislocated shoulder   fixed it!
LR Beach
Willmott George stomach cut   13 stitches
Hebditch Walter died   no treatment
Thatcher Jonas   musket ball in trapezoid ex deltoid 6 stitches
Unknown   broken ankle no treatment
Unknown   no treatment
Unknown   no treatment

On the next page (page 7) it reads:
LR Army Camp   All wounded badly dehydrated
5 Unknown   bloody flux salt water and starvation
Thomas   side wound   6 stitches
Unknown   leg wound bandage
Unknown ? Seth?   broken skull   bandage
Unknown   loss of r eye   no treatment
Unknown   broken leg splinted

I am confident that **LR** will be Lyme Regis which is about 30 miles west of here. Working backwards, that makes the **B** on page 4 Bridport and I'm guessing that **FA** is Forde Abbey, which is a big house near Chard. Uncle Robert has promised to drive me over next weekend as it is open to the public.

These two pages look like a doctor's treatment list. Could it be from the Civil War?

Love Caddie

From Rachel Greenleaf
To Caddie
Date: Monday 25th July
Subject: Mystery man

Well done. I'm sure you are on the right track. Can't be Civil War, though. Remember, the Isaac Newton quotation!

If you Google Forde Abbey you will see list is likely to be from Monmouth's rebellion, sometimes called the Western Rising. Better still, go to the County Record Office in Dorchester. They will have a copy of History and Antiquities of the County of Dorset by the Rev John Hutchins. That will tell you about FA. Owner Edmund Prideaux seems to have been well involved.

Keep me informed.
R

Chapter 15
On the March
15th June 1685

It was before dawn when Monmouth's raggle-taggle army began to break camp on the hilltop above Lyme. Officers shouted to wake the bleary-eyed soldiers and strode through the field, knocking down the temporary shelters with their swords. When Ethan was woken by the noise his first thought was that they were under a surprise attack by King James's army, but Andrew Crompton reassured him of the latest news. Monmouth had at last made up his mind and they were going to move out immediately. Andrew and Ethan reported back to Monmouth's headquarters and were given their orders for the day. Ethan was pleased that he would not be required until later and rode back to the camp to help Lucy prepare the sick soldiers for their journey in a hospital cart. It was several hours later that a line of soldiers dressed in a variety of uniforms and armed with muskets marched from the field to the beat of a solitary drum. A ramshackle peasant column carrying their assortment of farm implements followed these half-trained troops. The whole army began to wind its way from Lyme towards the coaching inn at Hunter's Lodge on the road that runs from Axminster to Bridport.

Andrew, riding with Lucy and Ethan, told them what he had heard of the long and bitter arguments through the night between Monmouth's staff officers as to whether they should march on Exeter or towards Bristol. Eventually it had been decided to move northwards, roughly in the direction where Lord Grey had reported Lord Albemarle's troops to be marching. Monmouth was confident that thousands in Somerset would rally to his flag. Others, and there was growing pessimism amongst his officers, were concerned about the fighting ability of the new recruits. They felt that their army, without cavalry cover, would have little chance against trained soldiers.

June continued to be hot and dry. The foot soldiers frequently dropped out of line to fill water bottles and take impromptu rests. The officers shouted a mixture of encouragement and abuse, but still the column was painfully slow. Andrew Crompton was under orders from his uncle, Colonel Lord Grey, to keep the column moving. As he was busy all morning, Ethan and Lucy took the opportunity to discuss their situation. Ethan was enthusiastic about his new responsibilities to the Duke. He had to report to Monmouth every morning and evening to see if there was anything he should be doing. He suggested that while he was away Lucy would be wise to stick close to Andrew. 'He seems to be a good fellow and friendly enough,' he said 'and at least with him we'll have some of Otto's food every day. If it rains at night we can all cram into his tent.' He thought for a while. 'You'd better be careful now he knows you're a girl. He thinks you are very pretty.'

Ethan's compliment cheered Lucy up, though she was a little disappointed that he had added nothing himself. She was beginning to have doubts whether it was such fun pretending to be a boy. Things over the last two days had happened so fast she'd had little time to think about her position. She had been pleased that she could help the wounded, but had no wish to be involved in a battle. Even the skirmish at Bridport had shown her that the consequences of battle were far more horrid than she could deal with. Now, as their horses ambled over the heather, she was feeling quite grubby and a little scared. She missed the warm welcome of Anne Langley's house in Bridport, but shuddered when she remembered the suffocating life at Forde Abbey.

Before she could express any doubts to Ethan, he began to talk of her success with the wounded. 'Andrew and everyone here thinks you're wonderful, and before I left Lyme I heard the soldiers talking about 'the boy healer,' but of course I didn't know then it was you. How do you know what to do?'

Lucy shrugged. 'I don't really. As I told you, my father is a very clever doctor in London and I have often watched him and helped him at work. All I've done is use my common sense, but I really don't want to do any more operations like I did on that poor man with the musket ball in his shoulder.' The memory made her feel queasy. 'I do like to be useful. The trouble with life at a place like Forde Abbey is that women are just expected to be ornaments.' She paused and then added fiercely, 'I want to do more with my life than be an ornament.'

They rode in silence for a while as Ethan could think of nothing helpful to say. He needed to distract Lucy in some way. Then he had an inspiration. 'Let's see if we can find the men you helped yesterday on the beach. Andrew said their cart was somewhere near the rear of the column. I'm glad they haven't been left behind. If they were picked up by General Churchill's men I expect they would be executed as rebels.' Ethan was aware that he was babbling, but his suggestion seemed to have a positive effect on Lucy who cheerfully accepted his idea. They turned their horses round and trotted comfortably back down the marching column.

They found the hospital wagon near the rear of the line. George Willmott was in high spirits. He showed her his scar with great pride. Though still raw it didn't seem to her to present any signs of putrefaction. George told her about the others. 'Jonas has gone off with Goody Hebditch, dead Walter's ma. He told me to let you know his shoulder's already feeling better. The lad with the eye out, his missus took him home. The others are around here somewhere.' *I'll put a record of their progress in my logbook tonight*, Lucy thought.

With Ethan's help, she arranged a canvas screen over the cart to provide some shade from the sun and at the next stream both of them filled up the men's water bottles. Some of the diarrhoea victims complained that they were hungry and begged her to fetch them rations, but she told them forcefully that they were not to eat till suppertime tomorrow. The men grinned at her vehemence. Even though she was obviously very young, they seemed to accept that she knew what she was doing.

Early in the afternoon as they reached the top of the hill everyone shuffled to a halt. Looking down on the valley of the River Axe, Monmouth's scouts had seen a company of enemy foot soldiers drawn up to block their advance. Word spread through the waiting ranks that there was to be a battle. Gradually the officers urged the men into attack formation and the line advanced on the enemy, who they understood to be Albemarle's militia. From their position at the rear Ethan and Lucy had a good view of what was happening. As the two armies met, and the first shots were exchanged, the militia broke ranks, turned and ran. They dropped their weapons and ammunition pouches and anything else that might slow them down. Monmouth's soldiers waved and cheered as if they had won a mighty victory. Had the cavalry then ridden round the flanks they would have cut off and surrounded the retreating soldiers. As the Devon militia were almost all sympathetic to Monmouth's cause nearly a thousand half-trained fighters could have been added to his forces. Monmouth was no general though. He was happy for his army to make camp where they were. He did send out one patrol to collect the abandoned weapons and others to encourage the fleeing soldiers on their way. Ethan was surprised to see these men returning to camp driving cattle and sheep, which were then slaughtered and cooked. Andrew assured him that Monmouth had promised the farmers that all supplies would be paid for when he became King, but to Ethan this foraging looked like theft.

Next morning, Ethan, riding Tor, was once more travelling on his own. As they were close to Forde Abbey Monmouth had given him a letter to take to his master, Sir Edmund. 'Tell him he is welcome to join our victorious army in Taunton in two days time.'

When Ethan arrived at Forde, he left Tor at the stables. 'I've had to re-shoe the left fore, Sir,' he told his boss. Geoffrey Ostler sucked in his breath sharply and made a disparaging tutting noise. Tor was one of his favourite horses and he immediately checked the hoof to see if there was any damage. Ethan made his way to the house. In the front hall one of the servants recognised him and asked what he wanted. Ethan explained his mission. 'The Master's away.' The footman looked flustered. 'I'd better tell Mistress you're here.'

As Lady Prideaux descended the stairs to meet him she had a defeated look about her. Ethan took off his cap and stood awkwardly holding Monmouth's letter, waiting for her to speak. 'My husband is not here.' She held out her hand and Ethan gave the letter to her. While he waited in silence she broke the seal and read it. 'Tell His Grace that Sir Edmund was arrested yesterday and is at this moment on his way to London ...,' she paused a moment, '... to the Tower. Tell him he can expect no more help from this house.' With that she turned away and walked slowly back up the grand staircase.

Ethan decided there was no need to hurry back to Monmouth with his negative message. Although he was concerned for Lucy, he was sure she would be safe under Andrew's protection, particularly as she had already built a reputation as a healer. He decided to spend the rest of the day at Forde and to leave for Taunton the next day. He found Olly on his own in the loft. The boy told him that George Fox hadn't touched him since he had hurt his shoulder. He also recounted how, the day before, a troop of militiamen had turned up at the Abbey with a warrant and had taken Sir Edmund away. Lady Prideaux had spoken to all the staff and warned them that they might themselves be in danger. She had given permission for any of them to leave if they wished to, but no one had.

When Ethan looked into the stables he found Tor was being groomed and petted by Geoffrey, who gave him an evil look and muttered something about him being an irresponsible good-for-nothing. However, he didn't seem to have found anything specifically wrong with the animal. 'I shall need him tomorrow when I return to the Duke,' Ethan told him. Geoffrey did not think to question the order. Satisfied that he had no further responsibilities, Ethan decided to spend the rest of the day trying to ensure his life in an army camp would be more bearable.

At lunchtime he cornered the housemaid Evie, and explained to her that he badly needed some clean cloths for bandages and also some changes of clothes for a girl roughly Evie's age and size. Evie, who had taken a fancy to Ethan, was immediately suspicious and wanted to know more about this girl. Poor Ethan, who wasn't a natural liar, had quickly to invent a nurse, daughter to Colonel Lord Grey, who was helping with the wounded. He explained that her clothes had been lost in the ship crossing over from Holland. Evie was satisfied that the daughter of a Lord could not possibly have designs on a stable boy like Ethan and promised to help. He scrounged two hay sacks and a saddlebag from the tack room and, with Olly's help, 'borrowed' some of the clothes left behind by lads who had gone off to join Monmouth. His heartfelt story of near starvation persuaded Cook to bake him some biscuits and when she wasn't looking he collected some old glass water bottles from the pantry. He did feel bad about taking from such a generous woman without asking and deep down he knew this was little better than stealing. Just before he left the kitchen Cook gave him a large square of soap *for that poor lady the girls told me about,* and when she urged him to take anything else he needed for *those unfortunate wounded men*, he felt less bad about the glass bottles.

Evie and the other chambermaids who lived in the attics of the big house had collected armfuls of old clothes, including a smart green riding jacket and skirt which Lady Prideaux had handed on to her maid. None of the girls, however, had the nerve to wear these, so they were happy to pass them on to *the young Lady Grey* Ethan had mentioned to Evie. A group of girls came down to the stables to hand over their offerings. Finally with a flourish and a giggle Evie produced a worn petticoat, which she told Ethan was still warm as she herself had only just taken it off. The other girls had been well prepared for this joke and Ethan, embarrassed, blushed and became completely tongue-tied. Then inspired, he solemnly told the group that he felt sure that all the wounded men would feel much better when they knew where their bandages had come from and gave Evie a smacking kiss, to great cheers.

Early the next morning, while Geoffrey helped Ethan saddle Tor, Olly bundled up the clothes and supplies. It was a heavily laden horse that set off to return to Monmouth's army.

Chapter 16
The Clubmen
16th June 1685

Lucy was irritated with Lieutenant Crompton. For the past two days, while Ethan was away, he had fussed over her quite unnecessarily and he was always whistling tunelessly. *Where is Ethan?* She thought. *He promised he would only be away a day. He should have been back yesterday. He's so unreliable.* Also the dirt of an army on the march was getting to her. Her skin felt greasy and itchy. Andrew had ordered Otto to provide her with water for washing every day, but this morning he was late and she had shouted at him. The hot bath in Bridport seemed an age away and she felt altogether grimy and unhappy.

Knowing that it was her time of the month that made her irritable did not make Lucy feel any better. She was determined not to take it out on the wounded men, but Andrew Crompton, *so annoying*, was a different matter. She was walking beside the cart carrying the wounded men when he rode up whistling again, probably for a chat. One scowl from her and he decided he would be better employed encouraging the rest of his troop. *Where is that infuriating Ethan?* She thought.

***

Knowing roughly the speed Monmouth's army was travelling, Ethan had worked out that he should overtake them somewhere between Chard and Taunton. The baggage was likely to be travelling slowly, but the Duke and his staff would want to make an impressive entry into Taunton as they hoped many recruits would join them from there. The sacks stuffed with old clothes and the worn saddlebag with the glass bottles bumped rhythmically against Tor's flanks. Ethan felt well fed and rested. The sun was again shining and to his eye the grass was about ready for the second hay crop. He realised he was looking forward to seeing Lucy again and knew she would be really pleased with the soap he had managed to get for her.

He was about five miles from Taunton, and had already passed many of the stragglers and camp followers of Monmouth's army, when he saw a solitary horseman ahead. The man was sitting still, apparently waiting. As Ethan drew closer, with dismay he recognised the rider. It was his old enemy Colonel Henry Venner who sat there, fat, red-faced and sweating in his heavy army jacket. Ethan's carefree mood left him. Venner had promised he would get even with Ethan for what he considered his impertinence. The boy had no doubt that he was here waiting for his chance. He looked around for help but the two of them were alone on the road.

'You stop right there, bumpkin,' Venner ordered, placing his horse in front of Tor. 'Taken your time, haven't you? I've been waiting all morning for a chance to teach you a lesson.'

Ethan wondered how he might pacify the angry man. 'I've an important message for His Grace. Please let me through.'

'Your important message, I expect, is to tell the Duke that the lily-livered coward Prideaux is too scared to come and join us. I can pass that on.'

'Sir Edmund has been arrested and sent to the Tower,' Ethan retorted getting some of his nerve back. He tried to edge Tor round in front of Venner's horse, but with a touch of his spurs Venner blocked him off again.

'What's in those sacks? Been stealing again have you, pig-boy?'

'These are bandages for the wounded men. There's bound to be many casualties if we have to fight.'

'Quite the little saint, aren't we?' Venner sneered. 'What does a country oaf like you know about warfare anyway?'

Ethan couldn't see how he was going to escape from this situation. Venner seemed determined to punish him and he was armed, while Ethan had nothing to defend himself with. Once more he tried to edge Tor forward.

Venner drew his pistol, pointed it at Ethan and pulled back the hammer. 'I told you to stop there.' He still hadn't made up his mind what to do with the boy. He had expected him to be terrified when he was stopped. A bit of humiliation, some taunting, to put him firmly in his place, would have been enough to restore the Colonel's dented pride and sense of worth. But Ethan showed no sign of being frightened. Before Venner could make up his mind what to do, Ethan dug his heels into Tor's flanks and struck Venner's horse on the muzzle with his fist as he passed. Totally unprepared for this, Venner fired his pistol at Ethan just as his startled horse reared backwards. The bullet missed the boy but carved a red furrow down Tor's neck. The horse screamed and bolted.

Ethan was an excellent horseman but he had difficulty controlling a panicky Tor and all the baggage he was carrying at the same time. Tor had swerved off the road and started to gallop up a steep hill. As Ethan heard Venner's horse coming quickly up behind him he decided to ditch the sacks and saddlebag, throwing them into a clump of bushes. He was then able to concentrate on Tor. Venner may have been fat, but he was an experienced cavalryman. Glancing over his shoulder Ethan could see that he had drawn his sword and was gaining on him. He knew that he was riding for his life.

The path steepened as it neared the top of the hill and passed through a narrow passage between two large rocks. To his dismay Ethan saw that the way ahead was blocked by a criss-cross of tree trunks. He managed to pull a frightened Tor to a halt by the pile of logs and turned to face Venner. At the moment Ethan thought he was about to be hacked down, he saw someone leap from an overhanging rock and knock the panting officer from his horse. Before he had time to react to this he felt a crack on the side of his head and everything turned black.

***

Ethan tried to open his eyes and sit up. That was a mistake. He groaned, deciding to keep his eyes firmly shut. His head ached where he had been hit. Perhaps he should first try and work out his situation, lying where he was with his face pressed into the dirt and his mouth as dry as a piece of old parchment. Behind him he could hear people talking, though too quietly to understand what was being said. His arms seemed to be tied behind his back and his shoulder hurt, *probably where I hit the ground.* His first thought was that the enemy must have captured him, but as he slowly sorted the low murmur of voices into comprehensible conversation he wondered if it might be a band of gipsies who had attacked him. *I can't have been out for long as the sun still has a good heat in it,* he thought. From where he was lying he could hear the occasional moo of a cow, and he could smell cattle and horses. This made him remember the injured Tor. *It's time I woke up and found out what's happening,* he thought.

Ethan, squinting into the bright sunlight, could see he was lying on the edge of a considerable grass bowl with a ruined building over to his right. Later he was to discover that this was the bailey of Castle Neroche, a mediaeval fortress knocked down by Oliver Cromwell after the Civil War. He groaned again and struggled to turn over.

'Jason. This one's woke up.' A boy not much older than himself wandered over and prodded him with a musket. *I hope that's not loaded,* Ethan thought.

A second, older man carrying a club, *probably Jason* Ethan guessed, wandered over to join the boy. He straightened Ethan out with the toe of his boot so he was lying on his back. 'What do you want here?' he said in a gentle Devon burr.

The boy helped Ethan to sit up. Besides Jason and the boy he could see over thirty other people, men, women and children, huddled together at the far side of the enclosure. All of them held weapons of some sort. In addition there were over sixty head of cattle and a dozen horses. 'Can I have some water?' he asked.

'What do you want here?' Jason asked again.

I'd better say something as I'm in no position to argue, Ethan thought. 'I was escaping from one of Monmouth's soldiers who was trying to kill me.'

'This him?' With his foot Jason pushed Venner's body into view. Ethan was pleased to see that his enemy too was tied up. In addition he was gagged and looked furious.

'Yes. That's Colonel Henry Venner, and he's a truly horrible man.' Ethan felt his best chance of escaping with his life was to distance himself as far as possible from Venner. 'My name is Ethan Jolliffe and I work as a stable boy for Sir Edmund Prideaux at Forde Abbey. He had heard talk in the army camp of the Clubmen, groups of farmers who banded together to protect their animals from foraging soldiers in both armies, named after the weapons they invariably carried. He guessed that he was being held not by enemy soldiers or by gypsies but by local farmers. They had certainly chosen a good place to conceal their cattle. Unless you knew about Castle Neroche you wouldn't guess that this nondescript little hill could be such an effective hiding place. 'My father, Nathaniel Jolliffe, used to live by Forde Abbey. He now farms in Dorset. We have over thirty milking cows.' He hoped that this would firmly put him on the side of the farmers.

Jason was still suspicious but he did shout over to the others. 'Any of you heard of a Nathaniel Jolliffe?'

An old man left the group and walked over to join them. 'I used to know a Nathaniel Jolliffe as lived near Chard. Left the area to go farming in the East somewhere.'

'My mother's name is Sarah,' Ethan butted in.

'Ah, that's right.' The old fellow looked as if he was gazing back in time. 'Pretty lass with lovely curly hair like chestnut coals. This young fellow's got his mother's hair.'

For the first time Ethan was delighted with the colour of his hair. He felt a wave of relief as Jason helped him to his feet and untied his hands. 'Could I have a drink of water?'

This time his request was met with a nod and the young boy dashed off. The others stood around in awkward silence until he arrived back with a can of water, which Ethan quickly downed. 'How's Tor. He's my horse.' The musket ball fired by Henry Venner had not appeared to go very deep into Tor's shoulder, but the horse had obviously been extremely frightened by the experience. 'Can I see him?'

More than anything else Ethan's concern for his horse convinced Jason that the boy did not represent a threat to the Clubmen. 'Don't you worry about Tor. Old Arthur's put a salve on his wound and fixed him up proper. Arthur's the best horseman in Somerset.' He beckoned to Ethan. 'Come and meet the others.'

When Ethan explained that he was merely a messenger between Sir Edmund and Monmouth, many of the Clubmen questioned him about events. He was able to describe the Duke and tell them what had happened in Bridport and Axminster. There was general regret that Sir Edmund had been sent to the Tower, but Ethan got the impression that this tough group of farmers were not particularly interested in one side or the other, but they would go down fighting to protect their livestock. 'I had two sacks of old clothes and a saddlebag which I had to throw into a hedge at the bottom of the hill when I needed to escape from Venner,' he told them.

Jason, who appeared to be the leader of the group of farmers, sent the young boy to collect them. 'What do we do with him?' He jerked over his shoulder with a thumb pointing at Venner. 'We had to gag him because of his filthy language. 'Twern't very pretty at all.' There was a general discussion among the men folk and a consensus that it would be unwise to let him go. 'I'll finish him off then,' Jason said. He turned to Ethan. 'What do you think, lad?'

Ethan hated and feared Colonel Venner but he couldn't face the idea of cold murder. Though Jason had volunteered to do whatever was necessary Ethan sensed that the idea of killing a prisoner did not sit comfortably with any of them. If Venner was released too soon he would quickly return to Castle Neroche with the army foragers, who were probably even now scouting for food, and the farmers would lose their cattle. A free Venner would be a constant danger to him, yet he would be difficult to keep as a prisoner for any length of time. The furious colonel had already sworn revenge on the clubmen as soon as he was back with Monmouth's army. Ethan then remembered that camp gossip in Lyme had recounted how General John Churchill had reached Bridport with the Royal Dragoons and was marching north to cut off Monmouth's force. He explained this to the farmers. 'Why not find General Churchill's soldiers and hand him over to them as a rebel prisoner? There may even be a reward for turning in a ranking officer.' This idea was discussed by the men and well received. Two of the younger farmers, probably hopeful of being the ones who received the reward, volunteered to do escort duty the next day.

Venner was soon forgotten. Ethan, who was still feeling groggy from his hit on the head, was persuaded to stay the night. He checked up on Tor. Arthur had put a generous amount of salve on the wound and the horse seemed none the worse for his ordeal. Though Jason insisted that secrecy was still essential and had ordered that no fires should be lit, they suppered well on cold pork and apple sauce liberally washed down with scrumpy cider.

Chapter 17
To Bristol and Back Again
19th June – 3rd July 1685

Lucy felt miserable. Andrew was off drilling his soldiers somewhere in the camp and she still had no idea where Ethan was. He had promised to turn up yesterday but there had been no sign of him. First thing that morning she had changed some of the bandages on her wounded, but there were only three men in the cart who still needed any help from her. She decided to walk into Taunton just to give herself something to do. The town was buzzing with people, most of them wearing leafy twigs stuck in their hats. Over a thousand new recruits had joined Monmouth's army and signed on as the Blue Regiment. She saw that the Duke himself was speaking to the crowd from the back of a cart. She pushed though until she was somewhere near the front. A chattering gaggle of over twenty young girls were pushing forward to present banners to him. Lucy noticed that most of the girls were around her age. The Duke of Monmouth gave each of them a chaste little kiss on the cheek as he took the flags and handed them on to one of his aides.

The final banner fixed to two poles was unfurled and held over his head to great cheering. She read *Fear Nothing but God*, which she recognised as Monmouth's motto. Under the embroidered writing there was a picture of a crown and the Latin *Jacobus Rex*, which she knew meant James the King. She assumed this referred to James Monmouth not James II currently on the throne. As the flags flapped in the wind, the vicar of Taunton stepped forward and with wild cheering from all sides proclaimed before God that Monmouth was the rightful King.

Behind Monmouth's cart Lucy spotted Ethan's red hair in the chattering crowd. In some desperation she dropped a shoulder and elbowed through the mass of people towards the spot where she had last seen him. It wasn't Ethan but a younger, taller edition of him. She knew Ethan had hoped to meet his brother Daniel in Taunton and guessed this must be him, smartly kitted out with military blue jacket and white trousers. *He's far too young to be a soldier,* was Lucy's immediate thought. 'You must be Daniel,' she said to him. 'I saw you out of the window at Forde Abbey with Ethan. I'm a friend of his. My name is Luke.'

'Hi, Luke.' He gave her a shy smile; so much less confident than Ethan's usual cheerful grin. 'Where's Ethan? I've been looking for him.'

'I don't know where he is at the moment, but he promised to meet me at the hospital cart as soon as he returned from Forde.' Lucy explained her own work with the wounded. Suddenly it seemed unnecessary to go on pretending to Ethan's brother that she was a boy. 'My name is really Lucy not Luke,' she blurted out. 'Ethan thought I would be safer if I dressed as a boy.'

If Daniel was surprised by this revelation he did not show it. 'Hi, Lucy, then.' He smiled again.

'I'll take you to our camp. Ethan should be there by now. I must get back to my hospital cart, as that's where he will look for me. Will you come with me?'

'We're camped over the other side of town, father and me, with the Blue Regiment. That's made up of all those who've just joined and we signed on yesterday. A sergeant has been teaching me how to fire a musket,' he told her proudly. 'I know Father would like to see Ethan. Can I bring him along too?' He looked worried for a moment. 'Am I allowed to tell him you're really a girl? I don't like lying to him.'

'As you like,' she said with a shrug. As more and more people knew she was Lucy rather than Luke, her disguise seemed less and less important. They agreed to meet at the White's regimental camp some time in the afternoon.

Ethan was waiting for her by the hospital cart. She had planned to be pretty curt with him when eventually he turned up, but his anxious face and then the look of such relief when he saw her completely took away her irritation. He took both her hands in his, and then immediately dropped them, remembering she was still a boy to those around. He had taken over one corner of the cart with his bundles. Pleased with himself he showed Lucy the sacks of old clothes and rags he had collected from Forde. He emptied the saddlebag, proudly presenting the glass water bottles, and then with a flourish ... the bar of soap. Although Lucy was managing quite well in the mucky conditions of camp, she was absurdly grateful for his thoughtfulness. She felt tears beginning to well up in her eyes and brushed them away savagely.

'When Evie heard there was a girl nursing here she sent this.' Ethan presented her with the green velvet riding skirt and jacket. 'I told her you were

Lord Grey's daughter and that you had lost all your clothes coming over from Holland. All the maids collected these clothes to use as bandages, or I'm sure you could wear them if you wanted.' Lucy could see he was getting tongue tied and decided to dig a little deeper.

'This Evie, is she your girl friend?' She was surprised to find she was a little jealous of Evie. 'Tell me about her.'

Ethan blushed, remembering the smacking kiss he had given her. 'Oh, she's just one of the chambermaids. I think she fancies me a little, but to me she's just one of many friends.' He decided, however, not to mention the kiss or the joke about the petticoat.

Lucy was not yet satisfied. 'Is she very pretty?'

'She is quite pretty, but not as pretty as …' Ethan paused. Although he had little experience with girls, he did recognise Lucy was fishing for a compliment. He decided it was time to regain the initiative, '… as pretty as some of the other girls.'

Lucy decided to use some of the material she had been given to make a flag to mark the hospital cart. In this way anyone wounded would know where to come. She asked Ethan to find a good stick to act as a flagpole. Using an old white shirt for the background of the banner she cut two short lengths from a torn red neck scarf. Sewing these on top of the shirt she created a passable imitation of the flag of St George and she and Ethan were fastening it to the cart when Daniel found them.

Nathaniel, who had searched in the Bible through the book of Leviticus and had found nothing in it against women wearing men's clothing, was surprisingly happy about Lucy's disguise. He understood that it might be necessary for her safety and commended her work with the sick. When Lieutenant Crompton arrived and joined the group, the conversation naturally turned to what would happen to their army next. On his return, Ethan had reported to Monmouth the news of Sir Edmund Prideaux's arrest, and he had overheard a bitter argument between all the staff officers as to whether they should turn and face Albemarle's troops, or march on London or north to Bristol. These were the same arguments that he had heard at Lyme Regis and Axminster. Ethan did not understand all the military implications, but it seemed obvious that Monmouth needed to be a more decisive leader. Even now with six thousand men in his army all he seemed to do was dither.

In the end it was to be Bristol. The Jolliffe family agreed to meet regularly under the sign of the red cross, and for the next seven days the army marched optimistically north to capture the capital of the West. Then came the rain; days of it. Lord Feversham, King James's general with the royal army, arrived in Bristol ahead of Monmouth. Rather than risk dreadful casualties by an all-out assault on England's second city, Monmouth's high command decided to withdraw. Their next plan was to head for London. When General Churchill's forces blocked this road, the plan was again changed. Now the idea was to return to Taunton and try to regroup. With constant drenching by the rain, the morale of Monmouth's army was rapidly sinking. Already two thousand of the peasant soldiers had returned to their farms to deal with a potentially ruined harvest.

By the time the dispirited army arrived at Wells some of the soldiers, particularly those who doubted Monmouth's religious conviction, were ready to mutiny. A rabble of religious fanatics, Ranters, Diggers, Levellers and Fifth Monarchists, had collected outside the cathedral and was being whipped into a destructive frenzy by some anonymous, shaggy-haired preacher who railed against the church, the bishops and the King and implored the crowd to tear down this temple of the ungodly. Many in the crowd had originally joined Monmouth's cause because he had promised to repeal the Act of Uniformity, which compelled all Englanders to follow the rites of the Church of England.

In Wells they realised they would merely be replacing one high-church king with another. Some no doubt were driven by a genuine religious fervour, but many more used this occasion as an excuse to exorcise their military frustration. A junior officer reported to Monmouth what was happening at the cathedral and he immediately saw all his attempts to woo the gentry of England to his cause being dashed by this display of anarchy and ill-discipline. He promptly dispatched Lord Grey with some of his cavalry to investigate and bring the riot to an end. At the cathedral the first victims for the religious zealots were the statues of the 12 apostles on the beautiful west front of the cathedral. These were quickly pulled from their niches and smashed on the ground. By the time Lord Grey arrived the rioters had broken through the west door into the nave and were tearing up the prayer books, smashing the stained-glass windows and stealing any silver or brass objects they could find. Some of the men had dragged a barrel of beer into the body of the church, and quickly drunkenness was added to religious fervour in the destructive mayhem.

Monmouth, worried that he had not heard from Lord Grey, told Ethan to ride to the cathedral and to report back on the situation he found there. The great west doors had been flung open and inside the boy found an orgy of violence and profanity. Lord Grey, who had become separated from his troopers, was standing on the steps of the high altar with drawn sword holding the crowd of rioters at bay. Ethan pushed through the crowd and climbed the steps to stand beside his commander. 'His Grace asked me to find out how you were getting on, Sir,' Ethan said with a nervous laugh. A battered hymnbook was thrown from the crowd, catching him on the back of his legs. Other missiles and jeers followed.

Grey, despite his perilous position, seemed to be enjoying himself. 'Go and tell the Duke that I have the situation well in hand. I expect any moment that God will send a regiment of angels to protect me. Go quickly, boy, for this is an unhappy mob we face.'

Ethan decided he could not leave his commander alone and unsupported. He climbed the last two steps and turned to face the rioters. 'I will stay with you, Sir.' He risked a small joke. 'Now you have double the forces, you have twice as much chance of success.'

'Where is your sword?' Grey asked him.

'I do not carry a weapon,' Ethan answered, 'but if we are really lucky none of this lot will realise that.'

Whether it was Ethan's courage in standing next to Grey or his obvious extreme youth that impressed the mob, he was unsure, but from that moment the crowd seemed to lose interest in the altar and its two guardians. The brass lectern was tipped over and an orgy of chair-smashing followed. After some minutes a column of Monmouth's trained infantry, with bayonets plugged into their musket barrels, stormed into the cathedral from the south transept door and drove the rioters up the nave and out of the west end.

'Thank you, Ethan.' Lord Grey shook his hand. 'Standing beside me may not have been wise, but it was certainly brave. I could well owe you my life. We must report back to the Duke and let him know what has happened here.' Surprisingly they both found their horses still tied to the railings outside the west end of the cathedral. As they trotted up the main street of Wells, Grey asked him, 'What did happen to Colonel Venner? I last saw him in Taunton swearing vengeance on you. He left the camp and has not been seen since.'

Ethan could not think what to say, so he remained silent.

Lord Grey looked at him keenly. 'No matter. Another time will do.'

On several occasions during the short campaign that became known as the Western Rising, Lord Grey and his cavalry were accused of cowardice. In later years Ethan would recount this incident, always vehemently swearing to the Colonel's personal courage.

Twelve days after leaving Bridgwater a forlorn army trudged back into the town. The arguments now were whether to make a stand and fight or to flee. Though few in Monmouth's army by now held out much hope of success, Fate was to give him one last chance to be King.

Chapter 18

From: caddie@gmail.com
To: Rachel Greenleaf
Date: Tuesday 26th June
Subject: Logbook

Hi Rachel,
Went to town library today. Hutchins is unbelievably detailed, but unfortunately **FA** is in Somerset! Got plenty of info on Monmouth.
    Page 9 of logbook has a short list:

Gleanie   Guinea fowl
Maggoty   Fanciful
Coupie down   Crouch down
Pummy   Pulped down apples

Uncle Robert says these are all Dorset words and their definitions. *Dearest Daughter* can't have been a Dorset person, I guess.
    Page 10 is even stranger:

A says he thinks I am pretty. Is it a sin to enjoy that?

E says nothing. He almost complimented me today. I wish he would speak up.

Page 11 is another list:

Medicines from GS for DJ
Woundwort/Yarrow   draws out poison
Sphagnum moss   acts as absorbent
Medicines from GS for JJ
Madragora   to reduce pain
Hemlock   could have been used
*   but GS says no*

I don't understand how any of this fits together yet, but it's getting late. Onwards tomorrow.

Love Caddie

Chapter 19
The Battle of Sedgemoor
5th and 6th July 1685

'Gentlemen, Gentlemen, please!' Monmouth for once raised his voice and banged with his fist on the table. He was in the upper room of the Angel Inn in Bridgwater where he was meeting with his senior officers. The Duke was still wearing the purple and scarlet overjacket that he had worn when landing at Lyme, but this was now dirty and torn. The fatigue lines round his eyes and his ashen face were evidence that this campaign had not been easy for him. 'We must have an orderly discussion. This bickering and arguing will achieve nothing.' Monmouth looked round his war council and shook his head in exasperation. 'If we cannot agree a course of action amongst ourselves, what chance have we of convincing our army?' He looked to Lord Grey. 'Ford, you are my second in command. What do you think we should do next?'

Although Grey had fought alongside Monmouth since they soldiered together in the Dutch wars, he had lost confidence in himself and his ability to command men after the debacle of Bridport. Instead of the easy familiarity he had previously enjoyed with Monmouth, he now fell back on formality. 'My Lord, your army is tired and in no fit condition to fight Feversham's army. I believe we should fall back on Taunton and regroup there.'

'You mean we should run away again?' Nathaniel Wade sneered. 'We should be much closer to the channel ports in case we have to escape. Is that it?'

'Are you calling me a coward?' Ford Grey half rose in his chair, ready to challenge Wade.

The others turned to look at Monmouth to see how he would react. He laid a hand on Lord Grey's arm and persuaded him back to his seat. 'Ford is my friend, Nathaniel, as well as my second in command. This is not the time for us to disagree amongst ourselves. You may well command the senior regiment in my army, but I have warned you before, I will not have these slurs thrown at any friend of mine.' There was an uneasy silence while he paused to let the rebuke take effect. 'What is your suggestion, Nathaniel? Give me a better plan.'

'We must fight, Sir. These constant retreats mean that our army is frittering away. Some of our regiments are down almost to half strength. The further south we retreat, the more men we lose. Tomorrow when the army is well rested we should march out, find Feversham's army and crush it. If we retreat towards Taunton, I suspect Colonel Buffet's Blue Regiment will all slide away home. Isn't that so, Buffet? What's the morale like with your lot?'

Buffet shuffled uneasily in his chair. Of the regimental commanders, he and Abraham Holmes were the only two who had not been former companions of the Duke in Holland. He was nervous about standing up to one of Monmouth's friends; however, he wasn't prepared to accept this insult to his men without some riposte. He stood and faced Nathaniel Wade. 'Are you now calling my men cowards too? You have had it easy, Wade. Your Red Regiment is made up of experienced soldiers who have all come from the Dutch wars. The reason the Reds have lost so few to desertion is that there is nowhere else for them to go. The rest of us have had to train volunteers, some straight from the farm, and been given very little time to do it. Yes, some of my men who joined the Duke's colours in Taunton have deserted and returned home without permission, but so have Holmes's and Matthews's. I honestly believe at this moment those who are here will fight. However, I concede that in one thing you are right. If we go south to Taunton I will lose more.'

He paused and then sat down, satisfied that he had done enough to defend the reputation of his regiment. 'I can, however, tell Colonel Wade where Lord Feversham's army is. Andrew Paschall is the Rector of Chedzoy, a village we passed through three days ago. He sent a message to Captain Izzard, one of my officers, to say the Royal army left Somerton this morning and is setting up camp in the village of Weston Zoyland not three miles away. Paschall believes they are three thousand strong and intend to blockade Bridgwater.' He fell silent, relieved to have given an opinion without openly disagreeing with either of his superior officers.

'We are not strong enough to attack Feversham directly,' John Foulkes continued. Foulkes commanding the White Regiment, had served with Monmouth in the Dutch wars and was respected by all present. 'We have almost no artillery and his troops are well trained and equipped. We should decide at this critical moment how best to maintain the impetus of your cause, Sir.'

Monmouth knew Foulkes to be a thoughtful and intelligent officer, not headstrong like one or two around the table. 'What do you suggest, John? Our ultimate aim must be to reach our support in London. How is that to be achieved?'

'We know that there is considerable support for your cause in Cheshire and the North West of England. We should bypass Feversham's army and travel back to Keynsham, cross the Avon there and then head north. There we can regroup and regain our strength. After that, a march on London avoiding any of King James's soldiers would not be impossible.'

'With Feversham's cavalry already patrolling the main roads we will never sneak past unseen,' Wade growled. 'I expect that is why he has moved his army forward.' He looked belligerently around the table. 'Now we know where the bastard is, let's attack him.'

Monmouth ignored this outburst. 'Jan, we haven't heard from you. What is the state of our cannons?'

Captain Jan van Straubenzee, a Dutch artillery officer who had sailed from Holland with Monmouth, smiled. 'As it is since we landed, Sire. We have had no chance to fire our guns yet. We still have our three small cannons. Each will fire a three-pound shot. We have gunpowder and are ready to fight, but My Lord Feversham's army will considerably outgun us. He has four- and six-pounders, at least twenty guns that I know of.'

'You live somewhere around here, Holmes. Describe this moor to me.' Monmouth turned to the only one of his high command who had yet to speak.

Abraham Holmes had little recent military experience but excellent local knowledge. He spoke with a gentle Somerset accent. 'Sedgemoor is mostly a vast peat bog, Sir, though it will be dry enough now it's summer. The whole area is criss-crossed with drainage ditches called rhines, dug by Dutch engineers thirty or more years ago to control the level of water on the moor. These are about eight feet across. Some will have water in them and some will be dry. The village of Westonzoyland where Lord Feversham has camped and the other villages of Chedzoy and Middlezoy are built on little islands of sand and clay in the heart of the moor.'

'Can you reach 'em by road?' Wade butted in rudely.

'Since the earliest times, these villages have been linked by primitive tracks, but I'm sorry, no roads. Even in the summer, movement across the moor will be slow. I believe Sedgemoor will make attacking difficult and defending easy.'

'Thank you, Colonel.' Monmouth looked around the table. He was no nearer knowing what was best to do next, and retreat, despair and exhaustion had left his war council venting like a volcano ready to erupt. 'There it is, Gentlemen. Four options. We retreat south, head north, attack across the moor or build up the defences of Bridgwater for a siege. I have already sent out parties to collect wood and stone for strengthening the walls here. But as for a siege, I am not encouraged by the lacklustre support I have received by the mayor and townspeople. I shall not make a decision about further action immediately, but I would like each of you to go back to your regiments and count the number of soldiers you have who are fit to fight and we could put into battle. All of you report back here at 5 o'clock and I will tell you what I have decided.'

At the same time that Monmouth was meeting with his commanders, a local farmer called William Sparke had spent the early part of the afternoon on top of the tower of Chedzoy church, armed with a spyglass, studying the position of the King's army. He saw that Lord Feversham had centred his defence on the village of Westonzoyland and sheltered his camp behind the broadest of the Sedgemoor drainage ditches called the Bussex Rhine. His artillery, supported by the cavalry, was guarding his right wing, controlling the Bridgwater to Taunton road perhaps to prevent Monmouth making a breakout northwards. A detachment of dragoons guarded Burrow Bridge crossing the River Parrett on the left. But, as far as William Sparke could see, the centre seemed to be surprisingly unprotected. Through his spyglass Sparke detected that the small cattle bridge made of a few rough planks that stretched across the Bussex Rhine was only lightly guarded.

He quickly sketched a map of the positions of the royal force and at 3 o'clock sent his young servant Benjamin Godfrey to tell the Duke what he had seen. Monmouth climbed the tower of St Mary's Church in Bridgwater to see the situation for himself. Encouraged to see the truth of Sparke's report, he asked Godfrey to investigate the royal army more closely. Godfrey returned before 5 o'clock to say that many in the royal army seemed to be drunk on cider and discipline seemed to be very slipshod.

So far Monmouth had provided little effective leadership to the Western Rising, but now, like a ruined gambler who can see no other way out from his parlous position, he decided to risk all in one last desperate throw of the dice. He ordered Ethan to summon all the army commanders immediately back to his temporary headquarters.

Once his war council was gathered together he laid before them an extraordinary plan based on the information Godfrey had brought him. There were to be no more retreats, no breakout to the north, no siege of Bridgwater, but a night attack on Feversham's army, across Sedgemoor, to surprise and defeat the enemy in one glorious victory. He ordered that all troops were to be ready to march by 11.00 p.m. The whole enterprise was to be conducted in complete silence. Surprise was everything. Benjamin Godfrey had agreed to guide the army along a narrow grass causeway parallel to the Taunton road that would avoid Feversham's cavalry patrols and artillery. Godfrey knew a place they could cross the first of the drainage ditches called the Langmoor Rhine. Several large stones marked this crossing and even in the dark he was confident this would not be difficult to find. Once over the ditch the infantry would be drawn up, while Lord Grey led his cavalry to capture the primary crossing place of the Bussex Rhine, the cattle bridge called the Upper Plungeon. The Duke had copied out Sparke's rough map onto the wall of the inn. He pointed out all the main features of his plan to his stunned company commanders who had grown to accept the Duke's indecision. No one had anything to say. 'Victory will be ours before the royal army even knows it is under attack,' Monmouth told them. 'There will be just sufficient moonlight for us to see our way and I am told it is likely that there will be a heavy mist lying over the moor. That and the darkness of night should provide a blanket of secrecy for our enterprise. Don't forget surprise is everything, Gentlemen, make ready your troops. We will leave at 11 o'clock. Remember the motto on our banner: *Fear Nothing but God.*'

If any of the officers present thought that the Duke was unwise to lead his untrained army down an unknown path and across a boggy moor in that most difficult military manoeuvre, a night march, no one spoke out loud of his unease.

The centre of Bridgwater quickly became a chaotic scene as news of the planned attack spread. The whole town was loud with preaching. Fanatical ministers, who had followed the army to Bristol and back, shouted their message of death and destruction for all papists and idolaters from the back of carts, from windows and even standing on upturned beer barrels. Each preacher gathered his little crowd of followers to listen to his ranting, while the less godly supporters took advantage of the confusion to get drunk. The officers frantically tried to drive their soldiers back to their respective regiments camped on Castle Fields to the north of the town. They were well aware that time was short for those with muskets to make ready for battle. Their men had to prepare fresh cartridges by filling little canvas bags with gunpowder, as reloading their matchlocks with powder horn and ramrod was a clumsy business for poorly trained troops while exchanging fire with an enemy. The officers also had to issue fresh lengths of slow-burning match to each musketeer, as the previous days of rain would undoubtedly have dampened the old matches and they could ill afford any misfiring on the first attack. Those without muskets had to grind the accumulated rust from their swords and scythes or other weapons. Gradually the market square emptied as the ragbag army were persuaded to return to their regiments.

Ethan asked Monmouth if he could visit the camp to say goodbye to his family. Monmouth gave permission but made the boy promise that he would be back by 11 o'clock. 'I need you here, boy; I must have your word on it.'

Ethan found his father and brother with Lucy by the hospital cart. This was now empty as all those who had been sick or injured in the recent retreat from Bristol had either returned to their regiments or deserted the army altogether and had gone home. Lucy still had the red cross symbol flying limply on the flagpole. 'Is there to be a proper battle?' she asked Ethan nervously.

'Aye, lass,' Nathaniel answered her. 'Daniel and I are with Colonel Buffet's Blue Regiment. We are to be second into the assault just behind Monmouth's Own. It is likely to be a bloody affair. But, if God wills it, we will triumph this night.'

Ethan could see that Lucy was scared about the outcome and in particular her responsibility to deal with all the possible wounded from a full-scale battle. He tried his best to reassure her. 'The Duke has ordered all the supply and ammunition carts to line up in the town's main street. There is no need for you to join them. You stay by the cart here, and I will come back to you as soon as I can. I think it's time you went back to your uncle in Dorchester.'

Nathaniel asked the others to kneel with him on the grass. He prayed that God would keep his family safe from the present immediate danger and then left with Daniel to join the Blues.

Lucy was frightened by Nathaniel's words. She had enjoyed using her little knowledge to help the few sick soldiers who had been brought to the cart and believed she had been useful. A battle, however, was a different matter. She had been tired out by the miserable march to Bristol and back and dreaded being alone again when Ethan left. 'I have to get back to the Duke,' he told her, 'I gave my word that I would.' He was torn between honouring his promise to the Duke and his desperate wish to comfort her.

Starting to panic, for once Lucy lost her self-control completely. She threw her arms around him and started to cry. 'Please don't leave me,' she begged. 'I'm scared that something awful will happen to one of us.'

Ethan prised her arms from around his waist and held her by the shoulders. 'Stay here,' he told her fiercely, 'then I know where you will be. I promise, promise, promise I will come and find you as soon as I can.' He kissed her clumsily on the cheek and ran back into town. Lucy climbed onto her cart and sat frightened and desperately miserable, alone.

At 11 o'clock a single drum roll signalled the moment for Colonel Wade to set out with Monmouth's Own. He was followed by Colonel Buffett with his Blue Regiment, composed of volunteers raised in Taunton including Nathaniel and Daniel Jolliffe. Monmouth, riding his black stallion Ulysses, watched his army march in silence off to battle. Lord Grey, also mounted, sat beside him, with Ethan on Tor behind the two of them.

For the first hour things went surprisingly well for the Duke's untrained troops. A night attack is a difficult tactic even for highly disciplined forces. Thanks to the heavy mist lying like a duvet over the moor, the royal cavalry, the Oxford Blues, who on Feversham's orders were patrolling the Bristol road, failed to spot their advancing enemy. However, Benjamin Godfrey was unable to find the stones that marked the spot where it was easy to cross the Langmoor Rhine. For some while, Monmouth's army crashed around in the dark as those behind piled into those who had been halted by the ditch. Eventually Godfrey discovered the stepping-stones and the men struggled across the ditch. By 1.00 a.m. Lord Grey's cavalry and Monmouth himself leading the Blue Regiment were all over the Langmoor Rhine and drawn up in battle order. The possibility of triumph was so close, but what happened next almost certainly guaranteed disaster.

While Lord Feversham was asleep in Westonzoyland, Lord John Churchill (recently promoted to General Churchill) had sent a cavalry patrol on to the moor to guard the centre. A trooper spotted Grey's advancing cavalry, a musket was fired and a trooper galloped back to the Royalist camp to raise the alarm. Any success had depended on Lord Grey taking his cavalry over the moor at full speed to secure the Upper Plungeon before the royalists could defend it. But already he was too late. So far only one warning shot had been fired, but almost certainly, without the element of surprise, the battle was lost. When Lord Grey's troop reached the right flank of the royal army, a Scottish voice from Dunbarton's Regiment challenged them across the Bussex Rhine, 'Wha's theer?' One of Grey's captains answered the challenge by saying they were scouts from Lord Albermarle's troop.

When the cavalry arrived at the cattle bridge again they were challenged. 'Who are you for?'

One of Grey's troop replied, 'We're for the King.'

Again the challenge, 'Which King?'

'King Monmouth.'

'Take that with you then,' and this time a withering volley of musket fire followed. As at Bridport, Lord Grey's ill-trained horse fled in panic. Unable to control their mounts the troopers rode back across the moor straight through the two columns of advancing infantry, confusing both of them, and on back to Bridgwater. Of all the cavalry, only Lord Grey pulled up and returned to find the Duke of Monmouth.

As soon as John Churchill heard the alarm he rapidly moved the army's artillery to cover the main crossing point over the Bussex Rhine. As Lord Grey's cavalry fled, the Red and Blue Regiments continued to advance in line. Churchill's artillery opened up using the glowing musket matches of Monmouth's massed infantry as their target. The canister shot, thousands of musket balls fired from the cannons cut swathes through the helpless peasant army. By good fortune Nathaniel had slipped in the mud just before the guns fired. This accident probably saved his life. Daniel, who had been marching beside him, was one of those struck by the first fusillade. A musket ball hit him high on his left leg. The impact knocked him over. Immediately Nathaniel, who has been trying to keep a protective eye on his son, scrambled over and knelt beside the injured boy and attempted to staunch the bleeding.

A second broadside from Churchill's cannon swept the advancing soldiers. It was starting to get light and still not one of Monmouth's army had crossed the Bussex Rhine.

A third volley from the cannons was too much for the troops, most of whom had never faced enemy fire before. The remnants of the Blue Regiment backed away from the spitting death across the ditch and retreated. Monmouth, half-pike in hand as he sat on his horse, looked at the disaster unfolding and turned towards Lord Grey. 'All is lost. These fellows will soon run.' He summoned Ethan who had been close to him the whole night. 'For your constant help, I thank you, boy. Lord Grey and I will ride north to the coast to try to find a ship to take us to France. You had better hurry back to your farm. There will be a sad ending to this night's work.' The Duke of Monmouth turned his horse to the North West and rode off into the mist without a backwards glance at his suffering army. The second and third of his infantry regiments still marched forward towards the guns. Ethan wanted to find his father and brother, but thought he would be unlikely to succeed. There was nothing else for him on the moor. Glancing once more at the carnage in front of him, he gently turned

Tor and began the short ride back to Bridgwater, determined to find Lucy.

Chapter 20
Flee? Whither Shall We Flee
6th July 1685 Early in the Morning

At last the black sky began to lighten in the east, bringing an end to that ghastly night. A watery sun started to burn off the mist that had lain like a damp hand all over the moor through the hours of darkness. Long after the Blue Regiment had retreated, the others, the Red, the Green and the White, had continued to push forward against the guns because no one had told them otherwise. In the end, the peasant army showed much more raw courage than their departed royal commander. It is difficult to believe that Monmouth either deserved or earned such blind loyalty.

Nathaniel had dragged the wounded Daniel forward to find a little protection in the ditch that had proved to be such a barrier to the Duke's army. He was surprised how little water there was in the ditch and thought that better military intelligence before the battle might have led to a direct assault being successful. He had ripped off his shirt to bind up the wound on Daniel's leg and had succeeded in staunching the bleeding.

The soldiers of the King's army stayed safely behind the Bussex Rhine until all resistance had petered out. But by the light of the early morning sun the first royalist infantrymen picked their way over the Upper Plungeon and onto the moor. From Monmouth's army, over one thousand men had died that night compared with a mere eighty out of the

King's army. Nathaniel could hear the occasional pop of a musket being discharged, as wounded men were executed. He glanced back over the rim of the ditch, back the way they had come, looking for a possible way of escape. The savage actions of Feversham's soldiers already on the moor convinced him that neither he nor his son would find any mercy in that direction. If he and Daniel stayed put, they would be quickly found and in all likelihood butchered where they were. He decided that a bold approach would be their only hope. Crawling though the puddles in the bottom of the ditch he dragged Daniel behind him and then pulled him up the far side. Nathaniel then picked up his son and carried him towards the enemy soldiers. Shirtless and with a body in his arms he obviously did not represent a threat to anyone. The artillerymen, sitting smoking their pipes round the guns, allowed him to approach. No one was prepared to shoot an unarmed man. 'He's only a child. Please help.' Perhaps too his plea to them was another reason they both survived.

A young officer ordered that they be escorted to the rear. Lord Feversham had decided that Westonzoyland church should be used for prisoners and Nathaniel and Daniel were the first to be locked in. Later that day five hundred other survivors joined them in their temporary gaol. Some of the women from the village brought buckets of water to the exhausted and thirsty men. One of these whispered to Nathaniel describing a small door on the north wall of the church that was unguarded. All day their guards had told them stories about hanging gibbets being erected on the edge of the moor and he had no doubts that he and Daniel would be strung up shortly.

Daniel was weak from loss of blood but his father persuaded him that he could walk; that he had to walk. They practised up and down the north aisle of the church and when he could see no more light through the west window Nathaniel slipped out of the little door that in the past was used by the priest to enter the vestry unobserved. The door was unguarded just as he had been told. As boldness so far had served him well Nathaniel decided to continue with boldness. With Daniel leaning on his father's shoulder the two of them passed through the ranks of soldiers, sitting round their campfires laughing and smoking as they discussed their day's work. The enemy had been utterly smashed, there was no need for guards now. The two Jolliffes walked straight through the middle of the army and out the far side.

Nathaniel was determined to put as much distance as possible between them and the battle site before dawn. Though Daniel was wounded and tired and he too was exhausted, he drove them both on across the barren marshland. Daniel whimpered with pain as his father dragged him through drainage ditches and carried him on his shoulders wading over the River Cary. His aim was to reach the sanctuary of the Polden Hills before dawn, but exhaustion overtook both of them. Just before it was light they came to a small wood on a rise in the ground and Nathaniel agreed that they could lie up for a while. Safely hidden in a scooped-out hollow under a fallen ash tree Daniel rested while his father planned how to get them both back to Dorset and Corton Farm.

***

It was still dark when Ethan rode into Castle Field. He had no difficulty spotting the red cross flag among the few carts left abandoned when the army had marched onto the moor the previous night. At first their cart appeared to be empty. He could not see Lucy anywhere. Then he found her frightened and cold hiding between the wheels under the cart.

'Thank God you're safe,' she cried, scrambling to her feet and flinging her arms around him. 'An hour ago some of the cavalry rode into the camp here shouting that our army had been smashed.' With her arms wrapping him tight she was talking into the curve of his neck. She babbled faster and faster as the dam of tension broke. 'There's been a stream of soldiers coming and going, some shouting and swearing, others looking worn out and just collapsing on the ground. We haven't had any wounded yet and I didn't know what to do.'

'Monmouth has lost and gone back to France.' Ethan felt a surge of tenderness for Lucy. To feel the curve of her body pressed against his thrilled him in a way that was totally unexpected and overwhelming. Though he was enjoying holding her close, he knew there was much to do. He hoped there would be a chance for some more of that later as he unpicked her arms from around her neck. 'Listen, Lucy, we are in huge danger. We must get out of here straight away and get back to either Forde or Corton as quickly as we can. Enemy patrols will be here as soon as it's light and we must be far away by then.'

'What about the wounded?' she asked.

'The wounded will have to look out for themselves,' he said brutally. 'There's nothing more you can do. Remember that green riding outfit I brought you? Put it on. You're to be a lady from now on. I think you'll be more at risk being a boy than a girl. Come on. Hurry up,' he ordered her as she stood dithering. Ethan had had plenty of time to make plans as he rode back from the battlefield, and it didn't take Lucy long to get a grasp of what was necessary. She dug around in one of the sacks for the clothes he wanted her to wear. While Ethan went to saddle Becky she pulled off and discarded Peter's trousers and leather jerkin and put on the velvet riding skirt and jacket. She found one of the water bottles and washed her face and rinsed her hair. She hoped that made her look a little more presentable. Ethan led up Becky and, gathering up the saddlebag and two of the water bottles, they abandoned the rest of their belongings and rode swiftly out of the camp. They crossed the Parrett by the town bridge as Ethan guessed the river would provide some protection from the enemy advancing over the bloody field of Sedgemoor.

There was a faint glow in the sky. Though Ethan had no clear idea how to find his home he hoped that if he headed towards the rising sun they would eventually come to places in Dorset he recognised. Becky seemed fresh and frisky and the short gallop back from the battlefield had not tired out Tor, so they made excellent time covering the miles.

Around midday they stopped for the first time at a small farm building not far from Yeovil. 'The horses need a rest and so do I,' Ethan said. 'I'll see if

I can scrounge some food.' The cottage was a low thatched building made of cob with deep recessed windows. Outside there was a broad, raised stone slab on which Lucy thankfully sat down while Ethan knocked to try to raise someone. The farmer's wife, who met them at the door, seemed nervous and suspicious, but the boy and girl both obviously exhausted seemed harmless enough. She refused to let them inside, but brought them some bread and milk with a raw egg beaten into it. She told them they could rest for a while in the barn round the back.

Ethan told the woman about the great battle and Monmouth's flight. 'My father and young brother are still on the moor and I don't know what has happened to them.' The woman admitted that her own son had gone to join the Duke's army. 'I hope that some stranger will show him some kindness,' she said sadly.

Though Lucy was an experienced rider, apart from the gentle meander from Dorchester to Forde it was a long time since she had ridden any distance. After twenty miles hard riding, her muscles ached and her thighs were sore. Becky too had been trotted and cantered further than she had ever been before. 'I don't think I can make it all the way to your farm today,' Lucy warned Ethan. 'If we ride more slowly for one or two more hours this afternoon, I should manage the rest tomorrow.'

***

When Monmouth and Lord Grey left the battlefield they headed straight for Downside, the home of Edward Strode just to the north of Shepton Mallet. The Strode family had been Monmouth's strongest supporters and the Duke knew he would not be turned away now. They pushed their horses hard and covered the twenty-five miles in less than three hours. Edward Strode, woken by the unexpected sound of horses arriving at the front of the house, welcomed them in. Within a further half hour Monmouth and Grey were sitting down to an early breakfast of ham and eggs with toast and beer.

'You are welcome to stay here, My Lord, for as long as you choose,' Strode told him. 'But I fear my loyalty to you is well known and I would expect a visit from the dragoons later today. The King's men will be expecting you to head for the nearest coast at Weston or Bristol. My advice is to rest awhile and as soon as you are ready head for one of the ports on the south coast. You should be able to find a ship at Poole or Weymouth. There are plenty there who favour your cause.'

'Thank you, Edward.' Monmouth finished his mug of beer. 'Your advice is good. We will leave as soon as our horses have regained some energy. I would not wish to put your family in danger a moment longer than is necessary.'

'Sire, James, my friend, I wish there was more I could do for you. From here it is less than fifty miles to Weymouth. You should be there well ahead of any pursuit.' He pressed a small leather bag into Monmouth's hand. 'Here are fifty guineas. It should help you with the ship. There's only one other thing I can do. If the soldiers arrive at Downside I will tell them you have headed west.'

After a short sleep Monmouth and Grey set off again. This time they travelled south on the Yeovil road heading for the Channel ports.

***

Late in the afternoon the same day Ethan and Lucy had travelled another seven or eight miles beyond Yeovil. Lucy was exhausted and felt she could not go any further. They left the road and, hiding themselves and their horses in the trees that bordered the track, they lay down to rest. Sometime later Ethan was woken by the sound of horses coming down the road from Yeovil. Without waking Lucy he edged forward to see who it was, keeping himself well hidden by a blackthorn hedge. Two horsemen drew alongside and Ethan recognised the men who had been his commanders for the past three weeks, the Duke of Monmouth and Lord Grey. He came out from behind the bushes and stood on the verge of the road. Lord Grey had immediately drawn his pistol and pointed it at a potential enemy. 'Well met, Sirs,' Ethan said. 'I had thought you'd already taken ship to France. It must be God's good fortune that allows us to meet here.'

Monmouth looked tired but managed a wan smile. 'You can put that up, Ford,' he instructed Grey who reholstered his pistol. 'Well met indeed, Master Ethan. Perhaps not so much good fortune as we are going to the same destination from the same starting place. Lord Grey and I are strangers in this part. Can you direct us towards Weymouth or Poole?'

'I could take you there myself, Sir,' Ethan answered. He then remembered Lucy asleep in the wood. 'No, I'm sorry. I regret I have a companion who can go no further and we must spend the night near here. I can, however, give you directions.' At that moment Lucy emerged from behind the hedge, leading Becky and Tor. 'This is my companion Lucy Wells, Sir. I am seeing her back safely to our farm near Dorchester.'

'Good day, Mistress Wells.' Monmouth gravely took her hand. 'My mother's name was Lucy.'

Lord Grey, who had up to this moment said nothing, leaned across to Monmouth. 'Remember, I told you in Taunton of the boy healer, the one the soldiers were talking about? Later I saw him at work in one of the cavalry camps and thought then he was devilish pretty. My nephew told me that he had discovered that this was no boy. I believe I can recognise in Miss Lucy our boy-healer.'

Lucy blushed but said nothing.

'Is that true, Mistress Wells?' Monmouth asked and Lucy nodded. 'Lord Grey told me of your work with the wounded. It did much to improve the morale of the men and on their behalf I would like to thank you.' He paused for a moment and then continued. 'Our enemies will not be far behind us. Lord Grey and I must ride on, but if you can direct us, Ethan, we will once more be in your debt.'

'We are near to Melbury, Sir. The Strangways family, who live there, are no friends to your Grace's cause. Do not leave this road until you are well past Melbury House. Then if you go down the Chantmarle Lane and across country you will miss out Dorchester and should also avoid any royalist patrols. The paths are narrow, but I think to be lost is better than to be captured.'

'Well said, Ethan. We will do as you suggest. Now, Lord Grey and I must away. God's speed to you both.' With a wave of the hand the two men started to move off.

'Wait,' Lucy called out and the two men halted their horses. 'Sir, if you will have us, Ethan will be your guide and together we can provide a more suitable escort for you.'

It was Lord Grey who answered. 'It is true, Lucy, that it will be a great help for us to have a guide. But have no doubt, if you ride with us you put yourself at considerable risk. Also, be certain we cannot afford to delay because either of you are weary.'

Ethan and Lucy had a brief discussion and Lucy then answered for both of them. 'I am not too tired, Sir. Ethan says it is about twenty miles from here to his home. There we can all spend the night. It will be an honour for us to go with you and we are prepared to take the risk.'

They set off together, with Ethan and Monmouth leading. 'My mother will be pleased to give you food and shelter for the night,' Ethan told the Duke. 'We should be there late but before dark.'

This was quickly agreed to be an excellent plan. Now that some definite decisions had been taken, all the party, but particularly the Duke, seemed to be reinvigorated. 'Your father, Ethan, will he mind my coming?' he asked. 'Does he believe in my cause?'

'I last saw my father and my young brother Daniel approaching the guns on that horrible moor. Whether they are still alive or not, I've no idea. I do know that he would expect me to offer you our hospitality.'

'In God's truth, what have I done?' Monmouth muttered to himself. He turned back to Ethan. 'I shall pray for their safe deliverance. I can do no more now.'

They all rode on in silence, thinking their different thoughts. Lord Grey, riding next to Lucy, handed her some of the bread and cheese that the cook at Downside had given them. She accepted the offering with a smile. He broke off another hunk of bread and gave it to Ethan. They passed down narrow lanes and farm tracks and saw no one on their journey. By the time they reached the old Roman road at Winterbourne Abbas, both Lucy and Becky were exhausted and near to collapse. Monmouth noticed she was swaying in the saddle and took his horse alongside Becky. 'Ethan says it is less than five miles now, Lucy. You have done really well. This is a day you will look back on with pride all your life. My horse is strong. Now you must join me on Ulysses.'

Lord Grey helped her slide from Becky's back across to Monmouth's horse and she settled on the broad rump behind Monmouth's saddle, putting her arms around his waist. Grey gave her a drink, a mixture of water and wine, from his bottle and took hold of Becky's reins. Monmouth continued to talk encouragement to her as the tired horses plodded up to the top of the Ridgeway. From there they followed an old Iron Age track until Ethan was able to point out Corton Farm below them.

Sarah Jolliffe ran out into the courtyard when she heard the horses arriving. Ethan dismounted stiffly from Tor and she threw her arms around him. 'Thank

God you are safe.' She hugged him tightly. 'Where are your father and brother? Are they well?'

Ethan tiredly disentangled himself from his mother. 'I last saw them around midnight, Mother. They were well then, but since that time there has been a great battle near Bridgwater. I don't know how they've fared. We have ridden near fifty miles to get here.' He led Sarah round Tor to the horses behind him. 'Mother, this is His Grace, the Duke of Monmouth, and Lord Grey. In Father's name I have told them they can spend the night here. Like me they are tired and hungry.'

Monmouth dismounted and took one of Sarah's hands. 'Madam, we would indeed welcome some food and a place to sleep as your son says, but you should know that to give us shelter puts you and your family at risk.'

Sarah did not hesitate. 'In my husband's name you are welcome, My Lords.' She looked over to the girl who had been riding pillion behind Monmouth. 'Who is the lass, Ethan?'

'This is Lucy Wells, Mother. She has been my travelling companion. I will explain how we met later.' Monmouth held up his hand to Lucy to help her dismount, but the girl collapsed into his arms.

Sarah quickly realised that this was not the moment for talking. 'Josh and Kate!' She called forward the twins who had been hiding behind her. 'Look after their lordships' horses, and Tor and the other pony as well. Give them a good rub down and plenty of hay and water.' She led Monmouth towards the door. 'My Lord, welcome to Corton Farm'.

Chapter 21
The Sacred Trust
7th July 1685

Ethan put Lucy's arm around his neck and half carried half supported her up the stairs. He laid her gently on his bed in the attic room. By the time he returned downstairs Sarah had given the two guests some warm water to wash and sat them down by the kitchen fire, each with a mug of ale. Monmouth had taken off his jacket and boots and sighed with content.

'Mother, can you please look after Lucy?' Ethan asked. 'She's too tired to move.'

Sarah was busy at the stove. 'Ethan, you come and sit down. You look worn out. I'm busy cooking for our guests.' She turned to her daughter who had come in from the stables. 'Kate, you go and see to the girl. You'll know what to do.' Kate hurried off, pleased to be part of the drama.

'I've no time to sit, Mother,' Ethan told her. 'I must ride into Weymouth immediately to see what ships there are in the harbour. It is vital that His Grace leaves tomorrow before news of the battle reaches here. Any delay puts him in more danger.'

'No, Josh will go,' Sarah said. 'He has ridden to Weymouth many times before. He can take the pony as your horses look as exhausted as you do. Even if he's delayed he will find his way home as there will be plenty of moon tonight.' She turned to Monmouth. 'My Lord, tell the boy what you need to know. He is only twelve but he's a clever lad. Because he is young no one will suspect him. He will be in no danger.'

Monmouth, who was almost as tired as the others, looked as if he would disagree. He had no wish to put anyone else at risk on his behalf. While he paused, Lord Grey interrupted, 'Make yourself ready, Joshua. We need to know what ships are in the harbour, what size they are and if they are ready to sail. We also need to know whether there are soldiers guarding the port.' Lord Grey got up from his chair and patted Joshua on the shoulder. He was not often seen to smile, but he did so now. 'Hurry now, lad. This is important work you do.'

Upstairs, Lucy hadn't moved. Kate was thrilled at the responsible job she had been given. First she pulled off Lucy's boots and socks, and then she loosened the velvet jacket. She had brought a bowl of warm water from downstairs and with a cloth began to wash Lucy's hands and then her face. Lucy opened her eyes. 'Help me out of this jacket please.' The two of them struggled to take Lucy's arms out of the sleeves and she lay back down with a sigh. 'My legs hurt.' Kate began to wash her feet. 'Please help me take this skirt off. I think my legs are bleeding.' Kate had never seen a riding skirt before and directed by Lucy she found the buckles, undid them and dragged the heavy material off her. The insides of Lucy's thighs were rubbed raw.

'I must ask Mother what to do,' Kate said in a panic and fled downstairs. Sarah handed her a jar of ointment and told her sharply to get on with it. This was no time for feebleness in the Jolliffe household. Kate's hands were shaking as she gently wiped the salve onto Lucy's wounds. It obviously relieved some of the pain almost immediately. When Lucy closed her eyes Kate thought there was little more she could do. She pulled a rough blanket over the now sleeping girl and crept downstairs.

Later that night Sarah sat by the fire waiting for her youngest son to return. It was dark outside and all four of the escapees from Sedgemoor were asleep. It was after midnight when she heard the sound of the pony's hooves, still a long way off, as Josh trotted the last mile back to the farm. Ten minutes later the boy came into the kitchen.

Joshua was bubbling with excitement. 'Weymouth is swarming with soldiers, Mother. I've never seen so many. I was stopped twice by guards on the road going in and asked to explain what I was doing up so late. I came back on the Dorchester road so I wouldn't have to go past the same men, but there were guards there too. There were three ships in the harbour, but soldiers were standing at the end of the gangplank on each of them. It looked as if they were waiting for him.'

Sarah gave him a mug of warm milk and told him to go to bed. She wondered how much danger her family was really in and what to do next. She put another log on the fire and sat for a while. The longer the Duke stayed at Corton the more likelihood there was that he would be captured. It also meant more danger for all those at the farm. About four in the morning she woke Ethan and explained the situation to him.

'He must leave at once, Mother. Poole harbour or possibly Lymington might not yet be guarded. I shall escort him as far as Poole.' Sarah protested at that, but she could see that her son's mind was made up. She recognised in Ethan the same sense of duty that his father had.

Monmouth and Lord Grey were woken and immediately understood the need for haste. Despite still feeling the effects of yesterday's gruelling ride and lack of sleep, Monmouth managed to remain remarkably cheerful. Ethan, with the resilience of youth, seemed to have recovered completely. While he went to saddle the horses, Sarah cooked up some porridge.

Sarah had noticed that Monmouth had taken his saddlebag to bed with him the previous night. Ethan returned from the stables in time to see the Duke place the saddlebag on the table and open it. He drew out a small simple black box made of a sort of wood that Sarah had not seen before. 'I have one further request to make of your family.' He pushed the box towards Sarah. 'Give this to your husband when he returns and ask him to look after it for me. I give this as a charge to the Jolliffe family. When your husband is no longer able to honour it, the responsibility passes to Ethan. Will you do that, Ethan?' The boy nodded. 'The contents of this box are very important to me. In time I shall send for it. Inside there is also sufficient money for you to use in bringing it to me wherever I might be. Will you accept this charge on behalf of your husband?'

'We will, Sir,' Sarah answered without hesitation.

'It will be a sacred trust for the family, just like the chapel is,' Ethan added.

'To be caught with this box would be very dangerous for you. It must be well hidden so if the soldiers come searching they will never find it.' He glanced up at the Bible on the shelf. 'Give me that please, Ethan, and bring me a pen and some ink.'

Ethan placed the Bible on the table and went to fetch the pen and ink. Monmouth dipped the quill pen into the inkwell and next to the children's names on the first page carefully wrote in the margin *7th July 1685. The Day of the Sacred Trust* and underneath he signed the initials *JS* and then *R*. He thought awhile and then added *Semper Fidelis*. He turned the book to Ethan. 'What do you think, lad?'

Embarrassed, Ethan admitted that he couldn't read so Monmouth explained. 'This is today's date. Then I have used your words and called today the Day of the Sacred Trust. Those are my initials, James Scott, and the R is for Rex, Latin for King, though that is a title, I fear, will never be mine. This here is also Latin and from now must be a motto for the Jolliffe family. It means *Always Faithful*. That is how I shall remember you all.' He sanded the ink and closing the book handed it back to Sarah. Ethan could see that his mother was crying. He felt both a heavy weight but also exhilaration in the trust this great man had given his family. 'Now we must ride.' The Duke turned to Sarah. 'Say goodbye to Lucy for me. There is no need for her to be woken. Tell her I think she is an exceptionally brave girl and I again thank her for what she did for my soldiers.' He bent down to kiss Kate on the cheek and then Sarah. 'I shall pray that your Nathaniel and Daniel are safe, and I promise I will try to see that Ethan comes to no harm.'

Lord Grey, who had said little all morning, shook Sarah's hand and with that the two of them, followed by Ethan, left the house and rode off into the darkness.

At first they travelled slowly and carefully, partly because it was dark but also because the horses were stiff from their long journey the day before. Once on the Ridgeway they made better time and crossed the Dorchester road as the sun lit up the sky in the east. Where possible Ethan led them by tracks and narrow lanes away from the main road. They crossed the River Frome by the old packhorse bridge at Wool, which was fortunately unguarded. By now they were in a part of Dorset that was unfamiliar to Ethan. They overtook a carter on his way to Wareham market who told them it was less than fifteen miles to Poole, suggesting that the quickest way would be to ford the River Piddle upstream from Wareham and to travel across country.

By now both horses and men were tired and again and again they were forced to take a rest. At Upton they saw that the road into Poole was guarded and they narrowly escaped detection. The possibilities of escaping by sea from Poole were forgotten and the small harbour at Lymington became their next target. As the day wore on their stops became more and more regular. Monmouth was depressed and silent and neither Ethan nor Lord Grey could get him to think about his future. They saw enemy patrols with increasing frequency and were forced further and further inland. Near Ferndown, Monmouth, obviously near to exhaustion, suggested that they should surrender to the next patrol they saw. Lord Grey persuaded him to hide in a small wood while he went forward to see if he could discover somewhere for them to spend the night. Neither of them was to see Lord Grey again.

When it was dark Ethan started to prepare a bed of branches and leaves for the Duke, but Monmouth stopped him. 'You have done enough, Ethan. It is time for you to go home.' Ethan started to protest, but Monmouth gently stopped him. 'I promised your mother I would not lead you unnecessarily into danger. Your family has done enough for my cause. It is essential that you put as many miles as possible between yourself and this place by morning.' He fished in his jacket pocket and pulled out a golden guinea. 'This is not a payment. There is no way I can repay the services you have done me. Keep this as a memory of the man you helped who would have been your King. Take my horse, Ulysses. Both our nags are worn out and you will need him to get home safely. I will go from here on foot. Tomorrow I expect they will take me, but I believe my uncle the King will show me mercy.'

Ethan knelt and kissed the hand Monmouth extended to him. Without a word he turned away, leading Tor and Ulysses, and left the Duke of Monmouth sitting on a rotting tree stump.

Chapter 22
A Long Way Home
6th – 13th July 1685

Nathaniel struggled to make up his mind. If he failed to find medical help for Daniel the boy's wound could well become infected. However, unless he put a distance between them and that bloody moor, they would quickly be recaptured. From what he had seen, that was likely to mean death and he was determined that Daniel would not die.

From the little copse where they had spent the night he could see a tiny cottage almost entirely surrounded by rows of planted willow trees. He decided that help for Daniel was most urgent and made his choice. Leaving Daniel lying in their overnight hidey-hole he went to the cottage and knocked on the studded oak door. A bent old lady opened it and promptly slammed it shut in his face. Nathaniel knocked again. This time, an equally old man, with a face as wizened as a walnut, opened the door and stood there, scowling at him. 'What do you want?'

Throughout his life Nathaniel had tried to be an honest man, but he would certainly have lied if necessary to save his son. He decided that on this occasion the truth would serve him best. 'My son and I have escaped from the soldiers. He lies wounded in your wood. Will you help us?'

'You bin fighting for that Monmouth?' the man asked.

'Yes, fighting and losing,' Nathaniel replied.

'Best bring the lad in then,' and he closed the door.

Carrying Daniel on his back, Nathaniel returned to the cottage and knocked a third time. It was the old woman who opened the door. 'Come,' was all she said.

The main room, which opened up straight from the door, was dark after the morning sunlight. A square table dominated the centre of the room and it was here she indicated to Nathaniel he should lay Daniel. 'Take his breeks off then.' Nathaniel was getting used to the woman's clipped way of speaking. He unbuckled Daniel's trousers and slipped them off. The torn shirt he had used to stop the wound was dirty from the muddy ditches and soaked with blood. The woman untied the crude bandage and looked at the gash caused by the musket ball. She shook her head, sucking in her breath between her teeth as she prodded with her finger. Daniel groaned.

'She knows what to do.' The old man tugged at Nathaniel's arm. 'Best leave her be.' They went into a second room and the man took an ancient jacket from a hook behind the door and handed it to Nathaniel. 'You ought to be dressed if the soldiers come looking.' This was not a family who used two words when one would do. Nathaniel felt confident that they were not going to hand him over to the army immediately, but this didn't mean they were out of danger. 'I would like to thank you. My name is Nathaniel and my son is called Daniel. We farm in Dorset.'

'You be in the wrong place then. You and he both.' That seemed to be the end of the conversation for a while. Nathaniel still didn't know his hosts' names and he had to take on trust that the old woman knew what she was doing to his son. 'Come outside,' the man said and left the cottage, with Nathaniel following tamely behind. 'If the soldiers come, use this.' He handed Nathaniel a small sickle.

That won't be much use to hold off Feversham's army, Nathaniel thought. But the old man pointed to the nearest willow bed where he had obviously been working. 'Cut those withies there. My woman will hide the boy.' Nathaniel realised that the old man had summed up the situation instantly and produced an immediate and acceptable plan. He decided that the best disguise, despite his exhaustion, was to start working. He went to the willow bed and began to cut the thin wands and to stack them on the path. The old man was sitting behind the cottage smoking his pipe and weaving the split canes into a basket. Though Nathaniel was anxious to be heading for home he knew Daniel wouldn't make it unless he had first rested and been able to build up his strength.

Around 11 o'clock the woman brought out a mug of beer for each of them with some bread and cold meat. This was the first meal Nathaniel had eaten for thirty-six hours and the simple meal tasted like a feast. 'The boy's sleeping,' was all she said.

Nathaniel reckoned it must have been mid-afternoon when the soldiers rode up. He saw that the old man had slipped quietly into the house, so he chopped away at the willows.

'Seen any strangers here?' the young officer shouted to him.

'Nah.' Nathaniel reckoned that the old man's short sentences might well be worth imitating.

'We need to search your house.' The young man couldn't have been much above twenty years old and his three dragoons didn't look very interested in the job they had to do.

''Tain't my house,' Nathaniel said. ''Tis the Master's,' and with that he again began to hack at the willows.

It does not take long to search a two-bedroom cottage with one small outhouse. Within a few minutes the soldiers had come outside again and rode off. As they left, the officer shouted, 'Let us know if you see any strangers around.'

Nathaniel felt that the character he was playing would not have taken part in idle chitchat. He kept on cutting and said nothing. When the dragoons were out of sight he went into the cottage to discover why they had not found Daniel. The old woman carefully removed a stack of baskets from a pile in the corner. They appeared to have been stacked higgledy-piggledy, but when the last one was lifted clear and a length of reed matting was peeled back he saw his son sleeping soundly on a rug on the floor. She smiled. 'He'll get better now,' was all she said, so he went outside to cut some more willows.

For three days he worked at the cottage. Twice more soldiers came to the door but on neither occasion did they bother to go inside. On both occasions the old man answered their questions as tersely as he had answered Nathaniel's and this seemed to satisfy them. On the third evening the old man told Nathaniel, 'I be taking baskets to

Glastonbury market tomorrow early. Best the two of you come with me.' That was all.

The next morning a horse and cart had appeared from somewhere and the old man and his woman loaded it with baskets of all different shapes and sizes. They left a coffin-like space for Daniel against the side of the cart and the old woman slipped a rug in for him to lie on. Once he was in position she patted his face much to his embarrassment and stacked more baskets over him until he was completely hidden. 'He's a good lad,' she said to Nathaniel. 'Now you mind him well.' When Nathaniel tried to thank her, she waved a hand and went back into the cottage.

The journey towards Glastonbury was without incident, the old man puffing contentedly on his pipe. They passed several different groups of soldiers marching towards Bath and went through one guard post unchallenged on the outskirts of Street. In the town marketplace the old man stopped the cart and pointed south. 'Your home be that way. Follow the road to Yeovil.' These were the first words he had spoken that morning. Like his wife he was not interested in being thanked and Nathaniel was conscious he did not even know the names of those who had saved him and his son. The old man climbed back onto his cart, cracked the whip and set off, leaving Nathaniel and Daniel standing beside the market cross.

Daniel's leg was still very tender, but he limped beside his father uncomplaining. Nathaniel, though anxious to reach home as soon as possible, decided not to try to do too much walking each day. The next two days were remarkable for their lack of anything unusual happening. They passed to the north of Yeovil, fearing that the entrance to the town would be guarded. By now Nathaniel recognised the area and was getting more and more confident about getting Daniel back to Corton Farm. They lived either by begging for food or by stealing from farmers. This bothered Nathaniel, but he was prepared to sacrifice any principle for his son's safety. By the third day the pain of Daniel's leg had increased and a gland had swollen in his groin. Even a short walk made him sweat and out of breath. That night they slept in a barn near the head of the Cerne Abbas Giant. This was less than fifteen miles from their farm. Even with short stages Nathaniel believed they should be home in two days.

On the fourth day since leaving the willow-cutter's cottage they arrived at the River Frome on the outskirts of Dorchester. By now Nathaniel was carrying Daniel whose leg was so swollen he could put no weight on it. When they reached the old Roman aqueduct, which cut through the eastern corner of Poundbury hill fort, he could go no further. He carefully laid Daniel down. 'I'll have to go and get help, Dan. I'll leave you the rest of our water and get home as quickly as I can. If you lie in this old water channel and I cover you, no one will spot you. You should be safe as I don't think any water has flowed down here for a thousand years.'

Daniel managed to smile at what he thought was his father's attempt at humour. 'I promise I won't be going anywhere, Father. Be as quick as you can.'

Nathaniel slotted his son into the ditch that had once been an aqueduct and kissed him on the forehead. Finding some pieces of wood nearby he gently placed these in position to cover him. He then strode off up the hill, determined to fetch help from home as soon as possible. It was then that his luck ran out. A returning cavalry patrol coming down the road from Bridport saw him. Nathaniel ran, but the horsemen quickly overhauled and captured him. 'One more for the cells, lads,' a trooper called out. A defeated Nathaniel's hands were tied behind his back and he was dragged into Dorchester. He was desperate to think how he might get a message to Corton. If he failed, Daniel would die. His own fate concerned him not at all.

When the little column stopped for a moment in Dorchester High Street, he spotted an old friend from Upwey leaning against the wall. He knew he had to act quickly 'Mistress Homer.' The woman looked up and he saw that she recognised him. 'Tell Sarah her heart's desire is where we exchanged rings.'

'Keep your mouth shut, you,' the corporal snarled and clubbed him in the stomach with the butt of his musket. Nathaniel was forced to his knees. Annie Homer looked horrified. Nathaniel, gasping for breath, managed to shout out again, 'Please, Annie. It's urgent.'

For this he received a kick in the chest, which laid him out on the ground. It was a half-conscious Nathaniel who was dragged round the corner towards Dorchester gaol.

Mistress Homer was both shocked and intrigued. She was determined to get the message to Sarah Jolliffe without delay, partly out of friendship but also she revelled in being first with any piece of local gossip. She persuaded her husband to drive immediately to Corton Farm, where she passed on to Sarah the news that her Nathaniel was a prisoner, in a suitably sombre voice. 'The soldiers beat him up something terrible. It was awful. Before he was knocked out he said, "Tell Sarah her heart's desire is where we exchanged rings." I think that's right.' She repeated it in an even more doom-laden voice for greater emphasis. 'Your Nathaniel then said it was urgent, you poor dear.' She paused to gauge the effect of her dramatic story. 'It must have been terrible important because they knocked him down a second time before dragging him off.' Strangely, and rather disappointingly for Annie, Sarah was not weeping hysterically nor collapsing in a faint. 'What do you think it means, Sarah?'

'I have no idea, Annie, but thank you very much for bringing the message. You are a true friend.' And a mystified Mistress Annie Homer found herself gently escorted out of the door and sent on her way home.

Chapter 23
Rescue
11th – 13th July 1685

When Ethan said goodbye to Monmouth his father and Daniel were still someway to the north of Yeovil on their dreadful journey back to Corton Farm. Ethan was exhausted. He had only managed to snatch a few hours sleep over the last four days, but he was anxious to get home as soon as he could. Both horses, Tor and Ulysses were also worn out, so throughout the first night he led them on foot. He was aware that there was potentially still danger for him, particularly as the Duke's horse might easily be recognised. He decided to travel inland, keeping well away from the coast, as the purpose of most of the patrols seemed to prevent Monmouth escaping to France.

He travelled by night and slept by day, covering only a few miles each night. By the third day Ulysses seemed fresh enough to be ridden and he wearily pulled himself into the saddle and completed his journey seventy hours after he had last seen Monmouth. Lucy and Sarah welcomed him home with nothing but sad news. They had still heard nothing about Nathaniel or Daniel. Also, the previous day, it had been announced in Dorchester market place that Monmouth had been captured and sent to London for trial.

Joshua, who in the absence of all the men folk had been helping his mother run the farm, offered to rub down and feed the horses – an offer that Ethan was happy to accept. He slumped over the kitchen table while his mother heated up some food. 'I'm really starving, Mother, and haven't had a proper meal since I was last here.'

'Tell me what happened,' Lucy asked, so he told her of his journey to Ferndown, how Lord Grey had gone missing and how Monmouth had finally ordered him to go home. Sarah was relieved that one at least of her men folk was back safely. She hummed to herself while listening to the two of them chatting together. In her heart she gave a blessing to Monmouth that he had kept his promise to her.

'He gave me his horse Ulysses because he knew how tired Tor must be. He also gave me this.' Ethan brought out the golden guinea and handed it to Lucy to look at. 'I shall keep it always in memory of a good man.' Lucy handed the coin back to him and he gave it to Sarah. 'Will you keep it safe for me, Mother?' Ethan said. Sarah placed it carefully in her little treasure box.

'Last time I saw you, Lucy, you were worn out. How are you feeling now?'

'I was so exhausted that I slept for twenty-four hours. Kate and your mother have looked after me really well. Kate has been especially sweet. I'm still terribly stiff when I walk and I've some horrid scars where my legs were rubbed raw on Becky's sides, but,' and she giggled, 'I'm afraid I can't show them to you.'

Sarah pretended to be shocked by this but, as she had come to know Lucy, she had already grown fond of her. She trusted the girl and it was not difficult to see she was important to Ethan. Two mornings later a well-rested Ethan announced that he would have to take Tor back to Forde Abbey. 'I will take Ulysses as well and come straight home tomorrow. I need to tell Lady Prideaux that I must manage the farm here until father comes home. Are you coming with me, Lucy?'

'I never want to sit on a horse again,' Lucy said with spirit. 'I'll be happy helping your mother here. Do be careful. I'm sure there's still danger.' So once again Ethan left home.

Lucy and Sarah spent the morning working in the kitchen. Lucy was no cook and marvelled at how efficiently Sarah produced food with simple ingredients. Sarah gently quizzed Lucy while she worked, and she was happy to chat about her father in London and her uncle and aunt in Dorchester. She told Sarah what she knew about Ethan's activities over the last fortnight and her own attempts at nursing. 'When next we ride into town we must find your uncle and tell him you are safe. I expect he has been worried about you,' Sarah said. It was then that Annie Homer turned up, handed on her strange message and promptly left.

Sarah called the twins and Lucy together. Although she had presented a calm appearance to Annie, the news about Nathaniel had naturally distressed her. She sat the three of them round the kitchen table. *How strange*, she thought, *that I already think of Lucy as part of my family.* 'Children, thank God your father is alive, even if he is a prisoner. The soldiers seemed to have knocked him about a bit, but Annie Homer saw him in Dorchester earlier today and she didn't think he had been wounded in the battle. I will go to the gaol tomorrow to see if I can speak to him. Before he was hit he told

Annie to pass a message on to me. "*Tell Sarah her heart's desire is where we exchanged rings.*" He said it was urgent. I've tried to work it out but I'm so worried I'm not thinking very clearly. I have no idea what he meant.'

Lucy grabbed a piece of paper and a pencil and wrote down the mysterious conundrum. 'There are clearly two separate parts to this,' she said, drawing a pencil line after the word *desire*. 'Let's take the second part first. When you were married, did you swap rings?'

'No dear, we gave each other a betrothal ring when we first promised ourselves to each other.' She held up her left hand showing her ring finger. 'This is mine. Nathaniel doesn't wear his all the time because of the work on the farm. Let me think.' Her face scrunched up in concentration as she remembered back eighteen years. 'It was in the summertime. I was only nineteen years old and working in Dorchester. Nathaniel was working for Sir Edmund at Forde at the time. That was old Sir Edmund. He, I mean Nathaniel, came over especially to see me one Sunday. We went for a walk on the old fort at Poundbury and that was when we gave each other rings.'

'*Where we exchanged rings*. That's it. Poundbury fort must be where he's talking about,' Lucy said decisively. 'Now, what about the first part? What does that mean?'

'I don't know. It's nothing to me.'

'What do you want more than anything in the world?' Lucy insisted.

'Oh, that's easy. I want Nathaniel and the boys to be home safely.'

'Well,' Lucy said triumphantly. 'It can't be Ethan who's at Forde Abbey or Nathaniel who's in gaol. It must be Daniel. He's trying to tell you that Daniel is at this Poundbury place.' She thought quickly. 'Nathaniel wouldn't have left him if there hadn't been a problem. He must be hurt or something.'

'I must go to him straight away,' Sarah said and she rushed around collecting her cloak and a blanket. 'I do wish Ethan were here to help.'

'Wait a moment, Sarah.' Lucy had worried what she should call Ethan's mother. When it came about, it all seemed quite natural. 'Nathaniel wouldn't have passed on a coded message unless he had thought there was still danger for Daniel. Your husband has just been taken to gaol. If you go rushing there to pick Daniel up, someone will recognise you and you risk drawing attention to him.' She turned to the twins. 'Do you two know how to get to Poundbury?'

'I do,' Josh said. 'Pa took me there after market once. He showed me the old watercourse where he asked you to marry him, Mother. I'll go.'

'You'll do no such thing, Joshua.' She turned to Lucy 'It must be me. I'll not have another of my sons at risk.'

'No, Sarah. I'll go with the twins. Daniel knows me. We met in Taunton. If you get caught all of us will be in danger. This way there'll be very little risk,' Lucy interrupted, thinking fast. 'What danger could there possibly be with three girls and a small boy travelling with the pony and trap?'

'Why three girls?' Kate asked.

'Last time I saw Daniel he was in a tattered blue military uniform. It will be dangerous for him to travel in that. He'll be recognised as a soldier. I'll wear this dress you lent me, and take the green velvet skirt and jacket for Daniel. No one will suspect him if he dresses as a girl. He will be hungry too. Boys always are, but he probably hasn't eaten properly for days. Can you put a hamper together? We'll pretend we're having a picnic.'

Joshua went out to make ready the pony trap while Sarah gathered together whatever food she could find. Kate collected Lucy's green outfit from the attic and she proudly presented a straw bonnet, which she had found.

Lucy tried to reassure Sarah who was desperately worried what might happen. She was not as confident as she pretended to be, but she was certain that Sarah was exactly the wrong person to be rushing off on a rescue mission. They piled the bundles of blankets and clothes and the basket of food into the trap.

'Take the hill track to Winterbourne St Martin,' Sarah told Joshua, 'and don't go into Dorchester. There's likely to be soldiers in town.'

Joshua was determined to be in charge of the pony and cart, so Lucy and Kate walked alongside for the first mile while Hubert, the pony, pulled the light cart up the steep hill. Once over the Ridgeway they all climbed on board and rattled down the other side, skirting Maiden Castle and up to the Bridport road. There all the fun of their adventure quickly evaporated. At the crossroads they saw three newly erected gibbets with the bodies of young soldiers hanging off them. A group of dragoons were laughing and jeering.

'Are they dead?' Kate whispered.

'I think so,' Lucy answered, 'but don't look at them if it makes you feel odd. When we pass the soldiers,' she told both of them, 'try to smile and wave to them. We're all supposed to be having a good time. And Joshua, slow down. We mustn't look as if we're in a hurry.'

Joshua walked the trap past the soldiers while Kate bravely waved and smiled. They crossed the main road and were soon out of sight and onto the path that circled Poundbury hill fort. The course of the old aqueduct was still clearly visible in the long grass. 'I think the place Father showed me is just round the corner,' Joshua said.

The sides of the hill fort were too steep for Hubert to manage so Lucy suggested they tied the pony to a bush and search on foot. Of course it was Joshua, rushing ahead, who discovered Daniel's hiding place. He rushed back to the others shouting. 'I've found him, I've found him.'

'Be quiet,' Lucy told him roughly. 'There's no need to tell the whole world.' But she and Kate hurried over to where Joshua was pointing. They carefully removed the planks of wood to reveal Daniel as snug as a hamster in his nest.

The boy looked exhausted and frightened, but managed a tired smile. 'Hi, you lot. Lucy, you look much prettier as a girl. Where's Father?'

Lucy decided now was not the time to unload that bit of bad news on him. 'We've come instead. We thought it would be safer, but we must hurry.' She explained her plan to Daniel. 'Josh, see if you can bring Hubert and the cart any closer.' She turned back to Daniel. 'We will carry you over as carefully as we can when we've changed your clothes.'

Lucy and Kate gently lifted the injured boy out of the water channel and, with as much consideration as they could, peeled him out of his old uniform and struggled to fit him into the lady's riding kit they had brought. Lucy was appalled at the state of his leg, which looked red and swollen around the bandage, though there was no sign of new bleeding. 'It hurts,' Daniel whimpered. Kate tied the bonnet under his chin and they stood back to admire the effect.

'Not too bad,' Lucy said. 'As long as no one comes too close, you'll pass as a girl. Remember Daniel, if we meet any soldiers, we must smile and wave. We're not skulking home as if we've a guilty secret.'

By now Joshua had returned. 'I've managed to get Hubert just round the corner.' He looked worriedly at his brother. 'It's not far, Dan. Honestly.'

Lucy turned to Joshua. 'Let's put those planks back and hide Daniel's old clothes in the ditch.' The three of them then picked up Daniel's limp body and without too much of a problem carried him over to where Hubert was patiently chewing the leaves off the myrtle bush he was tied to. Kate lowered the backboard of the trap and together they eased Daniel in. 'You can lie there for the moment,' Lucy told him, 'but if we pass any soldiers you will have to sit up.' Daniel smiled his acknowledgement but lay exhausted and unmoving on the blanket while Joshua turned the pony round and the anxious group headed for home.

'Must we go past that horrid place again?' Kate asked nervously.

'I'll try to find a different route, but I don't know any other way,' Lucy told her. She knew if possible avoiding the soldiers altogether would be safer for them. She explained the problem to Daniel.

'If we continue along Poundbury Road for a little way we'll be able to turn up Tilly Whim Lane. I've been there with Father when we've been going to Charminster. It comes out at Winterbourne St Martin. You'll know the way from there, Josh,' Daniel croaked. All agreed that this was the best idea.

Kate and Lucy again walked alongside while the tough little Hubert pulled the increased load to the top of the Ridgeway. The jolting of the cart made Daniel occasionally cry out in pain, but for the final two miles he seemed to be sleeping. It was a tired group that finally pulled into the farmyard just before dark.

Sarah sized up the situation immediately and took charge. She helped Lucy carry Daniel to his usual bed, talking soothingly to her frightened son. 'It's good to be home, Mother,' Daniel murmured and closed his eyes again.

Sarah removed the old and dirty bandage from his leg and sniffed at the wound. 'There's some flow here,' she said to Lucy pointing to the pus on the cloth, 'but the wound smells reasonably clean. Tomorrow we'll fetch Goody Shipley from Cor Gate. She's a wise woman and will know what to do. I'll sit with Daniel tonight. The rest of you go to bed.'

Chapter 24
A Dangerous Pause
14th July 1685

Lucy leaned over the old woman's shoulder to see more clearly what she was doing. 'Don't crowd me, girl. I need the light to see what I must see.'

At six that morning Joshua had taken the pony and cart the half mile to Cor Gate and passed on his mother's message to the shepherd's widow. Mother Shipley had listened carefully to Josh and then collected an array of bottles and jars together in a basket and come over to Corton Farm. Sarah looked exhausted, but Lucy suspected it was tiredness of spirit rather than anything physical. *She'll feel better when Ethan gets back,* she thought. So it was Lucy who led the old woman up to the room where Daniel was lying.

'Make yourself useful, lassie, and hold these.' The old woman handed Lucy some jars and a leather bag that seemed to be filled with dried leaves. 'There's some poison in the wound, and the lad has a fever, but nothing Goody Shipley can't cure.' She started to clean round the hole in Daniel's leg with drops of vinegar on a piece of cloth. Lucy noticed the cloth was so clean it looked as if it had been newly boiled. The old woman peered carefully down at the boy's body. 'Looks as if his important bits are undamaged,' she cackled, 'if that's what you're interested in.'

Lucy stood up, blushing. She had never seen a naked boy before, other than her brother Ben, but she was extremely interested to see how the old woman was going to treat Daniel's wound. 'Give me that jar,' she ordered and Lucy handed it over. Inside there was a dark green ointment which Goody Shipley began to apply generously to the red gash on Daniel's leg.

'What's that?' Lucy asked.

'That is woundwort. Some call it yarrow. I cut the tops off the flower in summer, dry them and mix them with pig's fat. That will draw the poison to the surface. Pass me the bag.' Lucy handed it over. 'This is sphagnum moss. First I steam it to get rid of any bugs that might cause infection, then I dry it. When it's like this I lay it on the wound.' She carefully placed a handful of the dried moss over Daniel's leg. 'This will lift all the evil out of the leg.'

Some people might have taken this old woman for a witch, Lucy thought. It was not many years earlier that government witch-finders had toured the country, picking on any elderly widows who lived on their own. Suspicious or jealous neighbours had often reported these poor women to the authorities. Accusations of witchcraft were difficult to disprove and many innocent people, whose only crime was a wish to earn a few pennies by helping people with well-tried country remedies, had suffered the ducking stool or been burned at the stake. But to Lucy, Goody Shipley was impressively confident yet careful in what she was doing. Her treatment gave Daniel his best chance of survival. 'I shall be nursing him,' she told Mother Shipley. 'What should I do?'

The old woman gave her some detailed instructions which again all seemed logical and sensible. As she was repacking her basket she looked Lucy straight in the face for the first time. 'You will be coming to see me again shortly. I will have an answer for you then,' she said mysteriously. With that she shuffled off and Lucy was left alone with a sleeping Daniel.

Ethan returned the next day. Sarah immediately told him of Nathaniel's imprisonment and Daniel's wound. Ethan brought alarming news. 'That's not good,' he said. 'The soldiers are searching all the houses. I saw them in Portesham and they were coming this way. I was told they're taking to gaol anyone they find who is wounded. They also seem to have detailed knowledge about who's missing from each household. There will be trials at the assizes in Dorchester next month and they're using absence from home as evidence that men were with Monmouth.'

'We can tell them where your father is,' Sarah said miserably. 'They already have him in gaol. They mustn't find Daniel though. He won't survive if he's put in prison.' She started to weep quietly. Ethan slumped down in a chair, obviously exhausted from his long ride.

Someone's got to do something, Lucy thought. *And it looks as if it's got to be me.* 'If the soldiers do come,' she said, 'they mustn't know that Nathaniel's been away for three weeks. Sarah, you must tell them that he was visiting someone just yesterday and didn't come home last night. Tell them you are worried because Annie Homer told you she'd seen him in Dorchester being held prisoner. You must get a message to him today, Sarah. He mustn't tell anyone he was with Monmouth.'

'What about Daniel?' Ethan asked. 'If they find him and see he's been wounded, they will know he was at the battle. We must hide him.'

'We'll put him in the secret closet,' Sarah said. No one will find him inside that. The door in the panelling is so well made,' she said to Lucy, 'that unless you know it's there, you could never find it.'

'If they discover that Daniel's missing, they will guess he was with the Duke,' Ethan said. 'That won't help Father's case either.'

'I'll be Daniel,' Lucy said. 'Get me some of his clothes, Ethan. The sooner we are ready the better. They could be here at any time.'

'We must put the Bible and Monmouth's box in with Daniel as well,' Ethan said. He saw that Lucy looked puzzled. 'I'll explain later,' he told her.

It was an hour before the soldiers clattered into the yard, dragging behind them a sad-looking bunch of captives. By that time everyone at Corton Farm was prepared. Daniel was lying hidden in the closet with the Bible and the black box. Lucy, dressed in a mixture of Ethan and Daniel's clothes, was in the stables rubbing down the horses and Joshua and Kate had been firmly told that they were to call Lucy 'Daniel' and that this wasn't a game. It was all right if they wanted to look frightened. Their missing father would be a good enough reason for that. Sarah and Ethan waited in the kitchen.

The corporal in charge of the four troopers was a rough, crude man. The Dowager Queen's Regiment, known as Kirke's Lambs, had built up an evil reputation for themselves in Tangiers, the colony that had been gifted to England from Portugal when

Charles II had married Catherine of Braganza, the Portuguese princess. After the battle on Sedgemoor the reputation of Kirke's Lambs was worsened by their brutality to any rebel soldiers they had captured. Corporal Oakshott and his men, members of this regiment, had personally strung up fifteen young men on hastily erected gibbets, including some who were already almost dead from their wounds. Some days ago, frustratingly the orders had come through that there should be no more hangings without trial. They were to bring suspects to Dorchester for the assizes. Their present prisoners had been picked up from farms and cottages in rural Dorset. Some were wounded and all looked scared and exhausted. Sarah came out into the yard to greet the corporal and his men.

'We're Colonel Percy Kirke's Lambs,' the corporal said, proudly pointing to the badge prominent on his uniform. 'We have orders from His Majesty to sniff out any rebels involved in the recent Western Rising.'

'We are a God-fearing house,' Sarah answered him. 'There are no rebels here.'

'That's for me to find out,' William Oakshott said bluntly. He drew a piece of paper from his pouch. 'Your neighbours tell me there should be six people living here. Jolliffes.' He read down the list. 'Nathaniel, Sarah, Ethan, Daniel, Joshua and Katherine. I want to see them all now.

'I am Sarah. The dragoons in Dorchester took my husband yesterday. We don't know why. I shall go to visit the gaol later today to find out. He is no rebel though.'

'Ha! One more to be stabbed with a Bridport dagger,' Oakshott laughed.

Sarah shuddered, knowing he referred to the hangman's rope manufactured in the ropewalks of Bridport. There was little point in arguing Nathaniel's innocence with this brute. 'This is my son, Ethan,' Sarah went on. 'My other son, Daniel, is in the stables with the horses, and the twins are playing, I think, in the barn. Shall I fetch them?'

'No, he can,' Oakshott said, pointing a thumb at Ethan. 'You, woman, will fetch food and ale for my men.'

Ethan returned a few minutes later with Lucy and the twins in tow. In the kitchen he discovered Corporal Oakshott trying to kiss his mother and tear at her clothing. 'You leave her alone,' he shouted, leaping forward to attack the brute. One of the watching soldiers casually sideswiped the boy with the butt of his musket, knocking him to the ground where he lay dazed and groaning.

The disturbance was sufficient to make Oakshott break off molesting Sarah. The presence of young children seemed to have dampened any desire he might have had. 'Give us some food, woman,' he growled at Sarah. These men disgusted her but she straightened her clothing and busied herself collecting some cold meat. Lucy knelt on the floor to check on Ethan who was moaning quietly.

'Who are you?' Oakshott said, directing the question at Lucy.

'I'm Daniel,' she replied, 'and this, who you have half killed, is my brother Ethan.' The corporal took a piece of charcoal from his pocket and put a cross by their names on his list. 'These,' Lucy said, pointing to the twins, who were white-faced and shaking, 'are Joshua and Katherine who is known as Kate.' Two more crosses.

The next five minutes passed agonisingly slowly. Lucy told Ethan to stay down on the floor. 'We don't need to provoke them any further,' she whispered. Eventually the soldiers went outside, still eating the food Sarah had provided. Without saying anything further they mounted their horses and rode out of the yard, dragging behind them the miserable prisoners they had collected earlier.

Ethan got shakily to his feet. 'I'll just check that they've really gone,' he said.

Lucy led him over to the chair by the fire and sat him down. She gently rubbed the bruise under his right eye, which was already swollen, and colouring nicely. 'You stay here, Ethan. Daniel can go,' she said grinning and went out. She was back in a few minutes. 'They've gone. I went up the hill to the road and saw them go into the next farm.'

Sarah had already been upstairs to reassure Daniel that everything was all right. 'I told him that he must stay in the closet for a while to be on the safe side. I did leave the door open though. I've brought these.' Sarah placed the family Bible and the wooden box on the table.

Lucy was confused as to why there was so much secrecy over the Bible and a very ordinary-looking box. Ethan explained about Monmouth's orders to them while she had been sleeping in the attic. Together they opened the book at the first page. 'This is what he wrote,' Ethan said, pointing. The writing was strong and clear.

Lucy knew that Ethan had difficulty reading so picked up the book. '*7th July 1685. The Day of the Sacred Trust*,' she read aloud. 'What does that mean?'

Ethan explained about the box and the money. 'The Duke's final instruction was that a member of the Jolliffe family must bring the box to him when he sends for it.'

'*JS and R.* What's that?' she asked him.

'James Scott, his name, and he told us the R stands for King in Latin. The motto *Semper Fidelis* means 'Always Faithful'. He wants us Jolliffes to be always faithful to his trust.'

Joshua hadn't seen the box before. 'What's in it that's so special?' he asked.

'Go on. Let's look,' Lucy urged.

But Ethan was adamant. 'We know there's money, probably gold, in there. The rest's a secret. If father decides to find out when he returns, then that will be his decision. For now we must hide it somewhere safe in case the soldiers come back.' Sarah agreed and asked Ethan and Lucy to be responsible for finding a suitable hiding place. For the time being, it would be for the best if no one else knew where that was.

The two of them went outside to discuss the best hiding place. 'As the Duke called it a *Sacred Trust*, why don't we hide it in the chapel?' Lucy said at last. Ethan agreed and they walked round the house towards the little chapel dedicated to St Bartholomew. It took them a long time to find a place they were both satisfied with and then even longer to hide the box somewhere that even a thorough search would not discover. In the end they were both satisfied with their choice and, feeling pleased with themselves, they cleaned up the mess they had made and left the chapel together.

Chapter 25
A Hasty Burial
18th July 1685

Lucy was sitting in the kitchen reading her own notebook. It was hard to believe so much of what had happened in the past two weeks. She welcomed a short period of peace from the rushing around she had been doing and the usual hurly-burly of farm life. Sarah she knew had taken some food to Nathaniel in prison and had promised to leave a message with the Beavis family and Ethan was fetching the cows in for the evening milking. She never knew where the twins might be but she guessed they were away playing with friends. She had looked in on Daniel ten minutes earlier. Though getting stronger and now able to move around the house, he still spent most days lying on his bed in the back room.

A shadow fell across the table as someone in the doorway blocked out the sunlight. 'Well, what have we here?'

Lucy recognised the hateful corporal immediately. His presence in the house meant potential danger for all of them. She stood up and tried to control her breathing. The last time he had seen her she had been wearing Daniel's clothes. Possibly a show of courtesy might help. 'Good afternoon, Sir. How can I help you?' She bobbed him a neat curtsey.

He swaggered confidently into the room towards Lucy. 'I'm Corporal William Oakshott. It's Mistress Jolliffe I'm looking for. My business is with her.' He looked shrewdly at Lucy. 'Who are you?' He narrowed his eyes as if trying to focus on the past. ' I'm certain I've met you before.'

Lucy tried to keep calm and began to think carefully. Even though she was now dressed as a puritan girl, the sergeant was close to recognising her. If that happened, all their deception would be uncovered and it would not be difficult for him to find the real Daniel lying wounded upstairs. 'My aunt is visiting her husband in Dorchester. Perhaps I can help you.'

'Perhaps you can, a pretty maid like you.' He came closer and she smelled again the stench of stale sweat that had sickened her on the previous occasion. 'How would you like to help your uncle?'

'Of course, I would. But what can I do?'

'I can arrange for your uncle to be set free if you will do a little service for me.' The corporal leered at her and Lucy was left in no doubt as to the kind of service he would expect. He carefully removed his pistol from his belt and laid it on the table. Lucy clasped her notebook to her chest as if this could in some way form a barrier between them. It did momentarily distract the sergeant. 'What's this then?' He reached forward to take the book. Beginning to panic, Lucy realised that if he looked in the book it could well make matters even worse. Though she had been careful to leave out most names, there was enough evidence in it for a clever prosecutor to incriminate Ethan, Daniel and their father. She snatched it away from the hateful man.

The book was just a distraction. That wasn't what Corporal Oakshott had come for. He made a grab at Lucy's breast with his left hand and pulled her body tight up against him with his right. She felt his fingers rucking up her dress at the back. Desperately she tried to push him away from her, but he was too strong. She kicked out with her feet but Oakshott just laughed. 'Proper little wild cat you are.' He leant forward to kiss her on the mouth, moving his hand from her breast as he did so. Lucy desperately tried to squirm away from his obscene embrace.

She was never quite certain what happened next. Most likely, she thought later, he caught his foot on the table leg. Whatever the cause, the result was he stumbled and half released her to try to regain his balance. With all her strength Lucy shoved him away from her and he fell backwards to the floor, striking his head on the cast-iron corner of the fireguard. She grabbed at the pistol from the table and pulled back the hammer, fully prepared to shoot him. Oakshott, however, didn't need shooting. He lay on his side absolutely still. The only movement she could see from the body was a thin trickle of blood seeping from his ear.

Lucy stood frozen for several minutes, holding the pistol in front of her and pointing it at Oakshott's heart. As her panic slowly subsided she came to understand that he wasn't going to trouble anyone again. She carefully uncocked the pistol and, laying it back on the table, sat down shaking with shock. Gradually she realised that Oakshott dead could cause as much trouble as Oakshott alive. She had to find Ethan.

Fortunately Ethan was milking in the lower cow byre. She grabbed at him, knocking over the milk pail between his knees, trying to blurt out what had happened. Ethan calmed her down, seeing the panic in her eyes, but not understanding at all what she was babbling about. He did understand that something terrible had happened in the kitchen and ran back with her to the farmhouse.

Corporal Oakshott's body was where Lucy had left it. Ethan took in the scene at a glance. Oakshott was not the first dead person he had seen, but this corpse was the first he had seen lying on his kitchen floor. He sat Lucy down and gently prised the story out of her. 'What are we going to do?' she said. It was that which was worrying Ethan. 'Who must I tell?'

This question at least was easy for Ethan. 'We tell no one, Lucy. If the army discovers that one of its soldiers has …' he hesitated. '… has died in this house we will all be in trouble.' He started to get his thoughts into some kind of order. It was obvious that he would have to come up with a solution as, for once, Lucy, still in a state of shock, was not thinking with her usual clarity. 'We have to assume that the disgusting corporal told someone where he was going. Even someone as vile as that probably has a few friends. When he fails to return tonight a search party will be organised and they will come here looking for him, probably tomorrow morning.'

'Can we bury his body on the farm?' she asked hopefully.

'They will come and search thoroughly. The disappearance of a corporal is a serious matter. Any newly turned over soil would instantly tell them where to look. The pond is no good for the same reason. If they do come questioning here they will drag that for certain.' He paced the kitchen for a while and then said. 'We'll put the body in the closet where we hid Daniel. We can secure the oak panelling so no one knows there is a cupboard, and after they have searched and left we can decide where the lout is going to be permanently dumped.' Ethan deliberately used crude and brutal language when talking about Oakshott in the hope that this would make Lucy feel better, even though he knew she had nothing to feel guilty about. 'Most important, Lucy, we won't tell any of the others about this. The twins are terrible actors and if they knew there was a secret like this they would give us away immediately. As it is, by behaving normally they will disperse any suspicion. There is also no need for Mother and Daniel to know. They both have enough worries. It'll be our secret. All right?'

Relieved that Ethan had done all the thinking, Lucy nodded, but the plan had to be altered immediately. As Daniel came down the stairs he saw the body by the kitchen stove. Ethan's instinct was to protect his gentle, kindly brother, but Sedgemoor had altered Daniel. He walked up to Oakshott's corpse and stirred it with his foot. 'Good. I don't know how he died, but whoever was responsible deserves a reward. This overblown garbage is a member of Kirke's Lambs. See here.' He pointed with his foot at the badge on Oakshott's jacket. 'Look at the emblem on those buttons. These are the monsters who went around shooting our wounded fellows on the moor. When they were ordered to stop doing that, they erected gibbets and hung them up so they could torture them with their bayonets instead. I hope he's rotting in hell.' He calmly spat in the corporal's dead face and looked defiantly at the other two.

'It was an accident, Dan. The brute attacked Lucy and she shoved him away. He hit his head and just died. We are going to hide his body in the closet in case they come looking tomorrow. We think it's best not to tell Ma and Josh and Kate, then they can act naturally if the soldiers come.'

The three of them lugged the corporal's heavy body up the stairs and into the north bedroom. They bent the corpse double and pushed it into one corner of the cupboard. 'Get some old nails from the shed,' Dan told Ethan, 'then it won't look like new work. I'll grab a bag of lime from the lower barn. If we cover the body with that, it should help to stop it smelling.'

Ethan nailed the panelling shut and rubbed some dust on the nail heads so they wouldn't shine. 'We must expect soldiers at some stage tomorrow,' he said. 'Lucy, if you could be away from the house it would probably be a good thing.'

'No. I want to be here. If they find the body it's important that I'm here to say what happened. Dan, you must be up and dressed tomorrow. Whatever you are doing when they arrive, they must not guess you are wounded.'

'There's a broken saddle in the stables. I can sit down to mend that and if I have to wait there all day it won't be too much of a strain. Let's tidy up downstairs.'

The three went back to the kitchen and the first thing they saw was Oakshott's pistol sitting on the table. 'We can't open the closet again. I have a loose floorboard in my room,' Daniel said. 'I'll put it under the boards and nail them down. I don't expect they will actually rip up the flooring. If they do, they will be looking for a body, not something buried in the dirt.'

Lucy noticed the damp patch on the rushes where Oakshott's body had lain. She bundled these together and took them outside to the place where the family burned their rubbish, while Ethan collected fresh rushes from the shed. A quick look round the kitchen showed them they couldn't do any more tidying. All they could do was wait for tomorrow.

***

It was around 12 o'clock the following day that the first soldiers turned up at the farm. Two badly dressed and ill-educated troopers with rifles slung casually over their shoulders sloped up to the kitchen door. Sarah had been delighted when earlier that morning Lucy had offered to help her with the cooking and the two of them were making meat pies, which Sarah could later take to Nathaniel in prison. Neither of the soldiers had been part of the original search party.

'Have you seen our corporal?' one of them asked from the doorway.

Sarah cleaned the flour from her hands and arms. 'Come in, please. What is that you are asking?'

'Our corporal's gone missing. He told the sergeant he was coming here yesterday and we haven't seen him since he left camp. He was spotted on the road near here yesterday afternoon. Did he come here?'

'I was away yesterday afternoon in Dorchester. Did you see anything, Lucy?'

Lucy was relieved that she and Ethan had decided not to deny ever having seen Oakshott. This lie might easily have been disproved. 'Someone did knock on the door when I was reading yesterday afternoon. It was a soldier who asked after you, Sarah. When he heard you were away he said he might call back another day. He was only here a few minutes and I am sorry I forgot to tell you.'

Sarah seemed totally unconcerned by this information. 'Never mind, dear. He may have wanted to tell me something about Nathaniel. If it is important I'm sure he will come back.'

The soldiers seemed uncertain what to do next. 'We need to have a look round so we can tell our officer he's not here,' one of them said.

'Certainly. Lucy dear, will you show the soldiers over the house? I can finish up here. I am sure Ethan or Daniel will show them the farm if they want to see that.'

Lucy led the two upstairs, first to the attic room, then to the three first floor bedrooms, then downstairs. The men did not show great interest in their search and she gathered from their comments that the corporal had been more feared than loved. Finally she showed them into the cellar where they pulled at various boxes and the stacks of firewood with slightly more enthusiasm but with as little success. 'It's too late for us to search the whole farm now,' one of them told Sarah, 'but I expect the Lieutenant will want to see the girl at some stage. She had better be here if he decides to come over tomorrow.' With that the two left.

'I wonder what all that was about,' Sarah said, putting the pies into the oven. 'What could he have wanted to tell me?'

***

A Lieutenant Craddock led the search party. In the farmyard he directed his men. 'You know what to do. Report to me if you find anything suspicious.' Ethan noticed that the soldiers had brought chains with them so he guessed that it had always been their intention to drag the ponds. 'Now, where is the maid who saw Oakshott two days ago?'

Lucy stepped forward. She was dressed in a simple linen dress and had borrowed a white cap. Sarah had been surprised when she had asked that morning if she could use it, and even more surprised to see her holding a prayer book in front of her in both hands. She addressed Lieutenant Craddock with her eyes cast down. 'It was I, Sir.'

'It was Corporal Oakshott who led a patrol of troopers here last week. Was this the same man you saw two days ago?'

'Lucy Wells is a visitor from Dorchester,' Ethan answered for her. 'She wasn't here when those soldiers came. You will see from the list that the corporal took that there were only five of us here that day.'

'Who are you then?' The Lieutenant fished a sheet of paper from inside his jacket.

'Ethan Jolliffe, Sir. This is my mother, Mistress Sarah Jolliffe, and those two playing in the yard are my brother and sister, Joshua and Kate. Another brother Daniel is presently working in the stables.'

'Check on this Daniel,' the Lieutenant ordered two of the soldiers. 'Make sure he is who he says he is and search the stables while you're there.' He pushed the paper back inside his jacket and turned to Lucy. 'Tell me about the soldier you saw.'

'There is little to tell, Sir,' Lucy said quietly. 'I was reading in the kitchen when he came in through the door and asked where my mother was. I pointed out that she wasn't my mother and that she was visiting her husband in Dorchester. He then left and I have not seen him since that day.'

Craddock looked at her. 'You've coloured up, Missy. There's something else the soldier said to you?'

Lucy hesitated. She had been quite proud of the blush and was careful not to overdo the effect now. 'He said he could help Mr Jolliffe out of prison if I did certain services for him.'

One of the troopers laughed. 'That's definitely Will, Sir.'

'What else?'

Lucy paused for some time and Ethan held his breath, wondering what she would say next. 'He said I probably had a pleasant enough body underneath all this puritan flummery, but not enough meat on me for his taste. He would come back to try me when I had gathered a bit more flesh. He laughed at me and then left.' Ethan gradually let the air out from his lungs and tried to relax. Sarah went over to Lucy and put her arm around her.

'I apologise, Miss Lucy. He should not have behaved like that.' The lieutenant looked at Sarah. 'Of course, the corporal cannot help your husband in any way. There is a judge coming from London and the law will decide what is to happen to him.' He turned to his soldiers. 'Now you lot, search the farm buildings, while I inspect the cellar again.'

The search went on for thirty minutes and nothing was found. No one bothered to look again in the long bedroom on the north side of the house. Lieutenant Craddock sat in the kitchen with a mug of ale Sarah had poured him as the various parties reported back their failure to find anything. Only the group dragging the pond had yet to return.

Sarah felt it was time to close this unnecessary affair. 'We are a God-fearing family, Sir. My husband has been wrongly arrested and now you are tearing apart our farm for no reason. It is not good for our children to see soldiers abuse us so.'

Craddock too felt it was time to finish things. His captain was a tough man and had ordered him to make a thorough search. He honestly could not sustain this any longer. He had one last thought. 'If you are a God-fearing family you must have a Bible here. Bring it to me.' Lucy had a moment of panic. The officer seemed intelligent enough and if he read what was inside, he might just guess at one of the secrets the family was desperate to keep hidden. Sarah went to the dresser and carefully lifted out the family Bible and laid it on the table. 'Now swear on the Holy Book that you did not see the corporal the day before yesterday.'

Sarah placed her hand on the Bible and looked at the Lieutenant. 'I swear that I only saw Corporal Oakshott on the first occasion when he visited my house.' She looked defiantly at the officer and prepared to return the Bible to the dresser.

'What about the girl and the boy, Sir?' one of the soldiers said.

Ethan stepped forward and placed his hand on the Bible. 'I swear by the life of Jesus Christ that I only saw the corporal alive in this house on the occasion he visited us two weeks ago.' He hoped that his prompt acceptance would mean that it would not be necessary for Lucy to take an oath, but Craddock saw in this little charade a way of persuading the captain that he had done everything necessary.

'Now the maid,' he said.

Lucy, looking as demure and unthreatening as she could manage approached the captain and curtsied. 'I cannot take that oath, Sir. I have already told you, I did see the man two days ago.'

'Oh, take any oath then,' the Lieutenant said shortly.

'I cannot do that either, Sir. You can see by my dress that I am a Quaker and it is against my religion to swear an oath. You will find in the Epistle of St James that he writes, *Swear not neither by heaven or by earth or by any other oath lest ye fall into condemnation.* I'll show you if you like, Sir.'

'It's true, Sir,' one of the soldiers interrupted. 'They are an odd lot those Quakers. They don't drink or fight as well as not swearing. Somehow I don't think Will Oakshott could have been a Quaker.' This produced a round laugh from the troopers in the room.

Lieutenant Craddock was about to say something when the final search party, wet and muddy, reported back that they had found nothing in the pond. He swiftly decided that there was nothing more to be gained from Corton Farm. 'Let me know if any of you hear anything more from the corporal,' he said as he led his troop from the yard.

'I didn't know you were a Quaker, Lucy,' Sarah remarked.

Chapter 26
The Bloody Assizes
26ᵗʰ August 1685

Over the next three weeks Lucy slipped into an easy routine at Corton Farm. There were no more visits from the army. Daniel, under the nursing routine established by Mother Shipley, was getting better every day, and she was enjoying helping Sarah around the farm. She saw little of Ethan who had thrown himself into taking care of the harvest. Some days Lucy would help him with stooking the corn or driving the cart to and from the fields, but on these occasions he was strangely silent and preoccupied. Every day Sarah would travel into Dorchester to visit Nathaniel in the gaol. She would take him pies and cooked meat to supplement the sparse diet provided by the authorities. Like many of the other prisoners he developed a bout of gaol fever, but though he looked drawn and exhausted after the fever had left him, at least he was still alive, unlike half of the other victims.

Around the end of July Lucy went with Sarah to her uncle's house in The Shambles. A neighbour told her that John and Mary Beavis had been away since the middle of June, she thought visiting relatives in Bristol. This neighbour lent Lucy the key to the front door and she collected one or two of her possessions, but was not sorry to leave the sad little house. In the market Sarah heard details of Monmouth's death in London that were brutal and disgusting. After a rapid trial and sentence, the public hangman, Jack Ketch, had botched the execution. No one knew whether this was accidental but he was reported to have taken eight blows with the axe to sever the head from the body. Ethan was even more sullen than usual on hearing this news and when he was working in the fields with Lucy she decided to ask him why he was so bad tempered these days. She made Ethan sit down on a pile of newly cut straw and challenged him.

'I feel that I let Monmouth down,' Ethan admitted at last. 'He trusted me to escort him to safety and I abandoned him when he needed me most. Do you remember the motto he gave our family, *Semper Fidelis?* I feel I broke his faith. What is worse, I heard that the Lord Chief Justice himself is coming to Dorchester to try the prisoners in the gaol here. He is already at Salisbury assizes. He is bringing with him that awful man, Jack Ketch, so he obviously intends to sentence people to death here. I can't bear the thought that father will be executed for treason. You know he is a good and honest man, but I am frightened that will count for nothing at his trial. I am now head of the family and I have no idea what to do.'

During her time with Monmouth's army it had not occurred to Lucy that she might have been at risk herself. Although the dreadful events surrounding the death of Corporal Oakshott had scared her, at the back of her mind she had assumed that in the end everything would be all right. The account of Monmouth's execution had shocked her into realising that she and the family were still potentially in great danger and that the lazy days of summer on the farm could be just an illusion. She should have realised that Ethan, who had quietly assumed responsibility for her trouble at the time of Oakshott's death, now needed her support? Her father had always told her to worry about those things she could do something about, but to ignore those she couldn't. She was not prepared to accept Ethan's gloomy resignation. It was time for clear thinking; something she was usually good at.

'When Monmouth was captured, the King's men must have interrogated him to get every bit of information from him they could. They probably even tortured him,' she said brutally. 'He didn't give us away then. You must know he didn't mention your part in his escape, or the soldiers would have been straight round to arrest you. If he didn't blame you or think you let him down, there is no need for you to whip yourself about it. Forget Monmouth; he's dead. What you have to do is think about those who are still alive. You are doing a great job on the farm and looking after your family. Daniel is getting better and your mother and the twins are managing. The only problem worth worrying about is how we can help your father.'

'You always see things so clearly, Lucy,' Ethan sighed. 'Perhaps that is because you are so well educated.'

She hadn't thought of that before. 'When this judge man ... what's his name again?'

'Judge Jeffreys,' Ethan said. 'He is the Lord Chief Justice. I think that means he is the most important judge in all England.'

'Well, when this Judge Jeffreys comes along, you will have to go and see him to persuade him your father isn't a rebel and has been wrongly arrested. You will have to see him before the trial, because judges never change their minds once they have made a decision.'

'I can't do that,' Ethan said. 'I wouldn't know what to say to him. Either I would dry up altogether or, what is worse, I would say something that would get Father into even more trouble. I couldn't bear that. Will you do it, Lucy?' She remembered with pleasure how she had managed the tense situation when Lieutenant Craddock and the troopers had come to the farm. She relished the idea of a challenge and she owed several debts to Ethan. *I hope by agreeing to this I am not giving in to the sin of pride,* she thought. 'As soon as he arrives in Dorchester I will go and see him to plead your father's case.'

A few days later rumours circulated in Dorchester market to say that Lady Alice Lisle had been sentenced to death in Salisbury assizes for harbouring fugitives from the battle of Sedgemoor. Judge Jeffreys had rejected all pleas for mercy. Things looked bleak, for it was also rumoured that he would come to Dorchester next.

The judge and his attendants arrived in town late on Thursday evening. Lucy, accompanied by Ethan, made sure she was in the town centre early on Friday morning. She naively hoped she might get a chance to see the Judge privately, but his procession from the judge's lodgings in West Street over the road to St Mary's Church was both formal and intimidating. Soldiers held the people back from getting too close to the Judge and Lucy and Ethan could only stand at the edge of the crowd and watch. After the service he again processed back to his lodging under escort. Lucy tried to persuade one of the soldiers on guard at the door to let her in to see the Judge, but the unhelpful man wouldn't give her permission. He told her to come back next day when the actual trials would start.

Early the next morning Lucy and Ethan left the farm for a further attempt to see the Judge. They waited for an hour outside his lodgings. When eventually she plucked up enough courage to ask the guard when the Judge would be coming out he laughed and told them about the private tunnel leading to the Shire Hall. He explained that the assizes had already begun in the Oak Room there.

Lucy was able to squeeze her way up the stairs and into the back of the trials room, which was tightly packed with people anxious to see and hear the famous judge. At first she could make out very little, but by pushing and shoving her way forward in a most unladylike way she managed to get into a position where she could see Jeffreys sitting on a low platform. The room had been decorated with scarlet banners on his orders. Her neighbours whispered that they feared this was a sign that he was in a hanging mood and looking for vengeance. His Honour was sitting on a high-backed chair with a broad oak table in front of him. He was wearing a full judge's wig and a scarlet robe, which matched the banners. He had obviously once been a good-looking man, but his face that morning was lined with pain and throughout the session he squirmed uncomfortably in his chair. Jeffreys had no need to raise his voice to make himself heard even at the very back of the room, as everyone was silent. This did not stop him shouting at the prisoners when he felt circumstances required it. To Lucy, whichever voice he used, he sounded mean and threatening. She looked across at the prisoner's dock where a scholarly looking man stood. He had dared to challenge one of the witnesses for the Crown and now looked fearfully across the court towards the Judge.

'You villain,' Jeffreys shouted at him. 'I think I see you already with a rope around your neck.' He turned to the twelve men, local shopkeepers and traders, who made up the jury. 'How do you see it?' he demanded. Not surprisingly they all muttered 'Guilty,' and Jeffreys ordered that the miserable man should be hanged in Weymouth Town Square.

I hope things get better than that, Lucy thought to herself, but it wasn't to be. A procession of sad-looking young men shuffled into the dock. Some were wounded, some were wearing the tattered uniforms that Lucy recognised from Monmouth's army, some were obviously unwell, and all were terrified. For the 68 who pleaded guilty to rebellion that morning, the sentence was death without bothering the jury. Thirty-eight pleaded not guilty and of these the jury dared to acquit only one. The others were also sentenced to death. As the day wore on, Judge Jeffreys became more vicious. By the afternoon, instead of a merciful execution he ordered that those who were found guilty by jury verdict should be hanged and then cut into quarters, with their heads and innards boiled. The heat in the cramped room became sweltering and some fainted both from the lack of fresh air but also from the horror of what they were hearing.

When the final group of the day was announced Lucy was stunned to hear one of the defendants named as Captain-Lieutenant Andrew Crompton. When her friend entered the dock with the other prisoners Lucy at first found it difficult to recognise him. All of the prisoners had the same weary defeated demeanour and tattered clothing. Andrew identified himself to the bailiff and pleaded guilty to the charge. He tried to stand tall, to face the Judge, but he had obviously suffered much during his month in prison. The Judge was obviously tired from his day in the hot stuffy courtroom. He leant back in his chair and shuffled uncomfortably on his cushion. Lucy had noticed that he had become more bad tempered and sarcastic as the day wore on. Unfortunately Andrew seemed to bring out the worst in him.

'You are the nephew of the traitor, the so-called Baron Grey of Warke, are you not?' Andrew nodded his assent. 'You miserable rebel,' Jeffreys shouted at him. 'Have you not the decency to cast your eyes down, but need to look justice in the face as though you are an honest man. Do you not see dishonourable death is at your shoulder?' Jeffreys rapidly worked himself into a lather and frenzy, as flecks of spittle sprayed from his mouth. Andrew, who until then had tried hard to remain dignified, paled before the Judge's onslaught. 'As one of those vipers who came over with the rebel Monmouth from Holland,' Jeffreys continued, 'your fault is most grievous. This court will make sure you pay your dues when you are dancing on nothing with a rope around your neck.'

Lucy listened to the Judge's outburst with increasing alarm. She realised that Andrew had little chance of mercy from the Judge, now she could see that Jeffreys wanted to enjoy his revenge in full measure. She screwed her handkerchief into a tight ball to try to stop herself from shaking as he continued his tirade. 'You will be taken from here to Lyme Regis, where this perfidious enterprise started,' Jeffreys continued. 'On the very beach where you first landed you will be hung from a gibbet and your guts ripped from your miserable body to be boiled in tar. Your head will be severed from your dead corpse and posted on the town wall as a warning to others.'

Lucy let out a low moan and felt herself near to fainting. Andrew looked over towards her and she thought she saw a flash of recognition in his eyes before he quickly looked away. She turned and pushed her way towards the stairs, determined to get out from that vile room as quickly as possible.

'You, girl, look where you're about. Mind who you're shoving.' She found her arms grabbed by a flabby old man with a red pockmarked face, who reeked of sweat and beer. Lucy gave him a push and broke free, making a dash for the stairs.

One of the women on the stairs gave her some support and helped her outside. 'Be careful of that man, lass,' she whispered. 'That's Jack Ketch, the public hangman, and he fears no one.'

Judge Jeffreys wound up the proceedings in the late afternoon by announcing that all the death sentences should be carried out on the Monday in two days time. 'Colonel Kirke,' he spoke to the army officer sitting near the bench. 'Please to arrange a military escort for all those sentenced to death. I shall give you a paper to determine at which of the towns of Dorset and Somerset each shall be hanged.' As he rose from his chair to leave the room, he spoke to Mr Henry Pollexfen, the Prosecutor for the Crown. 'Sir, hearing all these cases will cause us too much delay. We need to leave for Exeter on Thursday and there are still over 200 villains in the cells. Let prisoners know that if they plead guilty to the charges, my sentence will be one of transportation to the colonies rather than death. That should save us time.' With that he swept from the oak-panelled room.

Lucy was hungry and exhausted when she met Ethan outside. She tried to encourage him, but her account of the proceedings left both of them depressed. 'At least Nathaniel was not one of those condemned today,' she said. 'I shall go straight away now to the Judge's chambers to see if I can speak to him.'

The same soldier she had spoken to on Friday was again on duty. He looked as stern and inflexible as he had then, 'I can't let you in, Miss,' he told her. 'Anyhow, if I was you I wouldn't go near him this moment. His bladder stone has been vexing him all day, and he's in a filthy mood. You will get no charity from him today.' Lucy managed to squeeze out a few tears, which in the circumstances was not difficult. 'There, there, Miss.' The soldier couldn't cope with young ladies in distress. 'Come again early on Monday, before seven in the morning. I'll be on duty again and will see what I can do.'

Lucy's mind was racing. She managed a wan smile. 'Oh, thank you, officer.' She hoped that wasn't going too far. 'I will be there. Don't you forget.'

Back in the market square she again found a forlorn Ethan. 'I have an idea how to save your father,' she told him. 'You must do exactly what I tell you. You must go to the gaol and speak to him, however long it takes, even if you have to wait in Dorchester all night. He must not plead guilty when he comes before the judge, even if he feels honour bound to do so. We know from Daniel that he was not wearing uniform. He must say that he had nothing to do with the rebellion. I know it will be uncomfortable for him, but you must persuade him to lie. Say he had been visiting friends and was on his way home when the soldiers picked him up. Can you do that?' Lucy asked him urgently.

'I don't know,' Ethan said doubtfully. 'If he admits he was with the rebellion at least the Judge has said he won't be condemned. Anyhow, father likes to tell the truth.'

'Ahh, Ethan.' Lucy almost stamped her foot in frustration. She took a deep breath and calmed herself. 'Please believe me. I think I can save him, but it is absolutely vital that he does not plead guilty; that he says he was visiting a friend and that he was on his way home when he was arrested. Please make sure he says that for the family's sake.'

'I'll try,' Ethan said, trying to show a little more enthusiasm. 'What will you do?'

'I have to take the trap and go home immediately. I have something urgent to do there,' she answered.

Driving back to the farm Lucy rehearsed in her mind the next conversation that was necessary if she was to be successful. When she reached Corton she didn't drop down to the house, but continued along the road for half a mile to the hamlet of Cor Gate. She tied up the pony and trap outside the house of Goody Shipley and knocked on the door.

Goody Shipley shuffled over to the door to let Lucy in. The cottage was dark and smoky inside. The room was cluttered with rugs, bottles and jars, and the moth-eaten cat sitting in the armchair hissed at her. The old woman was smaller and more hunched than Lucy remembered and peered short-sightedly at the girl. Lucy noticed for the first time the wart on her chin sprouting hairs. Her heart sank. Had she made a dreadful mistake in coming here? Whatever help could this batty old crone be to her uncle? She was desperately worried now that she had made promises to Ethan that she would never be able to keep, and that her advice would lead to Nathaniel's execution instead of transportation to the West Indies.

'I told you I would be seeing you again,' the old woman smiled a toothless smile. 'I also said I would have an answer for you. What can I do for you now? What is the question?' She cackled with laughter. 'Is it a love potion you be requiring to get that numpty Ethan started.'

As a joke it isn't that funny, Lucy thought. 'He's not a numpty,' Lucy sparked angrily. 'He is kind, considerate, gentle and honourable, everything the ideal boy should be. And it's not a love potion I need.'

'My, my. Quite a show of feelings. I like spirit in a girl. What do you need from me?'

Lucy explained about her visit to the Shire Hall in Dorchester and how she had noticed the Judge's discomfort. How she had heard from the soldier about his bad temper because of the bladder stone. 'If you can give me something to get rid of the stone on Monday, I will try to give it to him before he goes into court and it might make him in a better mood. If I can put him in my debt, I can then ask a favour from him and save Uncle Nathaniel.' When she put her plan into words it did sound rather childish. 'Is it possible?'

'I do have some herbs that will dissolve the stone,' the old woman told her, 'but I am afraid it will take some weeks more than one dose on Monday to manage that.' She opened a cupboard in the bottom of an old dresser and reached for a small green glass jar. Lifting out the stopper she sniffed it and offered it to Lucy to smell. 'That's mandragora. Taken in the wrong dose it's quite deadly.' She cackled again.

'I don't want to kill him,' a startled Lucy exclaimed, 'just make him better.'

'I won't be killing him,' Mother Shipley told her. 'The stone will do that in not many years. If you give him two spoons of this, it will relieve his pain almost instantly. At least that will put him in a proper mood for the day. If he is worried about poison, you can drink it yourself. It will do you no harm either. Look.' She took a spoon from the dresser and poured out a spoonful of the pale yellow liquid and swallowed it. 'Mandragora relieves pain. I could have given you an extraction of hemlock or poppy, but this is more powerful and always acts fastest. This is the one you need.' She handed the bottle to Lucy. 'Mind you, not more than two spoonfuls, and not more than once a day.' Lucy thanked Mother Shipley and had just climbed into the pony trap when the old woman grabbed her wrist. 'There's two things that always puts a man in a good mood. For one of them he's too old and you're too young. The other is gold.' She slapped the pony on the rump and Lucy had to concentrate to control the animal. When she looked round, Mother Shipley had already re-entered her cottage.

On the way back to Corton Farm Lucy thought about the woman's final remark to her. *Of course, a bribe will help. All judges probably take backhanders,* she thought. *Where can I get some gold?* Then she remembered the box she and Ethan had hidden in the chapel a few weeks ago. *Ethan's sense of honour won't allow him to borrow whatever is in there, but a dead Monmouth won't need it now. If it helps Uncle Nathaniel, I am sure the Duke would have approved.*

Sarah had been waiting anxiously at home for news when Lucy returned. She told her that Nathaniel had not been one of the prisoners on the list that day. She explained that Ethan was staying in Dorchester until he had had a chance to see his father. Deliberately, she left out any detail from the ghastly scenes that had been played out in the courthouse and Sarah, probably for the sake of Joshua and Kate, chose not to ask.

Lucy made her way to the chapel, determined to act before Ethan returned. It didn't take her long to uncover the box from where they had concealed it. She sat on the floor and carefully unwrapped it from the leather protection. The little black box was not locked. Inside was a small leather bag closed with a silk cord. She opened it and spilled out a small pile of gold coins onto her skirt. She counted them, 49, and then put them back into the bag. This she put into her skirt pocket. Underneath the bag there was a piece of parchment. She knew that this was none of her business, but she couldn't resist having a look at it. The document was dated July 1648 and was written in a foreign language. She guessed this must have been Dutch because she recognised the words Den Haag written in the top line, the Dutch for The Hague. She took the paper across to the window so she could read it more clearly. It was already nearly forty years old and the ink was beginning to fade. There was a lot of writing and then four signatures. She recognised Charles Princeps written with a bold flourish and underneath in a crabbed and immature hand the name Lucy Walters. *This must be the marriage certificate of Charles II and Lucy Walters, which the Duke of Monmouth was talking about.* Underneath were two more names she could read, Mary Henrietta Stuart and Wilhem P. d'Orange. Those must be the witnesses. The rest of the writing was also in Dutch, so she skipped over it. *So Monmouth was the rightful King after all. This isn't much use to him now,* she thought. She then put the parchment back in the box. She took the little coin bag out of her pocket and jiggled it thoughtfully. Forty-nine gold guineas was a large sum of money. She wondered whether she should take it all, but decided that there was no doubt she could put the money to better use than any dead duke. She took one of the guineas from the bag and put it back in the box, *just for luck* she thought. The little bag with the remaining coins she put in her pocket and again carefully wrapped the box in Ethan's piece of old leather. This she hid once more just as she and Ethan had done some weeks earlier. The little bag of gold went into her bedroom under the mattress.

Chapter 27
Judge's Chambers
8th September 1685

Ethan halted the pony and trap next to the railings of St Peter's Church. The main street of Dorchester, usually so full of people and animals, was strangely silent at half past six in the morning. Lucy, sitting next to him, ran over the plan they had made together the previous evening. She wanted to check one more time some of the details with Ethan. 'You told your father that he was not to plead guilty.'

'Yes, I told you that already.'

'He is prepared to deny that he had anything to do with the rebels?'

'Yes, I said that as well,' Ethan replied, irritated.

'I'm sorry, Ethan, if this is boring you, but if I'm the one going in to see the Judge, I need to be sure our story is right.' She regretted immediately that she had snapped at him, but she was getting extremely nervous about what she had planned to do.

'Father will say he was going over to visit Farmer Pouncey in Charminster,' he said patiently. 'He was going to borrow Mr Pouncey's bull for breeding with our cows and needed to make the arrangements for collecting the animal. Mr Pouncey will confirm that if he's asked, as that bit's true. If anyone asks Mother she will say that he left home after lunch. Father knows that too.'

'We just have to hope that none of the troopers that arrested him are there to give evidence. It's six weeks since he was picked up, and the prosecutor hasn't used witnesses in many of the other cases. We should be all right on that.' Lucy looked nervously at the clock on St Peter's Church. Six forty five. Fifteen minutes more.

Promptly at 7 o'clock she presented herself at the door of the Judge's chambers. She was in luck as it was the same soldier on guard duty as she had spoken to the day before. Lucy had dressed carefully for the occasion. She was wearing the green riding habit that had belonged to Lady Prideaux and a straw bonnet to cover her straggly hair. She had chosen to make her appearance as simple as possible, as the effect she wanted to give to the Judge was one of wide-eyed innocence: attractive, but not available. She had no experience of trying to seduce older men, but was pretty sure she would be safe enough with an elderly judge at 7 o'clock in the morning.

The guard greeted her in a friendly enough fashion and told her the Judge was having breakfast in his room. She slipped him one of the gold coins, which she had taken the night before from Monmouth's box. It swiftly disappeared into his pocket as he led her inside and pointed to a door at the end of the corridor. 'Good luck, Miss,' he whispered to her.

She knocked on the door and was told to enter. She had prepared carefully what she was going to say, but her mind went blank as she saw the Judge for the first time without his wig. His short grey hair and lined face made him look tired and old. 'What do you want?' he snapped at her, looking up from his plate.

'My name is Lucy Wells, Your Honour, and I am staying with my uncle and aunt on a farm near here while I recover from a serious illness. I was in your court yesterday and I thought you looked unwell. My father is a doctor in St Bartholomew's Hospital and he heard it rumoured in London that you had a kidney stone. I know this must cause you great distress. Before I left London he gave me a small medicine cabinet in case I should again become unwell. In it there is a herbal tincture for the relief of pain which I have with me here. I am sure it will help Your Honour.' She hesitated, unsure how well her introduction had gone down with the Judge. *I must remember that this man is no fool. He is a cunning and vicious devil,* she thought. 'I realise that someone in your position must be careful of strangers, even those with as little guile as I have.' She tried her most innocent smile, and produced the little green bottle and placed it on the table. 'He assures me that two spoonfuls of this medicine will ease Your Honour's pain for the rest of the day. To show I mean you no harm, I am happy to take the medicine myself, as my father has told me it can cause no discomfort to anyone as long as the correct dose is taken.'

Jeffreys stared at her face and she had to concentrate hard so that she did not duck away from his gaze or look shifty or dishonest. Saying nothing he pushed a spoon towards her. She breathed a silent sigh of relief and, uncorking the bottle, she poured out a spoonful of the liquid and drank it. The taste was bitter, but she was determined not to grimace. She poured out a second spoonful and downed that also. Still the Judge said nothing. The silence began to unnerve her. Then she remembered what she had learned about the power of silence when her father had taken her to see a performance of Othello at the new Theatre Royal in Drury Lane. Jeffreys was using this to see if she would crumble. Eventually she pushed the bottle towards him.

'Would Your Grace like to take the medicine? I am confident it will make you feel better.'

Jeffreys reached out and grabbed hold of her wrist. 'What else do you want, Mistress Wells?' In his experience no one was generous to a judge without wanting something in return.

Lucy desperately tried to keep calm. She wanted to snatch her hand back from his vulture-like claw, but realised that any panic at this time would be a terrible mistake. 'I do have a request to ask Your Honour, but my first wish is for your good health.'

The Judge let go of her wrist and seemed to relax. That she had something else to ask of him seemed much more natural than that someone should wish him well for no reason. He picked up the bottle and delicately sniffed at the contents. 'This does not seem to have harmed you. You say it will ease my distress?'

'It is a herbal remedy based on mandragora and I can assure you it will help Your Honour.' Lucy managed to relax a little as the conversation was now going as she had planned.

The Judge carefully poured out a spoonful and swallowed it. He waited a while as if expecting some dreadful reaction. When none came, he poured a second spoonful. 'Two spoonfuls you say?'

'Yes, Your Honour. But to take more in one day would be dangerous. My father says there is enough for four days in the bottle, but the dose must not be exceeded, even if the pain returns.'

Judge Jeffreys shifted in his chair. It might be his imagination but he thought already he felt some relief from the unrelenting gripe in his groin and back. There was a knock on the door and the Judge's clerk poked his head in. If he was surprised to see Lucy he did not show it. 'Ten minutes until we should leave for court, Your Honour.'

Bother, thought Lucy. *I haven't even got to the important bit yet.* But Goody Shipley's medicine was beginning to work its magic. 'Get out, damn your eyes, and don't disturb me again,' Jeffreys shouted at the poor man, who rapidly disappeared. 'What is the favour you wish from me, my dear?'

Lucy swallowed hard. This was the bit she was even less certain about. She carefully pulled the little leather bag from her pocket and placed it on the table, making sure it chinked slightly as she put it down. She gently moved it across the table towards the Judge. 'There may be expenses which it is only right that my family should bear.' *I wonder what is the penalty for bribing a Lord Chief Justice,* she thought.

Jeffreys snaked a thin hand across the table and with practised speed disappeared the little bag into his pocket. 'Go on, my dear,' he said in an oily voice which to Lucy sounded much more creepy than his anger.

Lucy took the plunge. 'My uncle, Nathaniel Jolliffe, is due to appear before Your Honour here in Dorchester. He is falsely accused of being party to the recent rebellion of the traitor Monmouth. He is a simple farmer who was picked up by the militia when he was going about his farming business. I thought if Your Honour was prepared to order some enquiries, for which our family has happily been prepared to pay the cost, then justice would be well served.'

The Judge pulled a pad of paper towards him and, picking up his quill pen, started to write. 'Nathaniel Jolliffe,' he said as he wrote. 'Where was your uncle going when he was arrested?'

This answer Lucy had well prepared. 'He was going from his farm at Corton to visit a colleague in Charminster. I believe he is called Farmer Pouncey. It was something to do with a bull, but my uncle did not feel it was appropriate to tell me what. I am sure that either my aunt or Mr Pouncey will be happy to confirm this.' She paused as the Judge continued carefully writing on his pad. 'I am anxious that with the large number of prisoners before Your Honour still in gaol it might be difficult for my uncle to present his case properly. I am confident that as Your Honour now knows about this particular defendant, justice will be done.' She managed a smile that she hoped was winsome enough to melt his heart.

Judge Jeffreys thought for a moment. 'I will see your uncle after midday today. I shall be making necessary enquiries, but it will be the jury who decides his guilt or innocence, not I.' He stood up and reached for his scarlet robe that was hanging on a peg behind the door and put it on. Lucy helped straighten the black velvet collar. He next opened the tall black box on the floor and drew out his long judge's wig. 'Help me put this on.' She took the wig from him and standing in front of him, far too close for her liking, she put the wig on his head, accidentally brushing his cheek with her forearm as she did so. Jeffreys did not seem at all put out by this, but Lucy stepped back, uncomfortably.

'You will accompany me to court today,' he stated.

But Lucy couldn't wait to escape from the Judge's presence. One more bit of acting was necessary. 'I believe the courtroom is not suitable for a young girl like myself, Sir. At yesterday's hearing I nearly fainted. If you will excuse me I shall wait outside to discover what I hope will be the happy outcome of my uncle's case.' She looked critically at the wig and straightened it so that the parting ran down the centre. 'Very handsome, Sir,' she told the preening judge.

There was a knock and the clerk again put his head round the door. 'Your court is waiting, Your Honour.' He looked sourly at Lucy. 'I see you didn't need my help in robing today.' He held the door open and the Judge swept out.

Ethan was waiting for Lucy in the High Street when she eventually came out from the Judge's lodgings. 'How did it go?' he asked her anxiously. Then, noticing she was still shaking with the reaction to whatever had happened in there, he put his arms around her and held her tightly. After some minutes he felt Lucy relax and he led her back to the trap.

'Can we go to Poundbury, where we found Daniel?' she asked him. 'When we're there I shall tell you everything.' Ethan untied Hubert's reins and the little pony trotted up the High Street towards the hill fort.

Lucy told her story to Ethan as they sat on the grass looking down on the River Frome. He was horrified by what she said. 'What do you mean, you gave the Judge a bribe? Where did you get the money from?'

'I used Monmouth's gold.' Lucy told him defiantly.

'You shouldn't have done that. Why didn't you tell me what you were going to do?' Almost frantic with worry Ethan found he was shouting at her and tears came into Lucy's eyes.

'You asked me to help you,' she sniffed. 'If I'd said we should use the gold, you would have said no. I decided not to tell you. Anyhow, it is done now and the Judge took the bribe, so there's no point at yelling at me.'

They sat in silence while Ethan came to terms with what Lucy had done. He realised that she had risked a great deal for his family and that he had failed to recognise the tensions she had been under. 'What did the Judge say about Father?' he eventually asked. She briefly told him all that had happened in the Judge's chambers. 'I think you're very brave. I couldn't have done that. Thank you.'

Ethan knew it might be dangerous for him to go into the courtroom, as one of the many defendants might well recognise him and speak out, but he was determined to be there to support his father. Lucy agreed to stay by the pony and trap. By midday Ethan was squeezed in the back of the Oak Room standing as far away as he could be from the Judge and those in the dock. The defendants were brought up in batches of fifteen. After the clerk had read out their names, the men were asked to plead. In the first session after the lunch break all the defendants pleaded guilty and were swiftly sentenced to periods of transportation to the West Indies. The older the victim the greater the number of years appeared to be the Judge's criterion.

Nathaniel was in the second group. Ethan thought his father looked exhausted and near to despair. His name was the last to be read out from the register. He noticed the Judge look up from his writing as he recognised it. The first fourteen defendants all pleaded guilty to causing bloody insurrection. When it was Nathaniel's turn he raised his head to look at the Judge. 'Not guilty.'

'I will deal with the "not guilty" plea after I have sentenced the others,' Jeffreys announced to the court. The other victims were quickly dispatched to various terms of transportation. After they had been hustled out of the dock and down the stairs, Jeffreys turned back to Nathaniel who was still seated on the bench. 'What is the basis of your plea?' he asked him.

Nathaniel stood up, gripping the rail of the dock to steady himself. 'I am a loyal subject of King James and no rebel,' he stated in a firm voice. 'I was picked up by the army and thrown into gaol while going about my lawful business. While I accept that this summer was a time of great confusion throughout the West of England, it is a sad time for this country if honest citizens be arrested for no reason.'

'What is the evidence against this man?' the Judge asked Sir Henry Polexfen, the prosecutor. Up until that moment Sir Henry had had little to do. The stream of guilty pleas had meant he had barely looked through any of the cases.

'One moment, Your Honour.' Sir Henry shuffled through the pile of papers in front of him. Eventually he pulled one out from the stack. 'This man, Nathaniel Jolliffe, fled when challenged by an officer of the military. The officer, Ensign Curtis, deemed this behaviour to be suspicious and brought him in for questioning.'

'Did you run away?' the Judge asked Nathaniel.

Nathaniel smiled at the Judge. 'I did, Your Honour, but so might most people if faced by four charging cavalrymen with swords drawn. Before this moment I still have not been questioned.'

'That is what we are here for now,' the Judge answered sharply. He looked down once more at his papers. You live in Corton, I believe. What were you up to, five miles from home, when arrested by the military?'

'I was on my way to visit a neighbour to discuss a farming matter, Sir.'

'Who was that neighbour and what was the matter you needed to discuss?'

'It was William Pouncey who farms near here at Charminster. Every year I hire his prize bull to service my cows in the autumn. I wished to make the arrangement.'

The Judge smiled, something that had not occurred many times over the last few days. 'Why was your niece not aware of the reason for your journey?'

Ethan at the back of the room drew in his breath. This was not something he had briefed his father about. Nathaniel paused, uncertain how to answer. 'Your niece, Mistress Lucy Wells, when I spoke to her this morning, told me you had refused to say why you were going to Charminster. Why was that?'

Nathaniel paused to collect his thoughts, then appeared to relax. 'I did not think it seemly to discuss matters of cattle insemination with young maids. That is why I refused to tell her why I was going.'

'Have you discussed your testimony with Mistress Lucy?'

'No, Sir. I am prepared to swear an oath that I have not spoken one word to my niece since I was thrown into prison.'

The Judge looked across at the jury. 'This morning I sent one of the court officers to speak to Farmer Pouncey of Charminster. He does have a prize bull called, I believe (he looked at his note pad) Goliath. It is also his practice to hire Goliath to Farmer Jolliffe every year, and he was expecting him to come to make arrangements as in past years. In my opinion the Crown has failed to produce any case against this man. Foreman, how find you?'

The foreman, a local butcher who knew Nathaniel quite well and was aware of his absence throughout July from Corton Farm, made a show of discussing the case with his colleagues. They quickly arrived at a verdict and the butcher rose to his feet.

'We find the accused Nathaniel Jolliffe not guilty, Your Honour.'

'Quite right,' said the Judge. Then turning back to Nathaniel, 'the Court regrets your temporary incarceration, Mr Jolliffe, but as you rightly say these were troubled times in the western counties. You are free to go. Next cases please.'

Chapter 28
I am the Lord: That is my Name
9th September 1685

It was early evening and Nathaniel sat bemused in his farmhouse kitchen. The rapid change from hopeless despair facing the possibility of an immediate and violent execution, to elation at being reunited with his family, home and safe, was almost too much for him to take in.

'We must give thanks to Almighty God for your safe deliverance, my dear,' Sarah told him gently. Since Ethan and Lucy had brought him home in the pony trap she had guided and encouraged her husband, realising he would need time to adjust to his surprising freedom.

'Yes, indeed.' Nathaniel shook his head as if to clear his mind of the desperate thoughts, which still crowded there. 'Please will you fetch the Bible, Daniel?'

The whole family including Lucy were sitting round the table. No one had yet asked her the difficult questions about the part she had played in helping Nathaniel's release, but she knew that as soon as things were back to normal she was going to have to provide some answers.

Daniel brought over the family Bible and carefully laid it in front of his father. Nathaniel thought a while and then opened the book, searching for the chapter he wanted. When he found it he passed the Bible to Lucy. 'Please, Lucy, will you read Isaiah chapter 42 to us, up to verse eight?'

Lucy started to read aloud. As she did so she became aware of the raw emotions the passage generated in the room. Ethan was sitting with his head bowed and Sarah began quietly weeping to herself.

I the Lord have called thee in righteousness
and will hold thine hand and keep thee,
and give thee for a covenant of the people,
for a light of the Gentiles.
To open the blind eyes,
to bring out the prisoners from the prison,
and them that sit in darkness from the prison house
I am the Lord: that is my name:
and my glory will I not give to another.

Lucy recognised the passage where God promised through Isaiah to bring his chosen people out of their captivity in Babylon. She saw in this family a total confidence in God's justice. She handed the Bible back to Nathaniel, thinking that he would want to put it away, but in his turn he continued with the passage:

Sing unto the Lord a new song,
and his praise from the end of the earth
ye that go down to the sea, and all that is therein;
the isles, and the inhabitants thereof.
Let them give glory to the Lord,
and declare his praise in the islands.

He carefully closed the Bible. 'Now we must pray. Let us give thanks to the Lord for preserving this family safely in these times of trouble. Especially, God of grace and mercy, we thank you for sending Lucy to our family. Without her wisdom and her courage we would not all be here united in happiness. Give her the strength in the future to continue to use all these talents for the good of others, then to you will be the glory. Amen.'

Lucy swallowed back her tears. His words had affected her deeply and she knew now what she wanted to say, but Nathaniel had not yet finished. 'The judge in court called you my niece. I have only one niece and that is Jane, the daughter of my sister Anne. You, Lucy, I feel are more like a daughter to me than a niece. I hope you will be able to tell us the story of how you arranged for my release, though if you choose not to, I will respect that.' He smiled at Lucy. 'I must tell you that if you decide not to make all things plain, I will be questioning how you managed it for the rest of my life. It is for you to decide. I for one will not pry. You are now part of this family and as such are welcome to stay for as long as you please.'

'I called you Uncle to the Judge, may I call you Uncle now?' she asked shyly. When Nathaniel nodded she continued. 'Ethan knows my story and everything I have done has been with his help. As for how Ethan and I arranged your release, that you should know, though the story does me less credit than you might believe. Perhaps Uncle, if you were to look in the front of the Bible that would be a good place to start.'

Nathaniel opened the book at the title page where Monmouth had written his inscription six weeks earlier and together the family told him the story of all that had happened since he had left Corton Farm.

Lucy then told the rest of the family about the medicine from Goody Shipley and her determination to see the Judge in his chambers. 'I'm not proud that I stole Monmouth's gold or that I bribed a judge or that I persuaded you to lie, Uncle. I am proud that I helped you to be free, and by giving the cure to the Judge I may have put him in a better mood and been able to help others of the accused.' Lucy suddenly realised that she was desperately tired from the drama and tension of the day; not only tired, but ready now to return to her father in London. You have all been like family, kind and generous when I needed it. Now I believe my father needs me. I am recovered in health and must give him the love and care I owe him as a daughter. If you will all excuse me I would like to talk to Ethan alone. It is a lovely evening and now the corn is in we can walk round the top field.'

Sarah had been watching Ethan's face. She had seen his eyes following Lucy whenever they were in a room together and knew how important she was to him. She hoped the girl was not about to hurt her precious son.

***

The two friends did not go to the top field, but sat side by side on the pulpit rock on the hillside high above the farm in the late evening sun. It was a place Lucy had frequently come to when she needed to be alone over the last six weeks. Being alone had helped her to think. 'It is important to me that you of all people understand why I must return to London. Though I am weary today, being in Dorset for the last weeks has helped me to regain my strength. I owe you more than I can ever repay.'

'I don't want you to go,' he said. When she started to speak he put his finger on her lips. 'Don't say anything just now. It's my turn. I love you, Lucy Wells. I think I have loved you from the first time I saw your grumpy little face, under that dreadful haircut, come down your uncle's staircase. I love your energy and your compassion, your initiative and your courage. I love your prettiness. I know I am an unlettered stable boy and cannot contend with your astronomy and … what was it … logic, but I don't feel it is a sin for someone to love just because they are unlearned.'

He scrambled to his feet and stepped back off the rock onto the grass. 'I am not surprised by what you said about going back to London, though of course I hoped that this summer would go on forever. I have a gift for you, something by which you can remember our weeks together.' He pulled a dirty piece of cloth out of his pocket. 'This is very important to me, and that is why I want you to have it.' He unwrapped the package and handed her the gold coin, which Monmouth had given to him the night before his capture. 'This will make sure you never forget us.'

Lucy stood up beside him. 'Letters can be learned. You are not a numbskull, Ethan, and you won't be a stable boy forever. Why have I had to wait six weeks for you to say something warm to me? Why do you think I left Forde Abbey and the suffocating Lady Prideaux? Why did I put up with the grime and discomfort of army camp? Why did I endure that ghastly journey to Bristol and back? It was because I wanted to be with you, Ethan. I wanted to be with your cheerful smile and your kindness and generosity of spirit. When I left Forde Abbey it was because I guessed being with you would be more fun than being with Lady Prideaux. When I held you in my arms on the night of that terrible battle, I knew that not being with you would be unbearable.' She tilted her face up to him and put her arms around his waist. 'Kiss me, Ethan Jolliffe.'

Chapter 29
Goodbyes
10th September 1685

By the time Ethan and Lucy returned to the farmhouse, only Sarah was still up. She was pleased to see that Lucy looked less careworn than she had, and to her surprise Ethan looked smugly pleased with himself. A thought flashed across her mind, but she dismissed it. After all, Lucy was going back to London the next day. Lucy kissed her goodnight and went upstairs to her attic room, saying she needed to write up her logbook. Ethan too kissed his mother and went to bed.

The next morning Lucy went to Dorchester with Ethan to make arrangements for her to travel to London by stagecoach the following day. She would spend one night at the Rose and Crown, a comfortable coaching inn in Salisbury, and should arrive back in Chelsea the following evening. Lucy, who had managed the reverse trip three months earlier when she was still quite ill, was relaxed about her journey. But she quite enjoyed being fussed over by Ethan who was determined to make sure she was as comfortable and safe as possible. That evening, after supper, she asked if she and Ethan could speak privately to Nathaniel. She then told him all about her encounter with Corporal Oakshott and the following search of the property by the army.

'Thank you, Lucy, for telling me,' Nathaniel said. 'I have no wish for Sarah to learn this. She has been worried enough by my foolish decision to join with Monmouth.' He thought for a while. 'I think it best if Ethan and I brick up the cupboard tomorrow after you have gone. It was seldom used and I always found it an unpleasant little space. In a few months when all this political unrest has subsided, together we will plaster the whole wall and then we can pretend the whole affair did not happen.'

'There is one more thing, Uncle. I have been keeping a notebook for the past weeks. There are still parties of soldiers searching for rebels. Should my coach be stopped and the book fall into the wrong hands, it might be dangerous for all of us. I have given an account of how Corporal Oakshott came to die, acknowledging that none of your family had anything to do with it. I would ask you not to read the book as it has some private matters in it. But if you could keep it hidden and safe for me, I think to hide it here might be for the best.

'Come here, my child.' He swept her into his arms and gave her a long hug. 'I will do everything you ask and keep the book safe until you yourself come back to collect it. I will neither read it myself nor let anyone else read it, however much they ask it.' He smiled at his son. 'We shall all miss you, but I suspect Ethan most of all.'

The next day Lucy took the stagecoach to London.

Chapter 30

From: caddie@gmail.com
To: Rachel Greenleaf
Date: 31st July
Subject: Dearest Daughter

Hi Rachel,
I have managed to read the next two pages. There is not much written there and it makes no sort of sense to me. One is in Latin, which I am not very good at. It says:

Arcam nigram ducis in domo patris mei sub cantharo invenies.

I recognise *nigra* as black and *patris* as father. I think *ducis* comes from *dux* meaning a leader. I Googled 'cantharo' and all I could find was *cantharus*, a sea snail. Sounds to me as if the black leader has sea snails in his house. Poor chap. Any help?

Last page just says in the same handwriting:
E is no numpty and I am no maid.
Does this mean it was a boy writing after all?

Love Caddie

From: Rachel Greenleaf
To: caddie@gmail.com
Date: 31st July
Subject: Dearest Daughter

Caddie,
Really important I come down to Dorset asap. I am due some holiday. Would your uncle and aunt put me up for a couple of days? Look at the family tree. Maybe you will be able to work out who E is. Will explain all when I see you.

Rachel

From: caddie@gmail.com
To: Rachel Greenleaf
Date: 31st July
Subject: I need answers quick

Rachel,
They both say fine. Come as soon as you can. Give us a ring when you leave London – 01305 224765.

Caddie

Chapter 31
Unravelling the Past

Caddie was disappointed when Rachel asked if she could see Robert and Ruth as soon as she arrived. She felt Rachel was her particular friend and she felt possessive about the logbook she had spent so many hours deciphering. She tried hard not to appear sulky as they sat round the kitchen table with a cup of tea.

'Thank you for letting me come to stay this week end,' Rachel said to Ruth. 'I think there is a good chance that we can sort out all the Jolliffe family secrets once and for all. Caddie has done an amazing job with the logbook' (that made Caddie feel much better) 'and it could be that she has uncovered something that is really important. Caddie, did you have any luck with the family tree?'

Caddie unfolded her sheet of paper. 'I think E is likely to be Ethan Jolliffe.' She was thrilled by her discovery and had been aching to tell Rachel. 'He must have been about 16 or 17 at the time of Monmouth's rebellion. He married someone called Lucy Wells of Chelsea. I guess she might be *Dearest Daughter*, and if she came from London it would fit with her not knowing the meaning of those Dorset words. They had two sons called James and William. James was born in 1689 and William in 1691.'

Rachel nodded. 'Very PC names for the time.'

'Ethan must have been quite young to be a father, but he probably took over the farm in 1687 when his father Nathaniel died. He would only have been 18 or 19 then. How sad.'

'History is often sad when you put names and faces to it,' Robert said. 'What about the Latin, Rachel? None of us were much good with that.'

'Well, that's what I have come to see you about. If we Google the name *Lucy Walters* – she was the Duke of Monmouth's mother – you'll see details of what was known as the Black Box Affair.'

'I'm afraid we don't have the internet at the farm,' Ruth said. 'Caddie has either cycled into Dorchester or been to one of our neighbours' houses to e-mail you.'

Rachel had a quick flash of realisation what an effort it must have taken Caddie to contact her. 'Never mind,' she said, 'I'll show you on my I-phone later. It's another of these strange historical mysteries, which no one can explain. Lucy Walters always claimed that evidence of her marriage to Charles II was contained in a black box. I think even Samuel Pepys talks about it in his diary. Well, *arcam nigram ducis,* which you read in the book, Caddie, I think means *the Duke's Black Box.* I honestly think *Dearest Daughter*, who, if Caddie's right, sounds as if she might well be Lucy Jolliffe, is writing about Monmouth's black box.'

'What does the rest of the Latin mean?' Caddie was now as eager as Rachel.

'*In domo patris mei* definitely means in my father's house. This is a phrase Jesus uses when he was talking to his disciples. *In my father's house there are many mansions.* We'll have to work at that one. The last word *invenies* is the present subjunctive of the Latin verb *invenio*. I had to ask a colleague about that as my Latin wasn't good enough. He told me to translate it as *you may find*. There you have it. *Dearest Daughter* wrote in fairly simple dog Latin, *You may find the Duke's black box in my father's house underneath the sea snail.*'

'What about the last page, *E is no numpty and I am no maid*,' Caddie asked. 'Is that any help?'

'I don't think that means the writer was a boy as you first thought, Caddie,' Sarah interrupted. 'If you are right and E is Ethan and Lucy Wells is the writer, I guess it means she really liked Ethan and they had sex.'

There was a stunned silence and then all four of them roared with laughter.

'Well, they did marry, so that's all right then,' Robert said, defending his ancestors. 'Let's get back to the Latin bit. What if *domus mei* is not referring to Jesus's words but to Lucy's own father. What do we know of him?' He went to the dresser and took out the family Bible and laid it on the table. 'Here we are. *Lucy Wells, daughter of Dr Gideon Wells of Chelsea.* It sounds as if the box could have been hidden in Dr Wells's house in Chelsea.'

'I don't think so,' Rachel butted in. 'If the book was hidden in the secret room it is most unlikely that the box had been taken up to London. I feel it must be here somewhere. But, if so, why does she say *in my father's house*. I can't for the life of me work it out.'

'Let's take a break,' Robert said. 'It's a pity to come all the way down from London and not to see our beautiful Dorset countryside, Rachel. It is a lovely evening. Can I show you round the farm?'

'You've got an hour,' Ruth told them. 'Supper will be at seven.'

'Are you coming with us, Caddie?' Robert asked.

'I think I'll stay, if you don't mind. I've some tidying to do. Rachel, can I borrow your I-phone?'

'Sure. The Museum pays for my internet connection. Use it as much as you like.'

***

'I feel much better for a whiff of country air,' Rachel told Sarah as they sat down for supper. 'I really feel now I have shaken off the grime of the city. After supper I hope we will all be inspired to solve our little problem.' She looked up. 'Caddie, what is it?'

How is it Rachel always knows when I am trying to hide something? She couldn't suppress her excitement any longer. 'I've cracked it. I know where Monmouth's box is.' The others sat back and waited but Caddie was not going to waste this star opportunity. 'It seems a pity not to appreciate fully Aunt Ruth's steak and kidney pie with such a distraction. Also I need the table free to explain properly. Perhaps we can wait till after supper. Could I have a glass of wine, Uncle Robert?'

The conversation stuttered on. Sarah tried hard, questioning Rachel on the work she was doing at the Museum, but the talk was at best stilted. 'I had a letter from your father this afternoon, Caddie,' Robert said at last.

Caddie, who had been metaphorically hugging herself with the thrill of her discovery, wanted to know immediately all the news from her parents.

'It seems a pity not to appreciate fully Ruth's steak and kidney pie with such a distraction,' Robert managed to keep a straight face as he teased Caddie. 'And we don't want to be rude to our guest by discussing family matters over the supper table. I will show it to you when we have cleared up.'

Caddie realised that her ace had been totally trumped by her uncle and joined in the general laughter. No one, however, wanted to do the washing up straight after the end of the meal.

'I'll go first,' Robert said. 'Your father and mother are coming down here in a couple of days. They land at Heathrow early on Thursday morning and have hired a car and will come straight here. They will stay with us for a while. It will be a chance for your mother to reacquaint herself with Dorset, then all of you will be going back to your cottage in Hertfordshire.'

'Is Ben coming too?'

'Of course.'

'That's great.' Caddie's whole body seemed to relax and Robert wondered if he hadn't been a bit mean in not telling her immediately.

'Now you, Caddie. The steak and kidney is finished, the table cleared. What can you tell us?'

'Well, I decided to tackle this from two ends. First, the sea snail and, second, Dr Wells, though both strands come together very neatly. I Googled *cantharus* and Wikipedia could tell me very little except it meant a sea snail, but I did find some magnificent photos of various molluscs on another site. With them was a picture of a Greek two-handled drinking cup. I suppose it did vaguely look like the sea snail's shell, so I realised that *cantharus* could refer to more than just the snail. Then I went to Wiktionary. It's a sort of on-line dictionary,' she explained to her aunt and uncle. 'It's not something I have used before, but it did have another definition for *cantharus … a fountain or basin for worshippers to wash before entering a church.*

Now, if we get back to Dr Wells. Remember what he put on the title page of Lucy's book? Rachel, you told me that it was a pretty good definition of Bacon's Scientific Method. Then there was that quotation from Sir Isaac Newton. Also Lucy had tried to keep a record for her father of the medical bits she had seen or even dealt with. I didn't feel he was any old PhD, but a medical doctor. I asked myself where he might have worked and then I trawled through the London hospitals. The London Hospital wasn't founded until 1740 and Guy's was 1721. The oldest two were Thomas's, founded sometime before 1215, closed by Henry VIII and reopened in 1552, and Bart's, founded in 1123. Dr Wells could easily have worked in either of those.'

Caddie could see that her uncle had already jumped to the same answer that she had. Rachel, however, still looked mystified. 'I don't see ….'

'Tell her, Uncle,' Caddie said, very pleased with herself.

'The chapel just next to the house which has been the responsibility of my family for over 350 years is dedicated to St Bartholomew. *In domo mei* probably means in our chapel which has the same dedication as his hospital. What did you find there, Caddie?'

'Just to the right of the altar is a small stone basin shaped like a sea snail shell; well, a bit like one. I think these things are sometimes called stoups and were for holy water so the priest could wash his hands before the mass. I honestly think if we look under the stoup we may find Monmouth's black box.'

It was still light enough for them to troop out to the chapel. The little basin, not really shaped like a shell, was where Caddie had told them. 'If this is what Lucy meant,' Rachel said, studying it carefully, 'I think she was mistaken. I don't think this is a *cantharus*. They were traditionally near the entrance of a church, for the faithful to wash their hands. What we probably have here is a niche where the priest would place the reserved sacrament in a tabernacle. Of course that doesn't mean that Lucy didn't think this was a *cantharus*.' Below the basin were two thin rows of ancient green-glazed tiles. Rachel looked at Robert. There was no need for her to ask.

'There's only one way to find out. Tomorrow we will carefully lift those,' he said. 'My family are and have been the guardians of this beautiful little building for hundreds of years. It may well be our privilege tomorrow to unlock one more of its secrets.'

***

The next morning they had to wait as patiently as possible until Robert had finished milking the cows. Just before 10 o'clock the four of them were huddled round the altar in the chapel of St Bartholomew. Robert had a stone chisel and hammer ready, but before he could begin Rachel insisted on taking photographs. This, to Caddie, was one more piece of evidence that the eminent Dr Rachel Greenleaf was taking it seriously.

Robert worked painstakingly slowly. He was determined that even if this turned out to be a wild goose chase there would be no unnecessary damage.

Eventually six of the tiles had been lifted and Caddie took over with a trowel. The tiles were lying on a thin layer of sand and below that was soil. She rapidly scooped the debris into a bucket until she felt the trowel snag. 'I think I've hit something.'

Rachel knelt down next to her and used her fingers to scrape away more of the earth. There was something there, and it looked like a piece of old material. It certainly looked out of place under the floor of the chapel. Rachel stood up. 'Hold it a minute, Caddie. I must think.' She rubbed her hands clean of soil and fetched the inevitable pair of latex gloves from her pocket. 'I honestly didn't think we would find anything. Whatever it is we have uncovered, I am afraid I must insist now that we follow certain protocols. Boring, I know, but that's the way it's got to be. Ruth, do you have a cool bag?' Ruth nodded.

'Could you bring it with any ice bags that you might have in the freezer. I am sorry, Caddie, but I must do the excavation now. Robert, anything we find, though technically yours, must go to the laboratory to be properly preserved and examined. I hope you will give your consent.' Caddie could see that this was no game for Rachel. She was every inch the professional archaeologist.

The trowel Rachel produced from her trouser pocket was tiny. Centimetre by centimetre she removed tiny scrapes of earth until the piece of material (by now Rachel had told them it was leather not cloth) lay revealed. Slowly the depth of the object was uncovered and eventually Rachel was able, very carefully, to lift it from the hole and lower it into the cool bag. Sarah had brought along a quantity of tissue paper and this was gently packed round the object they had discovered.

'I'm sorry to be such a spoilsport,' Rachel said as she packed everything away, suddenly all serious and business-like. 'I must take this straight away to the museum lab. If I don't the whole lot may disintegrate into a pile of dust. Well done, Caddie. One hundred percent A1. I'm sorry but it is important that I take the diary too. I will try to make certain it is returned to you as quickly as I can. Thanks, Ruth and Robert, for your hospitality, but I'm going to rush off.'

Caddie felt disappointed and hurt. Rachel left behind her an enormous feeling of anti-climax. Caddie and Robert carefully refilled the hole, chatting aimlessly to each other without saying very much, and then Robert mixed a little cement and laid the tiles back where they had come from. The grouting round the six tiles looked fresher than the rest of the flooring. Apart from that the events of the last hour or two might not have happened.

***

In the morning two days later Caddie's parents arrived, to be met by an sparkling daughter and a beaming Uncle Robert. Ruth unfortunately wasn't feeling very well and was in bed, but promised to come down to see them later. After a snack lunch the family sat round the kitchen table together. 'You look well enough, Ellie,' Robert said to his sister.

'I am now,' she answered, 'but it was pretty ghastly at first. If Greg hadn't known the doctors at the Mission Hospital it might have been worse. Thank you so much for looking after Caddie for us. I hope she hasn't been too much trouble.'

'Mum,' Caddie, who was at the range making a pot of tea, looked at her mother with typical teenage exasperation. 'I am in the room you know.'

Robert stood up and went to put his arm around Caddie, a show of affection that certainly surprised his sister. 'We have loved every minute of having her here.' At that moment Ruth came into the kitchen and the usual kisses and hugs were exchanged. 'Sorry to hear you have not been well, Ruth. I hope you're feeling better now,' Greg Wells said to his sister-in-law.

'I'm not exactly unwell,' she smiled across at her husband who nodded to her. 'Robert and I are going to have a baby. It's early days still, but I'm confident that I'm pregnant.' Ellie folded her sister-in-law in her arms. She knew that, more than anything else, Ruth and Robert had wanted a child. 'Ever since Caddie came into our family I have been feeling different, sort of motherly, and I honestly believe that it happened because she has been here. If the baby's a girl, Rob and I want to call her Camilla Lucy. Lucy is a traditional name in the Jolliffe family. Will that be all right, Caddie?'

Caddie nodded. She was near to tears. Her emotions were a bit of a wreck at the moment. She had a sudden idea. 'If it's a boy, will you call him Ethan?'

'That's a strange name. Why Ethan?' her father asked.

'Oh, after Ethan Hunt in the Mission Impossible films,' she said and everyone laughed.

'After all, Ethan is as much a Jolliffe name as Lucy,' her uncle said quietly.

Postscript

Museum of London
15th May
CC2Y 5HN

Dear Robert and Ruth,

First, may I congratulate you on the birth of Ethan Robert. I read about his arrival in the Daily Telegraph and could not be more delighted. I thoroughly approve of your choice of name and hope that mother and baby thrive.

When I last saw you I promised I would let you know what happened to our discovery in your chapel. It has taken some while, but that is not unusual in our profession. There was nearly three months' work to stabilise the package. Had we not done that the whole lot might have disintegrated into dust.

The Diary. It has been thoroughly studied by experts and in the final page gives a clear account as to how your skeleton died. He was called William Oakshott and was not a very nice man. He was certainly the W.O. of Robert's pistol and the diary explains how the body and pistol came to be hidden at Corton Farm. I will give you details later, but am not free to do so yet.

*This letter will be a little disappointing for you, I suspect, for a very unusual reason. I have had to swear to the Official Secrets Act and am not permitted to tell you the details of what was in the package. It is thought by the very **highest authority*** *that to reveal the contents of the package at this time (I suspect that means following the recent royal wedding) is **not in the national interest**. Some faceless bureaucrat in the security services must even vet this letter. The following things I am permitted to tell you.*

1. Surrounding the package was a piece of coarsely tanned leather in poor condition made of cowhide. I regret I cannot tell you the name of the cow!

2. Inside the package was a wooden box made of teak. The wood was surprisingly well preserved and the box was undecorated and unlocked.

3. Inside the box were two pieces of writing. The first piece was on vellum and the writing was legible under UV light. I am not at liberty to reveal the contents, though I can say that any guess we might have made last August does not appear to be wide of the mark. It still has to be determined if the document is genuine or a forgery. The second piece of writing was a sheet of paper torn from a notebook. It technically belongs to you as it was signed by one of your ancestors and, I believe, when we get the chance to compare the two together, we will find that this page was torn from the book Caddie found. Here is a scanned copy of the note, though you will not receive the original for at least ten years.

I owe the estate of James Duke of Monmouth forty-eight guineas, which I have borrowed in order to bribe his honour Judge Jeffreys. I intend to try to arrange for the release of my

friend Nathaniel Jolliffe who is to be tried for treason.
Lucy Wells

There it is. Story complete. I shall of course write it up and I hope one day you (or your son Ethan) will be able to read and marvel at your family's history. Please give my love to Caddie and tell her that her vital part in the story will not be overlooked. One further matter. Inside the box was a Dutch guilder (solid gold) dated 1683. Of course this is rightfully yours and I have permission to return it to you, which I will do as soon as I can get to a Post Office. Of course it is your decision what you do with it. I appreciate it is part of Corton's heritage, but without Caddie's work and inspiration it would never have been discovered. Should she have it as a memento?

As for the writer of that logbook, for a young girl to travel with Monmouth's army, work with the wounded and to bribe the Lord Chief Justice of England must have taken nerve. Lucy Jolliffe nee Wells was some girl.

Yours sincerely,
Rachel Greenleaf

Historical Perspective

The facts about Monmouth's Rebellion are as accurate as I can make them, though there is no evidence that he ever visited Corton Farm; indeed, the timing from when he left the battlefield of Sedgemoor to when he was captured near Ringwood make such a visit almost impossible.

Charles II, still at that time a prince in exile, and Lucy Walters were both 18 years old when they met in the Netherlands. Charles was living with his sister Mary and her husband William, Prince of Orange. The story that there was a box containing evidence of Charles's marriage to Lucy Walters first surfaced in the 1670s. Lucy, who always claimed that she had been properly married to Charles, is supposed to have given a black box containing her marriage records to Bishop John Cosin before she died. This marriage was always denied by Charles II, who had good reason to do so. He married Catherine of Braganza in 1662 for political reasons. Throughout his life the Duke of Monmouth always claimed to be legitimate.

Charles and Lucy lived together as man and wife until he returned to England as King in 1660. Their second child, Mary (Monmouth's full sister), was a distant ancestor of the Spencer family and Princess Diana. It is perhaps an irony that one of the children of Charles II and Lucy Walters leads in a direct line to the Princes William and Harry.

Monmouth Beach where the Duke first landed is to the west of The Cobb in Lyme Regis. The present Cobb was reconstructed in 1820. The old coaching inn where Monmouth first stayed, known as the Golden Hart in 1685, is today called the Old Monmouth Hotel.

The historical facts about John Churchill, Duke of Marlborough, are, I believe, correct. The Churchills were an old Dorset family, and ironically a distant relative, also called John Churchill, leased Corton Farm from the Courtney family in the sixteenth century. He is mentioned on a brass plaque on the wall of the old Fleet Church ... *John Churchill, Gentleman, of Corton.*

Judge Jeffreys's lodging in Dorchester at No. 6 High West Street is now the Prezzo Restaurant. The Shire Hall where the Bloody Assizes took place is reputed to be the Oak Room Tearooms in Antelope Walk. The tunnel linking them is not open to the public.

The Battlefield of Sedgemoor can be visited three miles to the west of Bridgwater, though thanks to a more recent drainage ditch (the King's Sedgemoor Drain built in 1795) the Bussex and Langmoor Rhines dried up long ago and are no longer traceable. This has made the battlefield difficult to visualise. The church at Westonzoyland is where Lord Feversham kept prisoners after the battle, and the church tower at Chedzoy was where Farmer William Sparke spied out the royal army for Monmouth.

There are two famous novels about Monmouth's Rebellion. *Martin Hyde; The Duke's Messenger* by John Masefield published in 1910 and *Micah Clarke* by Arthur Conan Doyle published in 1889. Both can be downloaded for free, but are very dated in style. Also the second half of *Lorna Doone* by R.D.

Blackmore, first published in 1869, is about the rebellion.

Baron Ford Grey of Wark was pardoned by James II, though this is reputed to have cost him £40,000, a huge sum of money in the seventeenth century. His pardon was conditional on his agreeing to give evidence against other rebels. He re-entered public life when William and Mary came to the throne and was made Lord Privy Seal in 1701.

Corton Farm is privately owned and is half way between Upwey and Portesham, five miles south of Dorchester. Corton Chapel is also privately owned but is open to the public.

Forde Abbey near Chard looks much the same today as it did in 1685. The Abbey is privately owned but open to the public. The grand staircase that Ethan climbed and the Saloon where he met Sir Edmund are largely as they were in the seventeenth century. Sir Edmund Prideaux, having been imprisoned in the Tower, was eventually released when his wife (who was by no means as ditzy as I have portrayed her) paid a large fine or bribe of £15,000 to Judge Jeffreys (by then Lord Chancellor). Sir Edmund was given a discount of £240 for prompt payment.

Monmouth's brutal executioner, Jack Ketch, did indeed come to Dorchester for the Bloody Assizes and was responsible for carrying out many of the death sentences. He was imprisoned the year after Monmouth's death (1686) and died that same year.

The Bloody Assizes took place in Dorchester between the 5th and 10th September 1685.

Printed in Great Britain
by Amazon